Published by BSA Publishing 2020 who
assert the right that no part of this
publication may be reproduced, stored in
a retrieval system or transmitted by any
means without the prior permission of the
publishers.
Copyright @ B.L.Faulkner 2020 who
asserts the moral right to be identified as
the author of this work
Proof read/editing by Zeldos
Cover art by Impact Print, Hereford

BOOKS IN THE DCS PALMER SERIES

BOOK 1.   FUTURE RICHES

BOOK 2.   THE FELT TIP MURDERS

BOOK 3.   A KILLER IS   CALLING

BOOK 4.   POETIC JUSTICE

BOOK 5.   LOOT

BOOK 6.   I'M WITH THE BAND

BOOK 7.   BURNING AMBITION

BOOK 8.   TAKE AWAY TERROR

BOOK 9.   MINISTRY OF MURDER

BOOK 10.   THE BODYBUILDER

All available as individual or double 'case' e-books and paperbacks.

ALSO AVAILABLE: LONDON CRIME
A factual based book on the major London robberies and the 'geezers' who did the 1930-date.

THE PALMER CASES BACKGROUND

Justin Palmer started off on the beat as a London policeman in the late 1970s and is now Detective Chief Superintendent Palmer running the Metropolitan Police Force's Serial Murder Squad from New Scotland Yard.

Not one to pull punches, or give a hoot for political correctness if it hinders his inquiries, Palmer has gone as far as he will go in the Met and he knows it. Master of the one-line put-down and a slave to his sciatica, he can be as nasty or as nice as he likes.

The early 2000s was a time of re-awakening for Palmer as the Information Technology revolution turned forensic science, communication and information gathering skills upside down. Realising the value of this revolution to crime solving Palmer co-opted Detective Sergeant Gheeta Singh onto his team. DS Singh has a degree in IT and was given the go ahead to update Palmer's department with all the computer hard- and software she wanted, most of which she wrote herself and some of which are, shall we say, of a grey area when it comes to privacy laws, data protection and accessing certain restricted databases.

Together with their small team of favourite officers that Palmer co-opts from other departments as needed, and one civilian computer clerk called Claire they take on the serial killers of the UK.

On the personal front Palmer has been married to his 'princess', or Mrs P. as she is known to everybody, for nearly thirty years. The romance blossomed after the young Detective Constable Palmer arrested most of her family, who were a bunch of South London petty criminals, in the 1960's. They have three children and eight grandchildren, a nice house in the London suburb of Dulwich, and a faithful English Springer dog called Daisy.

Gheeta Singh lives alone in a fourth floor Barbican apartment, her parents having arrived on these shores as a refugee family fleeing from Idi Amin's Uganda. Since then her father and brothers have built up a very successful computer parts supply company, in which it was assumed Gheeta would take an active role on graduating from university. She had other ideas on this, as well as the arranged marriage that her aunt still tries to coerce her into. Gheeta has two loves, police work and technology, and thanks to Palmer she has her dream job.

The old copper's nose and gut feelings of Palmer, combined with the modern IT skills of DS Singh makes them an unlikely but successful team. All their cases involve multiple killings, twisting and turning through red herrings and hidden clues, and keeping the reader in suspense until the very end.

MINISTRY

OF

MURDER

CHAPTER 1

The River Thames ebb tide at Southwark leaves a forty foot shore of mainly soft, gooey mud behind it on the south bank. DCS Palmer had just found this out. He looked down to where his feet should be and saw as far as the end of his trousers and then mud. He quickly retraced his three steps back to a more solid part of the shore where DS Gheeta Singh stood. She gave a resigned shake of her head at the two clumps of mud that now housed his shoes.

'What did I say guv, just before you stepped forward?'

'You said *that mud looks soft.*' He wasn't looking at her as he said it; he was looking further down the bank towards the water lapping shore, where a team of white coated SOCA and Forensics officers, correctly clad in knee high rubber boots, were going about their business around a prostrate body which was laying half in and half out of the water. One of them had his attention brought to Palmer's arrival. He waved and pointed further along the beach where a line of planks laid on the mud gave dry access to the scene.

'Didn't notice those guv, did we?' said DS Singh. 'I would have thought the uniformed chaps on the gate might have mentioned it.' She turned and glared at two uniformed officers guarding the gate to the Victorian stone steps leading down from the pavement, where a small crowd of the public were gathering, their mobile phones recording everything and a smile on their faces.

Palmer made his way to the planks, followed by Gheeta. They took great care as they made their way along them as the planks had obviously been well-used, and were not slip-proof.

At the water's edge Palmer shook hands with Reg Frome.

'Sorry to disturb your peace Justin,' Frome smiled. 'Was he having forty winks when he got my call?' he asked Gheeta.

'I couldn't possibly comment,' she replied.

Palmer gave her an old-fashioned look.

Reg Frome, or to give him his correct title, Detective Chief Superintendent Frome was the head of the Yard's Forensic Murder Team, a team of forensic experts that were called in to work on any murder or suspected murder cases. He and Palmer came through the Hendon Police College at the same time, and had remained great friends and colleagues in the forty-odd years since. Resembling Doc Brown from the film *Back to The Future*, Frome's untidy shock of white hair and dishevelled appearance were his trademark as much as Palmer's trilby and Crombie overcoat were his.

'Why am I here, Reg? asked Palmer. 'And why are you and your team here? Just a bridge jumper isn't he?' He nodded towards the body.

'That's the first impression,' agreed Frome. He pointed to a police launch, stationary fifty metres out in the River, keeping the river traffic to the other side to minimise any bow waves disturbing the body. 'They spied him a few hours ago. Local Forensics were all tied up on the spate of knife murders in Hackney and Islington, and with the tide turning in the next hour or so we were asked to cover. Glad we were too.'

'Go on.' Palmer knew that tone of voice from Frome meant all was not as it seemed.

Frome squatted next to the body. 'See that.' He pointed to a small badge on the deceased's lapel.

Palmer bent and took a close look. 'NHS badge. Chap might have been a nurse or similar?'

'No, he's not a nurse.' Frome straightened up. 'His name is Jeremy Clive. A civil servant – he works, or worked, in the Department of Health in Whitehall.'

'How do you know that? Was he reported missing?' asked Palmer.

'No, his government pass was in his wallet. The facts are that about a hundred to a hundred and twenty people die in the Thames each year. Eighty percent are known suicides.'

'Okay, so what is so special about this one?'

'The badge.'

'The badge?'

'Yes, the badge. He's the third supposed suicide to have been pulled out of this stretch of the river in the last six months wearing that badge.'

'How do you know that? Your team wouldn't handle them, local Forensics would do it.'

'The Sergeant in the launch told me when we arrived that his men noticed the badge and remembered the other two. I got their names from the Marine Policing Unit records at Wapping and checked – all three worked at the Department of Health and Social Care.'

Palmer shrugged. 'Big department, Reg. Must be a couple of thousand workers in it at least, and it's only up the road in Whitehall. Could be pressure of work, stress, problems at home – any number of things could drive a person to jump.'

Frome took no notice and carried on. 'And all three worked in the same office at the Department of

Health and Social Care, the NHS Procurement Office, the office that decides which commercial companies get the medicine and equipment contracts. I thought that might warrant a little interest from you – too many similarities for me. Can't just be a coincidence surely?'

'The Procurement Office? So we are talking about big money then, aren't we? That does make it interesting Reg.' Palmer looked at DS Singh. 'I think we ought to take a look into these deaths Sergeant, don't you?'

Across the river on the north side, a man watched proceedings with interest. He watched until the police proceedings were over and the body taken away by the pathology officers in a blue body bag, and then he hurried away.

CHAPTER 2

Horace Jameson, Member of Her Majesty's Government for South Windsor, was in his office at the Houses of Parliament when a reception desk clerk rang through to advise him of a visitor.

'That's okay. Send him up, he knows the way.'

Jameson sat back in his seat and let out a long sigh, the sort of sigh a person exudes when really cheesed off. A minute later there was a light tap at his door.

'Come in Reggie,' he called out.

Reginald Compton, Senior Procurement Officer at the Department for Health, entered sheepishly, obviously relieved that the other two MPs that Jameson shared the office with were not there. He crossed to Jameson's desk and sat on the visitor chair placed in front of it. He was very agitated and slightly afraid.

'Jeremy Clive's body has been washed up on the South Bank. The police are there. I would never have got into this if I'd known all this was going to happen. That's Julie, Norman, and now Jeremy all dead. What the hell is going on, Horace? The police aren't stupid you know, they'll put two and two together...'

'And make five,' Jameson interrupted, giving Compton a reassuring smile. 'Reggie, will you stop panicking. I told you before, no way can any of this be traced back to us, no way.'

'Murder was not mentioned at the beginning – it was a simple money deal, no mention of murder. I don't want to be involved anymore. I'm out.'

Jameson rose from his chair and came round to Compton, patting him on the shoulder.

'No, you're not out Reggie. If you just stay calm and collected, nothing will happen. It will just be another suicide like the other two. '

'Three members of staff from one department jump into the Thames? That's bound to raise questions.'

'There wouldn't be any suicides if they'd taken the money and fallen in line, would there? Stupid people.'

'They had principles.'

'Silly principles – what difference does it make where a bloody drug comes from, eh? What difference would it have made to them which company supplies it? None, no difference at all.'

'It does when the price is four times more expensive.'

'NHS can afford it. For God's sake Reggie, they throw enough away on senior management who haven't a clue what they're doing. Just stay calm and all this will blow over.'

'No, I want out. No more, enough is enough.'

Jameson sat back down in his seat and blew out another large breath. 'Oh Reggie, do you realise what is involved here? '

'Involved? What do you mean involved?'

'Well, let's look at the facts. You are taking a backhander, and might I say a bloody big backhander, to make sure a certain drug is bought from a certain supplier. All you do is exaggerate that supplier's exemplary delivery time, his comparable price, and his high regard in other countries' health services that he deals with. And you make sure he gets the contract for supplying the NHS. What could be simpler?'

'Be a damn site simpler if any of it were true.'

'You have all the relevant paperwork, the references, the quotes. It's all there in black and white to support your decision.'

'And it's all fake – those references are all false, you know that. Three staff have questioned them, and those three staff are dead. What if I was ill and somebody else took over and checked back, eh? The house of cards would collapse. If anybody else but me was responsible for checking the paperwork, the whole scam would come tumbling down.'

'And with it your illustrious career, your holiday home in the south of France, your Panamanian bank account full of untaxed money. How would you explain that to HMRC, eh? Not forgetting that you will of course get an MBE or some sort of medal when you retire, you civil servants always do – and possibly a knighthood, and that gets you three hundred quid a day for fuck all in the House of Lords. You want to throw all that away? And what about your wife, Olive – you want to explain it all to her when the police call to arrest you?'

'Leave her out of it, she knows nothing about it. I've made enough, time to stop.'

'You can't stop, neither can I. You think it's easy, being on the Public Expense Committee and making sure nobody looks too closely at your department's choice of suppliers? Not easy at all. It's a wheel Reggie, a wheel we have to keep turning. If it stops, the cart tips over.'

'What if somebody else in the department smells a rat like those three did, and goes straight to the police? It was only luck that they came to me with their suspicions.'

'And then you to me. And do you know what that makes you? It makes you an accessory to the crime – an accessory to murder.'

That statement hit home with Compton. He felt a slight panic. 'You have a lot more to lose than me.'

'Meaning?'

'An MP taking bribes, mixed up in murder – you'd get a life sentence. You started all this, you have the contact, you got me involved with that bloody business trip to Romania. You had it all planned.'

'Did I? Did I really?' Jameson's mood and tone of speech changed to a threatening one. 'Listen to me Reginald Compton, I didn't force you to go on that trip – I didn't force you to get pissed and end up in a hotel room with two underage young ladies enjoying carnal pleasures.'

Compton was breathing fast as anger rose within him, 'I did not get pissed, as you put it – I was drugged, and nothing happened. The whole thing was staged, and I suppose you had no idea that the whole thing was being videoed through a one-way mirror either did you, eh?'

'None at all. It was brought to my attention afterwards, by a member of the Romanian Trade Delegation at their Embassy, that a senior civil servant in Her Majesty's Ministry had misbehaved whilst on a business trip. You should be thanking me for putting a lid on it. Or perhaps you would prefer the video to be aired? Try explaining it to Olive.'

'You bastard, I'll take you down with me.'

'Nothing will link me with that trip, it was offered and arranged quite legally and above board with the Ministry, the Romanian embassy, and the pharmaceutical company. They just wanted to show you their premises.

The Official Health and Safety Officer the department sent with you didn't find it necessary to cavort with girls in his hotel room. His report was very positive towards the company. Listen to me Reggie, just shut up and carry on doing what you are doing. If you rock the boat, there are people who aren't as understanding and as patient as me involved in this – I would have thought you might have realised that by now. I am not the top of the tree. These are people we don't want to upset, believe me – or do you want to be the fourth body floating down the Thames? Now bugger off, I've a meeting to go to.'

Compton stormed out of the office. He had a lot of thinking to do.

Alone in his office, Jameson sat and thought for a few minutes before making a phone call.

'I think we should meet. We could have a problem. I'll be at Luigi's about seven.'

CHAPTER 3

Palmer yawned as he walked into his office the next morning. He had watched *Deutschland 86* on catch up on the TV when he'd got home the evening before and binged through four episodes, until the banging on the floor by Mrs P. in bed above persuaded him to turn in. Then, in the morning, there was the explanation as to why his trouser bottoms were the colour of mud, Thames embankment mud.

Mrs P. had given him a weary look after he explained.

'Dementia, early signs.'

'No it's not. I just didn't realise it would be so soft.'

'I bet Gheeta didn't get her trousers messed up.'

'She didn't. She took the plank walkway.'

'I change my diagnosis – stupidity, not dementia.'

CHAPTER 4

At his New Scotland Yard office he looked at the pile of paperwork waiting on his desk and decided to give it a miss. He hung his Crombie on the government issue metal coat stand by the door, walked to the other side of his office and frisbeed his trilby towards the hat stand; then he walked back, picked it up off the floor and hung it on the hook. One day he'd get it right. He crossed the corridor into the Team Room where DS Singh and Claire, the team's civilian computer clerk, were working at two of the four terminals, the monitor screen scrolling madly as information was input.

They exchanged greetings and Palmer noted that Gheeta had already tacked up mugshots of the three deceased on the large white progress board on the wall at the far end of the room: Julie Hart, Norman Butwell, and Jeremy Clive. He recognised Jeremy Clive as the dead man on the embankment yesterday.

'So you think we should take a good look into this then, do you Sergeant?' he said, looking at the pictures. 'Is suicide out of the question?'

Gheeta swung round in her chair. 'Not entirely sir, but just seems a bit too much of a coincidence with three people from the same office jumping into the Thames in the last eight months.'

'Do we know that they actually jumped?'

'No, not conclusively. One brought up by a dredger, one caught on a Thames Water filter screen, and that one yesterday. The only certain thing is death by drowning, the pathologist reports were pretty definite. The coroner's verdicts on the first two were accidental death by drowning as well.'

Coroners are very reticent to give a suicide verdict except in cases where it is one hundred percent definite, the reasons being that the families of the deceased can tear themselves apart with guilt, and insurance companies usually have a suicide clause in the policy that lists it as a reason for non-payment. Coroners are aware of this and so avoid it. Coroners don't like insurance companies..

'Okay, so where are we at?' Palmer stood behind them, looking at their monitor screens.

'Just loading everything up that we can find on them – family, social life, career to date, bank accounts, security files...'

'Security files?' Palmer raised his eyebrows.

'Everybody working for HM Government is security checked by MI5, guv – background, political affiliations if any, police records. It's very thorough.'

'And you can download it?'

Palmer had brought DS Singh onto his department after noting her IT and cyber-expertise when she had been working in the Cyber Crime Unit and had updated his HOLMES programme in an hour, a job that outside contractors usually took two days to complete. Palmer was becoming more and more aware of the benefits his department would get from embracing new IT and social media functions, and had pulled strings and called in favours to have her transferred. Gheeta had grasped the opportunity with both hands; she had joined the force to fight crime and to be part of the Serial Murder Squad was her idea of heaven.

She had brought in computers and loaded them with every programme the department was likely to need: databases of known criminals, face recognition, NPR (

Number Plate Recognition), fingerprint and DNA records, and many more government databases that were supposed to be password-protected, which had not taken her very long to hack and access. Palmer turned a blind eye. If it helped him to solve a murder, then that was okay in his book.

'This MI5 database of personal files, I take it we need permission to take a look?'

'I couldn't possibly comment guv,' was DS Singh's regular reply to that question.

She had written a bespoke comparison programme that took all the information downloaded into it about a case and sifted and probed for a thread. Being a serial murder squad, the murders were always plural, and somewhere in the information downloaded would be a thread, something that tied the victims together; it could be ever so tenuous, but it would be there, something each murder shared – something they might not even have known they shared – but that thread would be there, waiting to be found.

'Okay, so at the moment we have no reason to doubt that we have three suicides. No evidence pointing to anything else. All we have is a strong suspicion that something is not as it should be at the Ministry of Health, which may or may not have contributed to three similar deaths of their employees.'

'Could be food poisoning.' Claire sat back in her seat. 'I've just noticed, the pathology report has the first two with pasta as their last meal.'

'Really? Well their deaths were four months apart, so they couldn't have had their last meals together. Be interesting if number three's stomach is full of pasta too. Either the Ministry canteen has pasta as a regular choice, or we might be looking for an Italian chef serial killer.' He chuckled to himself.

Gheeta ignored him. 'All three passed the MI5 check with no problems. Butwell and Clive were taken on from University, and Hart was a chemical analysis scientist. She worked over the river at the NHS Analysis Unit in Greenwich – all in all, a talented trio.'

'Okay, get as much information on them as you can and see if the computer can find a link other than the NHS and the Ministry. I think we need to quietly dig around in the Ministry and the Analysis Unit and see if we can ruffle any feathers.'

'If we are going to do interviews with the families we'll need some extra help, guv,' said Gheeta.

'Hold back on that for the present. See how we get on with the workplaces first. Don't want to upset any parents or relatives if we don't have to.'

Palmer's Serial Murder Squad was basically himself, Gheeta, and Claire. If the need arose where more officers were needed, he had a pool of detectives in the Organised Crime and CID units who he called on to help. They were all tried and trusted and liked working with Palmer. He was old school, called a spade a spade, listened to their input and treated them as equals, which they appreciated. So as not to tread on any toes, he only took them if they were off duty and available. With the force being so short-handed due to the twenty thousand cuts of the last few years, the last thing Palmer wanted to do was take an officer away from his day job and leave another squad short.

CHAPTER 5

The NHS Analysis Unit in Greenwich was a bright modern building on a small industrial estate off the Deptford road. Security was tight, and after showing their IDs Palmer and Singh were accompanied by a Government Security Officer up a flight of stairs to the offices above the laboratories and shown into that of the Director General, a Mr Grailing. According to the nameplate on his office door, Mr Oliver Grailing had an array of letters after his name signifying an academic and scientific career of note. He was late fifties, hair receding fast, portly and short, with thick lens glasses. He greeted them warmly and offered tea or coffee which they refused.

'Sit down, sit down please,' said Grailing, indicating leather sofas arranged along two walls. The sofas looked new, or maybe old but just unused. He sat behind his cluttered desk that reminded Gheeta of Palmer's. 'A terrible affair, terrible. One of my best scientists, Julie Hart – had a great career ahead of her. Terrible, terrible.'

Palmer nodded as though agreeing. 'Quite so. We've read the local police report and she seems to have been a steady, sensible girl.'

'Hardly a girl, Inspector. She was thirty-four.'

'It's Superintendent, Chief Superintendent, and any female under forty is a girl when you're over sixty.' He gave Grailing a withering look.

'Sorry, Chief Superintendent. But tell me, why are you so interested in her? I know it's a tragedy when anybody takes their own life, but it happens. So why the interest?'

'Suspicious circumstances, Mr. Grailing. But that is between you and us.'

It wasn't *between you and us* of course, but telling somebody that you are bringing them into what they perceive as a small trusted group often elicits more information . Palmer knew all the tricks.

'Oh.' Grailing was visibly shocked. 'Oh my... Well... How can we help?'

Palmer looked at Singh who took up the baton, her laptop recording every word.

'What was Miss Hart working on?'

'Quality control. Every drug that is in use by the NHS has to be quality checked every six months.'

'What for? What is a drug's 'quality' exactly?'

Grailing settled back into his chair and steepled his fingers in front of his chest, like a headmaster about to unveil the font of all knowledge to an eager student. Palmer thought to himself, '*oh God, please don't be one of these chaps who just likes talking about his own subject and rambles on and on and on.*'

Grailing blew out his cheeks and explained. 'Well, each drug that is passed by NICE – they are the government department who decide whether the drug gives value for money – every drug has to be basically taken apart every six months and its various ingredients checked, to make sure it corresponds to the ingredient mix that was sold to the NHS originally, both in weight, strength, and quality. Some of these drugs cost thousands of pounds, and a patient put on a course of them will be using tens of thousands of pounds of the limited financial resources the NHS has.'

'And this is what Miss Hart was working on?'

'Yes, as are many of the staff here.'

'What happens if a drug is found to be below standard?'

'The manufacturer is told and the Health Ministry Procurement Department is told to halt the contract until the pharmaceutical company that produces it has checked its manufacturing procedures and rectified the situation to our satisfaction.'

Palmer took the baton back. 'By which I take it you mean that a new batch of the drug would have to come here and be checked before the pharmaceutical company's contract was re-instigated?'

'Yes.'

'Do you have a list of the drugs Miss Hart was working on?'

'Yes, these tests take quite a time – we are very thorough, so she would only be working on a couple at a time.'

'If she found a problem with a drug, what was the procedure?'

'A stop notice would be sent to the Ministry and one to the company listing the quality problems.'

'Do you have copies of any of these notices she sent in the last, say, year?'

'They are sent by email.'

Gheeta saw an opportunity. 'From that computer?' she asked, pointing to one on Grailing's desk.

'No, no, Julie was a senior analyst – she had her own small office off the lab. I got copies emailed to me.'

'Is her computer still here?' asked Gheeta.

'Yes, all the analysts have their own laptops. It's in the store.'

'May we borrow it?'

'I don't see why not,' he smiled. 'I don't think you'll understand much of what's on it – scientific chemical analysis isn't very exciting.'

Little did he know it wasn't the scientific chemical analysis that Gheeta was after. It was the email or emails alerting Compton of a problem with a batch.

CHAPTER 6

It had taken a great deal of restraint from Gheeta not to start looking into Julie Hart's computer that evening at home, but protocol required a warrant before she could open up the contents. So the next morning she was in the office early, filled out the permission request and emailed it off to AC Batemans office. It would be approved of course – no reason why it shouldn't – so she opened up the laptop and fired it up.

Password-protected. Well, that was to be expected. She coupled a USB line to the laptop and her mainframe unit, tapped in a command, and watched as the laptop screen scrolled down at a rate of knots, hitting the password control app with twenty thousand variations a second. It didn't take long to break it. Too easy, thought Gheeta, just five letters: DRUGS. The front page opened with a list of apps and programmes on the left. The one Gheeta was after was 'Emails'. She opened the email page and input the names of the other two deceased, Butwell and Clive. Nothing came of the search. So Julie Hart hadn't had email contact with either of the Ministry chaps. The head of their department at the Ministry was Reginald Crompton – try that, she thought. Nothing again. Oh well, it had been worth a try.

Palmer came in with three coffees on a tray, followed by Claire.

'Somebody's keen today,' he said as he put a cup beside her. 'Milk, no sugar.'

Claire took off her coat and sat down at her terminal.

'Found anything?' she enquired.

Gheeta shook her head. 'No, not yet. Seems funny that she didn't have any contact with the Ministry.'

Palmer took off his Crombie and walked across the corridor to his office. He hung it on the coat stand, perched his trilby on top, and retraced his steps back into the team room.

'She probably deleted them. If she had found anything suspicious about a drug she would have passed her suspicions to the Procurement people and waited for a response. If the response was that it had been sorted, that was it – close the file and delete it.'

Gheeta raised her hands to heaven. 'Damn! How stupid of me, I haven't checked her deleted files.' She started tapping at her keyboard.

The screen burst into lines of fragmented data.

'What's all that?' asked Palmer, leaning forward.

'That is her deleted emails, guv. When you delete something it goes onto the hard drive and stays there until it is overwritten, and then it fragments itself. Don't worry, I've a cleaning tool that will sort it out. It's a new app from the PITO (Police Information Technology Organisation), my old team created it.' She went to her opening page and clicked on an icon, which she dragged and dropped onto the fragmented data. The screen scrolled down, and as it did so the fragmented lines of gobbledegook became legible lines of words, sentences, paragraphs and emails. 'Christ she's got enough emails here.'

'She was with the department for twelve years,' Palmer said.

'She must have had this PC all that time judging by the amount of information she deleted.'

The scrolling stopped. 'Right, now all we have to do is pull out any emails between her, Jeremy Clive, and Norman Butwell.' She tapped more demands into the computer and watched as it scrolled again. 'Nothing, nothing between them at all.'

Palmer was discouraged. 'That's a shame. There must be a link, got to be. Three people so closely linked by work don't turn up dead in a river without some kind of link between them.'

'Maybe, 'suggested Claire, 'they were all working on the same thing and that's the link?'

Palmer beamed, 'Of course it is – all three chanced on something wrong with the same product, or maybe the same supplier. Give Grailing a call and find out what Hart was working on at the time of her death.'

CHAPTER 7

'Who are we seeing?' Palmer asked DS Singh as they got out of the squad car in front of the Ministry building.

'Reginald Compton, Head of Procurement and Finance Monitoring. Sounded very jittery on the phone – couldn't understand why we were interested.'

'Well then, we had better tell Mr Reginald Compton why we are interested and see his response.' Palmer looked at the flight of stone steps leading up to the Ministry doors: Victorian architecture at its best, great columns of stone shouting empirical grandure. The wide stone steps they terminated in shouted sciatic pain. He really ought to get his back looked at and his discs sorted out. He'd been told by the doctor he had a slight trapped nerve that gave him a slicing pain in his right thigh when he jumped or stamped, and especially when he went up stairs. So the empirical great steps of the Ministry were not very inviting. However he managed to defeat them with a modicum of pain, and a slight grimace on his face.

They showed their pass cards and warrant cards to the security guards and were directed to wait whilst somebody from Compton's department would come down to accompany them upstairs to his second floor office. That somebody was a gaunt looking tall individual in an obviously ill fitting *off-the-peg* regulation civil service gray suit that matched his middle aged gray complexion. His worried expression peered from behind his plain NHS spectacles as he introduced himself as Alastair Prior, Deputy Procurement and Finance Monitoring Officer, which matched the name on his security tag hanging around his neck. Prior was a career civil servant, late forties, still living at home with his widowed mum and only one interest in life, his job. They took the lift to the second floor rather than a further longer flight of stone stairs winding up into the building which was a relief to Palmer.

Palmer hadn't much time for hanging onto the past that the British government seemed to like to do. When every parliament in the world – including the devolved British ones – voted on acts by pressing a button in front of them, the Great Mother of Parliaments in the UK had its MPs file out of the chamber through a lobby, to be counted and then file back in again – ridiculous in the twenty-first century. But then Palmer's republican views were well known. Mrs P. was convinced that if he'd kept them to himself, he'd probably have made it to Assistant Commissioner, if not all the way to the top.

Compton's office was a rather large affair, with a high ceiling and a rather large ornate Victorian plaster rose as its centre, with a chandelier hanging from it. Palmer noted Compton's large desk was tidy and clear of paperwork, which in Palmer's cynical mind meant Compton was either on top of his work or hadn't enough to do. Compton being a civil servant, Palmer plumped for the latter.

They exchanged pleasantries, refused a cup of tea or coffee, and sat down in two of a set of four leather button chairs as Prior made his exit. Compton sat behind his desk.

'I understand this is about Butwell and Clive?' he said.

'About their deaths sir, yes,' replied Palmer. 'Together with that of Miss Julie Hart over at the Analysis Department. You see, it struck us as a strange string of coincidences. All worked for this department, and all died from drowning within eight months of each other. Didn't that strike you as rather strange?'

'Miss Hart didn't work for this department, Superintendent. I didn't know the lady.'

'It's *Chief* Superintendent. No, she didn't work in this building, but her work was linked to your department.'

'I'm sorry, *Chief* Superintendent. But we had nothing to do with her.' Compton squinted his eyes, as though not understanding the line of questioning.

'Pestiment.'

Compton was obviously taken aback and tried to recover his composure. 'Pestiment?'

'Yes, Pestiment – an expensive drug approved by NICE as a blocker for Parkinson's disease, controls the involuntary shaking. My Detective Sergeant here is very good at exposing deleted emails on hard drives.'

'I don't understand, what has that to do with Pestiment?'

'Miss Hart had a problem with the drug – apparently she discovered that the main retardant in it was not at the level it should have been according to the NICE list, and she called your attention to it twice.' He offered the conversation to Gheeta with a wave of his hand.

Gheeta gave Compton a smile. 'Miss Hart emailed you in February, and then again in May of last year asking that you put a stop on the procurement of any further supplies of the drug Pestiment from European Pharmaceuticals, the company who supplied the drug, until they had sorted the problem out and had sent upfront samples to be tested and approved. You agreed.

We have copies of the emails.' She pulled them from her shoulder bag and placed them in front of Compton

Compton had a sudden memory recall. 'Yes, yes, now you come to mention it I do remember that. The company was very upset and immediately destroyed their existing stock and manufactured new. I think, from memory, Miss Hart passed the new batch.'

Gheeta nodded. 'Yes, she did. But being a conscientious scientist with a very responsible job concerning the health of the public, she kept checking every batch that came from European Pharmaceuticals. And would you believe,' she said with feigned amazement, 'another batch was found to be wrong just six months later. She emailed you about that too, just a month before her death. You emailed back and asked her to come here to present her findings to European Pharmaceuticals at a meeting you would arrange.'

Two more paper copies were placed in front of Compton. Palmer rose from his chair and walked slowly to the large windows that overlooked Whitehall. He spoke without facing Compton, knowing that Gheeta was registering Compton's body language.

'What happened at that meeting, Mr Compton?'

Compton shifted in his chair. 'I can't recall.' He searched for words. 'I think Miss Hart may have pulled out. I don't recall any meeting.'

'Perhaps the poor girl died before you could set a date for it?'

'I don't know, I really don't remember.'

'What about the two chaps who did work here, Norman Butwell and Jeremy Clive? What would drive two young men with good jobs and prospects to end up in the Thames?'

The perspiration was showing on Compton's forehead. 'I really don't know, they both seemed fine when they were here – perhaps they had issues with family, or something else outside of work?'

'Or an issue with Pestiment?' Palmer swung round and gave Compton the Palmer glare. The one that said: *I know you are lying.*

'H-h-how? They didn't have anything to do with the drugs.'

'No, but Miss Hart blind-copied both of them into her emails to you, so they certainly knew of her concerns. Amazing what a computer hard drive can tell you. Why would she do that, why copy the emails to them?'

'I... I have no idea.' Compton was obviously very uncomfortable.

Gheeta read from her laptop. 'Butwell was an account manager and Clive was an account auditor. Was one of their accounts European Pharmaceuticals by any chance?'

'I... I don't know offhand, I'll have to check.'

'I already have,' Gheeta advised him, 'and it was. Would you confirm that for us please?'

'Yes, yes of course. One moment please.' Compton left the room.

'What's he hiding, Sergeant? I don't think I've ever seen somebody as flustered as he is.'

'Something's rotten in this department guv, and he's involved in it somewhere.'

'How did you know Butwell and Clive were account manager and auditor on the European Pharmaceuticals account? Have you been hacking where you shouldn't be hacking?' He held up a restraining palm. 'Don't answer that – what I don't know I can't be held liable for.'

'No,' Gheeta laughed. 'No guv, no hacking. We know they were copied into Hart's emails about Pestiment, so why else would she do that unless they were part of the team? Just an obvious assumption that I think will be proved right when Compton comes back – unless he's done a runner.'

Compton hadn't '*done a runner*'; he came back in and retook his chair behind his desk.

'Yes, I can confirm they were both responsible for the European Pharmaceuticals account, in a financial way, of course.'

'What do you mean, *in a financial way*?' Palmer wanted to know.

'Well, if the faults with Pestiment were not rectified – and as I said before, they were rectified immediately – but had they not been, then a full audit of the account would have had to be done to ascertain what financial refund would be due to the NHS under the terms of its contract with European Pharmaceuticals. Clive would have done that and Butwell would have liaised with the company. But as I said, the matter was rectified immediately and the stock replaced. No low-quality stock ever went out to patients.'

Palmer called an end to the interview by walking to the door and telling Compton that he would be hearing from them. Prior was summoned from an adjacent office and accompanied them down in the lift and through to the foya without a word being spoken.

Neither Palmer nor Singh were happy as the squad car took them back to the Yard.

'Too many loose ends, guv.'

'Yes, and Compton's hiding something. Might be worth having a chat with the families – perhaps the deceased said something at home.'

Gheeta tapped at her keyboard. 'Butwell's is closest – he was a single guy with a flat in Hammersmith, parents live in Acton. I can detour that way in the morning guv, see if their son had said anything about work to them. I'll have a word with their FLO (Family Liaison Officer) beforehand to make sure they are up to questioning. Don't want to rekindle too much grief.'

CHAPTER 8

Reginald Compton was preying on Palmer's mind. He took the printouts of the case files on Butwell, Hart and Clive home, to sit quietly and read them through again. Something must be inside them to tie three 'death by drowning' coroner inquest verdicts together.

His thoughts of an uninterrupted review of the papers were quickly extinguished as he opened the front door to be greeted by Daisy, his faithful Springer who was always pleased to see him, and voices coming from the kitchen that told him Benji, his next door neighbour, was chatting with Mrs P.

Benji was Palmer's nemesis. Real name Benjamin Courtney-Smith, he was a portly, ex-advertising executive in his late fifties, who had taken early retirement and now had, in Palmer's estimation, too much time and too much money on his hands. A new car every year, and at least two cruise holidays to exotic parts. He wore designer label clothes befitting a much younger man, a fake tan, enough gold jewellery to interest the Hatton Garden Heist detectives, and all topped off with his thinning hair scooped into a ponytail, also befitting a much younger man. Palmer was unsure about Benji's sexuality, as his mincing walk and the waving of his hands to illustrate every word cast doubts in Palmer's mind; not that that worried Palmer, who was quite at ease in the multi-gender world of today. Of course he would never admit it, but the main grudge he held against Benji was that before his arrival in the quiet suburb of Dulwich village, Palmer had been the favourite amongst the ladies of the Women's Institute, the bridge club, and the various other clubs catering for ladies of a certain age. But now Benji had usurped his fan club; their fluttering eyelids had turned in his direction.

Palmer put on a smile as he came into the kitchen. 'Hello Benji, how are you?' He gave Mrs P. a peck on the cheek.

'I thought you had a rule never to bring work home,' Mrs P reminded him as he dumped his files on the kitchen table and sat down, as Daisy brought him one slipper from the hall in the hope her master might reward the effort with a treat. He gave her a pat. She was disappointed.

'I know, but this case is hiding something and I can't for the life of me figure it out. It's just so exasperating when you know there's a clue in there somewhere but can't see it.'

Benji flapped his hands as though swatting a fly. 'Oh I know just how you feel, Justin. I got stuck on a crossword clue yesterday – I'd got everything except this last clue: *something you put flowers into*. Three letters, got to be *bed*, hasn't it? *Flower bed*. But it didn't fit. I was getting so stressed I had to put it down and have a red wine.'

'Pot.'

'No, just a glass of wine. I don't smoke pot,' Benji giggled. 'I had a spliff once and was ill for a week.'

'Flower pot, *something you put flowers into*. Pot, flower pot.'

Benji was awestruck. 'Oh, yes of course! Oh, thank heavens for that – I was awake all night trying to solve that. Thank you Justin, thank you!'

Mrs P. shook her head in disbelief at the pair of them. 'Justin, Benji has bought me some supplements –

health supplements that I read about in the WI magazine.' She pointed to two jars of pills on the table.

'I take them myself,' said Benji. 'And even if I do say so myself, I don't look bad for my age.'

'You don't look that good either.' He patted Benji's stomach. 'That's a firkin, not a six-pack.'

'I'm working on it at the gym anyway,' added Benji quickly, steering the conversation away from his paunch. 'These pills just increase the body's own vitamins – and when you get to *your* age Justin, you have to give the body a little help.'

Palmer felt like giving Benji's body a little help out of the back door with his boot. Mrs P. saw the signals that a minor war was about to break out and quickly pointed to the jars of pills on the table. 'Two each of these every day with your breakfast, Justin – cod liver oil and omega-3. Mind you, I think we might double the dose on the omega-3 in your case as they are supposed to help the brain.'

'You must be joking!' Palmer scoffed. He had never taken pills in his life. 'Anyway, I think I've had enough of pills and drugs for one day with this damn case.' He rose from the chair a little too quickly and his sciatica stabbed him in the right thigh. 'Ouch!'

'Serves you right. How many times have you been told to get your discs seen to?'

'Haven't got the time.'

'More exercise, that's what you need – keep things moving. I'll get you a tracksuit and you can join our jogging club.'

Benji agreed. 'Exercise is the answer – nothing too strenuous, but jogging is just right. Gets the heart pounding.'

Palmer nodded. 'If it's the Women's Institute jogging club, I've seen them in the park – can't say they are likely to get my heart pounding.'

Benji giggled. Mrs P. was not amused.

'Some of the husbands come along too. And Benji leads it.'

'Then that's a definite no.'

CHAPTER 9

Palmer walked into the Team Room the next morning to
put the case files back. Claire was already at her terminal.
The big plasma screen on the wall was showing a central
London map.

'Blimey Claire, I thought I was early. You been
here all night?'

Claire laughed. 'No sir, my other half puts up
with a lot but I think an all-night shift here might disturb
the marital bliss a bit. I knew the pathology report on
Clive was due in this morning and I wanted to upload it
into the comparative programs, as I thought there must be
some link between our three victims. And Clive being the
last one, it could all hinge on him.'

'And...?' Palmer could tell by Claire's face she
had found something.

'Pasta.'

'Pasta?'

'Yes, you remember that both Hart and Butwell's
last meals had been pasta.'

'Mmm.'

'And you thought it was probably a regular dish
on the Ministry canteen menu?'

'Yes.'

'Well, the pathology report on Clive has his last
meal as pasta too.'

'Go on.' Palmer knew she'd found something.

'So I checked with the catering manageress at the
Ministry – pasta is a regular on the menu.'

Palmer's hopes sank. 'Oh.'

'Every Thursday.'

'So?'

'I checked the path lab reports on all the victims for the time the lab estimated they had been in the water and backtracked the days. Hart was killed on a Monday, Butwell on a Wednesday, and Clive on another Monday.'

Palmer pulled a chair up beside Claire. 'Interesting.'

'So they didn't eat in the Ministry canteen on the day they died – no pasta on the menu those days.'

'Okay.'

'If you check the screen,' she pointed up to it, 'the Italian restaurants within half a mile around the Ministry are flagged.'

Palmer could see the red flags on the map. 'So you think they might have all eaten at the same place prior to being killed.'

'Yes.'

'You could well be right. It's too much of a coincidence not to be relevant.'

DS Singh came in and unslung her shoulder bag, removing the laptop as they greeted each other.

'I couldn't be a FLO, not for all the money in the world.' She'd been around to Butwell's family home.

'Hard work with the family then?' Palmer asked.

'Butwell's father passed away a month after he was killed. His mother is trying so hard to hold it together but it shows. And of course when I show up asking the questions I need to ask, she begins to wonder why. She still thinks he died by accident after falling in the river, or by suicide. She has a guilt complex the size of Everest. *'I should have realised something was wrong, I should have noticed, a mother should notice these things.'* And her husband going too… all a bit much.'

'Did you tell her we were re-opening the case?' Palmer asked.

'No, I thought that if I did that then I'd have to say why. But we got one thing out of it which might help.'

'Oh yes?'

'She told me that she hadn't collected her son's things from West End Central yet. She couldn't bring herself to do it.'

'What things?'

'Stuff from his pockets – small change, keys bank cards and such, *including* his mobile phone.'

Palmer's eyes widened, 'That could be very interesting.'

'I thought so too,' said Gheeta, pulling Butwell's phone from her shoulder bag. 'So I picked it up from West End Central on my way here. I told her I would get her son's things for her and drop them round next week.'

'After you've had a look through it.'

'Can't do that guv, not without a warrant.'

'You go ahead, I'll get one from Bateman later. Oh and by the way, Claire's got an interesting theory about Italian food. Tell her Claire.'

Claire explained to Gheeta that Clive's post mortem had shown pasta as his last meal and that it couldn't have been eaten at the Ministry because it wasn't on the menu that day, and that the same applied to the others, so their last meals had to be eaten elsewhere, probably a local restaurant.

Gheeta looked at the red flags on the screen.

'So we start with the nearest one to the Ministry and see if they recognise the mugshots of the deceased.'

'That and check their reservations book,' said Palmer. 'With a bit of luck the victims' names will appear in that on the day they disappeared. What's the name of the nearest one?'

Claire checked her screen. 'Luigi's.'

Palmer put on his best Marlon Brando impersonation from The Godfather. 'Okay, we go to Luigi and-a we make-a him the offer he not about-a to refuse, eh?'

'Very good, guv,' complimented Gheeta.

'You like it?' Palmer reverted to his normal voice.

'Best Groucho Marx I've heard, guv. Very good.'

Both Claire and Gheeta tried in vain to hide their smiles. Palmer gave Gheeta a cold squint. 'Come on, we might as well walk – it's not far and I can work up an appetite. And guess who's buying the pastas then?'

Gheeta pulled a face. 'Seeing that the pasta has a habit of turning up in dead people's stomachs guv, I think I'll have the panazella instead.'

CHAPTER 10

Luigi's was busy. Outside tables were full catering for the limited time lunch hour eaters with small plates of caprese salad, focaccia rolls, risottos and various pastas, whilst inside the bigger menus and wine was the order of the day.

Palmer pushed through to the bar at the side. Heads turned as DS Singh, in uniform, followed him. A quick flash of his warrant card to a bartender wasn't really necessary as the manager who had been seating a couple at a reserved window table had clocked them entering and had quickly made his way over. Late-fifties, well-groomed and with a disarming smile, the manager looked every inch the archetypal hotel/restaurant manager: slim, tall, pencil moustache trimmed to perfection, and not a hair out of place on his sleeked-back coiffure. Palmer showed his card.

'Could we have a quiet word, sir? Somewhere private? '

'Of course.' The manager was a bit flustered and wanted Gheeta's uniform out of the customers' eyeline. Not good for business. 'This way, please.' He led them through a door behind the bar into what was obviously a very well-managed office; paperwork on the large desk was laid in fine order, and everything was arranged to give the impression of competence, which it did. He offered them the two chairs in front of his desk and took his seat behind it.

'How can I help?'

'Well, Mr...?'

'Giuseppe, just call me Giuseppe. Everybody does.'

He smiled. Palmer returned it. 'Well Giuseppe, we are investigating a fairly serious crime and think some of those involved may have been customers here.' Palmer wasn't going to elaborate further. The less people know, the less they can pass on. And in any case, this restaurant might well turn out to not be the one where the victims ate their last meals. 'Would you mind taking a look at some pictures and see if you recognise anybody?'

'Of course not.' He pulled a spectacle case from his waistcoat pocket, extricated the spectacles and put them on.

Gheeta opened her laptop, stood up and placed it in front of Giuseppe. She pulled up the mugshots one by one; each one got a 'no' from Giuseppe.

'I'm sorry, they don't ring a bell – but we get so many people here I could well be wrong. What I can say is they aren't regular customers – regular customers I do know.'

Gheeta was about to ask Giuseppe if he recognised any of the three victims' names but if he failed on the faces he wouldn't do any better on the names. But she had another idea.

'What about bookings? Do you take advance bookings?'

Giuseppe laughed. 'We have to. All the tables inside are generally booked up for lunch by eleven o-clock – most of the outside ones are too. Not boasting, but we are very popular, and with so many government offices in the area we have many civil servants and even politicians who eat here. We are very fortunate – not many restaurants in the area, mainly offices.'

'Do you have book for listing those bookings?' Gheeta was praying for a 'yes'.

'No, it's all on a computer programme. All the tables are shown, so we know when we are full and at what time there might be a vacancy.'

Gheeta could have cheered loudly. 'That programme is on a normal computer?'

Giuseppe nodded. 'A laptop, It's used solely for bookings.'

Gheeta nodded to Palmer, who knew exactly what she was after.

'My Sergeant will need a copy of that programme, sir – just so we can run through it and see if any names we are looking for come up.'

'A copy?' Giuseppe was worried. 'You mean a paper printout of all the bookings? Back to when?'

Gheeta closed her laptop. 'No, much simpler. I'll be able to download it all from your laptop onto a USB and work from that back in the office. It won't interrupt your programme – be done in two minutes.'

Palmer could see furrows of worry appearing on Giuseppe's brow, probably caused by him thinking about the data protection laws and the big fines for transgressing them. He wanted those names and stepped in.

'Other than that I can get on the radio and have one of my officers pop down with a seizure warrant and take the laptop away for checking. Should only be gone a week or so.'

'No, no we couldn't manage without it. What about data protection? We've jumped through so many hoops lately on all the new GDPR requirements, I don't want to get a fine or worse.'

Palmer's inkling had been right. 'Criminal investigation sir, overrides GDPR. You're in the clear'

'Okay, if you say so – download it then. Come with me.' He rose and they went into the bar where the small laptop sat on a pedestal at one end. Gheeta plugged a memory stick into a side USB port and the job was done in two minutes.

'That's it, all done.' She smiled at Giuseppe. 'The data will be destroyed if we find nothing to interest us.'

Giuseppe was relieved that the booking system seemed still to be working. 'Well, I have to say, I do hope you don't find anything, I would hate to think that Luigi's clientele included criminals.'

Palmer gave him an old-fashioned questionable look. 'I thought you said politicians eat here, sir?'

CHAPTER 11

The by-product of walking back to the Yard with Palmer was that he realised it was lunchtime. When he was working on cases his brain was so immersed in that case that food and drink went by the wayside, but walking in the sunshine and seeing the embankment populated by sandwich-eating workers on their lunch break clicked a message in his brain to ask his Sergeant if she wanted a sandwich.

Gheeta hid her amazement at the out of character request and plumped for a ham salad with mayonnaise, whilst Palmer had a beef and horseradish. Gheeta made sure that she only ate one of the two sandwiches in her box and offered the other to Claire in the Team Room when they got back.

'Here you are Claire, the boss thought you'd be so immersed in work you'd forget to eat – bought you a sarnie.'

Claire took a moment to believe that – even remembering to eat himself was not unknown in this squad, providing for another was...well, unheard of. But there was the sandwich. She took it.

'That's very kind of you, sir,' she thanked Palmer, who grunted something inaudible back and gave a Gheeta look that either said 'thanks' or 'I'll kill you' – perhaps veering slightly on the side of the latter.

'I'll get some coffees,' he said, feeling a bit guilty, and made his way from the team room up to the fifth floor, where senior officers and certain Home Office personnel had their opulent offices and their coffee machine: no money needed, and little pots that you popped in, pressed a button ,and out came a rather better cup of coffee than on Palmer's floor. The machine on his floor dished out a disgusting brew that was definitely not coffee, and then only when it had taken his money and sent a cup down before the brew, which wasn't often. So when he or Gheeta and Claire wanted a coffee, they went up to the fifth floor,

When he returned he could tell by the smiles on their faces that something had been found. He gave them their coffees.

'Seems like Julie Hart had covered her tracks, guv,' said Gheeta, pointing to her monitor screen which was showing Julie Hart's phone texts to Butwell that she had pulled off his mobile.

'Go on.' Palmer pulled a chair up and sat down, sipping the coffee.

'Well, on Butwell's phone there are a number of texts between him and Hart which are also copied to Clive, and it seems at first look that she had made him aware of a problem with Pestiment and asked what the procedure was to halt the contract, as he was the account manager for European Pharmaceuticals. He replied that she would have to clear it with Compton to put the payments on hold, and then if Compton gave the green light he would get Clive to audit the account and see what refund was due to the NHS for any substandard batches. Hart then forwarded the batch numbers from which she had taken substandard samples, and Butwell forwarded them onto Clive.

Palmer nodded. 'So all three of our victims were in the loop. All three knew there was a problem with Pestiment.'

'Yes, and from the very beginning. But we have to assume Butwell and Clive didn't get a stop notice from

Hart, so they would have thought the problem was sorted. So why were they killed?'

'Money.'

'Money, guv? What money?'

'I don't know, but both were on the financial side of the procurement process – one an accountant, the other an auditor – so it has to be something to do with money, some fiddling of the books maybe. Could be they found something not right in the European Pharmaceuticals accounts?'

'And being a pair of upright honest civil servants they would have brought it to the attention of Compton.'

'Yes, our Mr Compton seems to be popping up in a variety of scenarios, doesn't he? And none of them looking good for him.'

'He likes Italian food too,' Claire added. 'I've put Hart, Butwell and Clive into a search of Luigi's computer booking programme and they don't show up at all. However, the name Compton shows up quite a lot – most importantly he booked on the days our three victims died. Suspicious, eh?'

'Well, we don't know what we are dealing with here, but there's a pattern developing and it seems to be centring around Compton and European Pharmaceuticals. Sergeant, get a car to take you back to Luigi's and see if they have CCTV. If they have, get hold of the recordings for the days Compton booked. Keep the 'just helping with enquiries' thing going, and don't mention Compton by name.'

Gheeta rose, put her laptop in her shoulder bag and put her hat on. 'I'll add a couple of other dates in the request as well, just in case Giuseppe gets interested enough to have a look himself. We don't know that he isn't part of this caper do we?'

'Yes, good point,' Palmer agreed. 'And whilst you are doing that I'll get a warrant from Bateman to clear us for looking inside the phone and Luigi's booking computer. We don't want any clever lawyer claiming '*inadmissible evidence*' because we didn't get one if this develops into a crime and goes to court at some time. And another warrant to seize the account files of European Pharmaceuticals from the Ministry, I think I'd like a forensic accountant to have a look at those. If you recall the texts between Butwell and Hart, he said she was going to have to get a stop order from Compton. We are assuming that when he didn't hear anymore from Hart he thought it had all been worked out. But what if that wasn't so? What if he or Clive had found out something from the accounts and gone to Compton themselves?'

'Lots of '*ifs*' and '*buts*', guv.'

'I know, but there's a definite thread appearing and I have a feeling *there's something nasty in the woodshed.*'

'*Cold Comfort Farm*,' said Claire. 'Stella Gibbons, one of my favourite books. Gave me nightmares for months.'

She laughed. Palmer laughed too and nodded recognition as he left the office. Truth was he had no idea what Claire was on about, but knew that if he admitted so, ridicule would surely follow. He might not know his major authors, but he knew how to catch serial killers.

CHAPTER 12

'I've had Lucy from the Press and Media Office on my back, Palmer.'

AC Bateman wasn't happy, but then again he never was. 'The press has got hold of a story that we are investigating a drug cartel operating in the Health Service with two murders attributed to it.'

'They have it completely wrong then sir, haven't they?' Palmer smiled. 'As usual.'

'They do, but they need something or they'll publish that scenario, and the next thing will be a call from the Minister to the Commissioner, and she will want to know why we didn't stamp on it.'

Palmer and Assistant Commissioner Bateman tolerated each other. Bateman had wanted for a long time to combine Palmer's Serial Murder Squad, the Organised Crime Unit and the CID together in an effort to cut costs; in fact most of his time was spent in cost-cutting, as ordered by the Home Office, whose political masters seemed so stupid that they couldn't see the rise in crime was fuelled by the cuts in police manpower – obvious to the public, but not to the politicians. And Bateman being a career-motivated, fast tracked university graduate, who had never pounded a beat in his police life, was the sort of 'yes man' who fitted nicely into the political idea of an Assistant Commissioner.

Palmer, on the other hand, with his 'I speak as I find' temperament, was never going to be considered for a management role in the Met. But he was liked by the political elite because he solved crimes: a hundred percent clear up rate on the serial murders since the Squad became his kept him in their good books, and

liked by the media who trusted what he told them, and
this gave him the upper hand when Bateman repeatedly
tried to have him take retirement. No way, what would he
do all day except get in Mrs P.'s way? No, he was
wedded to his job, and there would be no divorce until he
wanted it.

Bateman continued. 'There's a press briefing at
four o'clock that I would like you to handle. Keep it to
'ongoing investigation' and don't mention any names or
Ministerial departments.' He turned his attention to
Palmer's case report he had quickly read before Palmer
arrived. 'It's all a bit inconclusive, Palmer.' AC Bateman
put his elbows on his large desk, steepled his fingers and
rested his chin on his thumbs. 'All circumstantial,
nothing that a good defence lawyer couldn't pull down –
and a company like European Pharmaceuticals will have
the top lawyers on retainers, you can bet on it.'

'I wasn't about to make any arrests sir,' Palmer
explained. 'But the jigsaw of evidence is coming together
slowly, and my next move will be to put pressure on
Compton. He's the link through all this – I don't know
what he's the link to, but whatever it is I don't like it. We
have three innocent people dead sir, and all had one thing
in common: Compton and European Pharmaceuticals,
and the link is provided by the restaurant's booking
programme and Butwell's phone texts. If I don't have the
permissions to look at them, any lawyer can shoot us
down. They are grade one pieces of evidence.'

'All right.' Bateman sat back. 'I don't agree with
the way you've done this, Palmer – the permissions
should have been obtained prior to seizing the properties,
but I agree on their importance. I'll sign the warrants, but

I won't backdate them, so an eagle-eyed lawyer might well pick up on that date discrepancy.'

Arsehole, thought Palmer. But that was the way of modern policing: everything done online or on standard computer templates, with in-built data recording systems that didn't lie about dates and times. He understood why Bateman had to stick to the rules, of course he did, it was self-preservation; but he missed the old days of paper warrants and permissions dated by hand, where you could leave dates blank and arrange your case timeline to suit your evidence and then date it – strictly illegal, but sometimes it was in the public interest to get a nasty piece of work put behind bars than to worry about a date or two.

'I'll take that chance, sir. I think we will have enough direct evidence once we get past Compton and find out what is really going on. Right, I had better check in with Lucy then.' He rose and left the office.

Bateman sat for a moment and then pulled open a desk drawer and took out a blister-card pack of Viagra pills. He looked on the back to see the maker: European Pharmaceuticals.

'No wonder the damn things don't work.' He threw the packet into the waste bin.

Palmer took the press briefing; he always told Lucy he hated doing them, but secretly he quite liked them – he knew most of the crime hacks that attended, and they knew him. They knew his style, and they knew he would give them enough for a story, and that it would hold true. There was an expectant buzz in the room.

He took the podium and signalled for quiet. 'Alright, calm down ladies and gentlemen. I'll give a statement and then take a few – and I mean 'a few' – questions.'

The journalists quietened.

'We have a situation of three bodies that have been taken from the Thames over the last few months – cause of death uncertain, but they all were employed at the Health Ministry in the same department. That's about it.' Brief, and leaving all roads open.

Lucy picked out the journalists to ask questions.

'Three bodies? We were told two,' said a young journalist who looked like he'd only recently got into long trousers.

'Well, if you come to us instead of some little nark who gives you the wrong info for a few quid you'll get it right son, won't you?'

There was a ripple of laughter from the older hacks

'What department at the Ministry?'

'NHS Purchasing'

'Is fraud involved?'

'Possibly, we are awaiting audits of the financials attached to the case.'

'How much money is involved?'

'Impossible to say until after the audit.'

'Why is the Serial Murder Squad involved if the cause of the deaths is uncertain?'

'There is a possibility the deaths were assisted in some way.'

'You mean they might have been murdered?'

'It's a possibility, but that is a possibility with every death isn't it? We won't know until a post mortem is carried out on the last body. The others have been cremated.'

'Are drugs involved?'

'Being the Ministry of Health, I would think there might – and I stress *might* – be drugs involved. The pharmaceutical kind, not the recreational kind.'

'Any arrests imminent?'

'Early days – we are following many leads and arrests are not being planned yet.' How many times had he used that sentence to the press?

Lucy stepped in. 'That's it, thank you. The press office will keep you up to date of any developments. Please remember this is an ongoing enquiry, and at present just that – an enquiry. So have respect for the deceased families – no contact.'

She knew that was a forlorn request, and had placed FLOs with each family to answer the tabloid door-steppers, warn off the paparazzi and take the phone calls – all of which would happen now as sure as night follows day.

CHAPTER 13

'What's that?'

Palmer was stood at the French doors that led from his back lounge into the large garden. He was enjoying a glass of Argentinian Malbec and had noticed something that wasn't there yesterday.

'What's what?' Mrs P. asked from her recumbent position on the sofa, where she was engrossed in a vegetarian cookbook.

'That hoop thing sticking up in Benji's garden.'

She put down the book and joined him. 'It's a basketball hoop.'

A long pole had appeared in the middle of Benji's lawn – the top six feet was visible above the eight-foot hedge that separated their gardens. On top of the pole was a wooden square with a metal hoop bolted on and sitting proud.

'I'd have thought netball was more him.' He flicked a look at Mrs P. expecting a rebuke, but none came. 'It's a bit near his greenhouse isn't it? I hope he's got it well anchored in the ground.'

'You throw the ball up and it comes down through the hoop, you don't throw at it – and in any case the wooden backplate will stop the ball going anywhere.'

'What's the point of it?'

'Good for the arms, the back, and the eye – and muscle movement, co-ordination...'

'Isn't there a pill for that? Be a damn sight easier.' He smiled at Mrs P. who glared back. 'How do you score it?'

'One point for every *hoop* – that is, when the ball falls through the hoop.'

The sound of a puffing Benji and a ball bouncing on his lawn could be heard. They watched as the ball appeared above the hedge on its way to the hoop. It missed the hoop, hit the backplate, and the whole lot slowly tipped backwards out of sight. The smashing of greenhouse glass seemed to last for ever.

Mrs P. held a restraining finger up towards Palmer. 'Not a word, don't say a word.'

'Wasn't going to.' But he couldn't resist. 'Do you get an extra point for that?'

CHAPTER 14

Reginald Compton was most surprised the next morning when the Ministry front of house security office rang through to say that DCS Palmer and one other were in reception asking to see him. He felt himself start to shake a little. What if they had found out about European Pharmaceuticals? What if they were here to arrest him? What if... what if... *what if*? He sent Prior down to collect them.

Compton had always suffered with anxiety and had been on Valium from the doctor for two years – in fact, ever since he got mixed up with Jameson and this damn European Pharmaceuticals scam. He pulled two Diazepam tablets from a blister pack and swallowed them with a swig from his bottled water. Calm down, keep calm, it's all going to pass over – just a normal police procedure that will be finished with and filed away in no time.

He met Palmer and one other at his door and indicated they sit down as Prior left them.

'Mr Compton, this is DS Atkins from our Forensics Unit – he's a Forensic Accountant. Now, at our last meeting you told me that were there any discrepancies on the Pestiment deliveries, then Jeremy Clive would have had to audit the account to ascertain if any refund was due to the NHS, correct?'

Compton shifted uneasily in his chair. 'Yes, yes that is correct. But there were no problems with the deliveries, so he wouldn't have had to audit anything.'

'Well, you see sir, we have uncovered a series of texts between Julie Hart and Mr Clive, via Norman Butwell, in which she is making him aware of her concerns over the quality of the Pestiment product, and asking what steps he would take if her suspicions were found to be true and the quality had been diluted. So, I want DS Atkins here to take a quick look at the Pestiment account to verify nothing out of the ordinary was done.

'It's all straightforward, just another tying up of loose ends – nothing to worry about, sir,' Palmer lied, noticing the glint of sweat on Compton's forehead. 'So, if you would ask for someone from Accounts – I believe they are two floors up – if you would ask for somebody to come and take DS Atkins up and make the relevant files available to him, I would be most grateful.'

'I'll be out of your way in no time, sir,' DS Atkins assured Compton with a smile. 'All I need to do is copy the European Pharmaceuticals and Pestiment account files onto a USB and I can then work on them back in the office.'

Palmer added: 'I have the permission papers here, sir. They allow me access to any computers or paper files I think relevant to the investigation.' He waved a paper at Compton.

Compton's pills had kicked in and he felt confident now. He phoned up to Accounts who sent a junior manager down to accompany DS Atkins up to the floor, with instructions from Compton to allow access to whatever he asked for. Compton then escorted Palmer down to the entrance foyer and they bade each other goodbye. Palmer left with a smile on his face; Compton went back up to his office without one.

Palmer had full confidence in DS Atkins, he had used the Forensic Accountant before on the recommendation of Reg Frome. Atkins had previously worked for Johnson Mathey and KPMG, and despite being one of their 'bright young things' he had become disillusioned with the work practices of those global firms, which, in his opinion, were based on greed, greed, and more greed. Rather than help clients save money, his seniors had instructed him to run up as many hours as he could on the account and book twice as many as he actually worked.

That didn't sit well with Atkins. He didn't look like an accountant is supposed to look: unkempt hair, NHS glasses, and a suit that hung on his slight frame like a loose rag on a pole. But appearances can be deceptive – dodgy financial figures and false accounting were his bread and butter, and had nowhere to hide once his penetrating gaze was turned on them.

CHAPTER 15

'Poor Mr Giuseppe is getting a bit paranoid,' Gheeta laughed as she unslung her laptop and recounted her visit for the CCTV. 'I think he thinks that we have him in the frame for some major crime. Bad news is that the restaurant hasn't got CCTV.'

Palmer was downcast. 'Damn.'

'The good news is that the bank opposite has an ATM outside.'

'An ATM?' Palmer couldn't see the link.

'Automatic Teller Machine,' explained Gheeta.

'I know what an ATM is Sergeant, but how does that help us?'

'ATMs have cameras guv, they show who is using them – it's a small but top of the range lens on the side of the unit, perfectly capable of recording clearly at a distance of up to fifty metres.'

Palmer smiled, 'Which is well over the width of a normal road and would pick up Luigi's entrance?'

'Correct. I had a word with the manager, and she is getting the ATM company to send me the files of the days we wanted to look at – should be with us tomorrow.'

'Well done, Sergeant.' Palmer rubbed his hands together. 'Let's hope we can see Compton with our victims – I know he's in this up to his ears, I just know he is. A couple of pictures of him with them and we can pull him in.'

Claire had been quietly tapping away at her keyboard. She sat back in her chair. 'I'm getting a thread here sir, a thin one but definitely a thread from European

Pharmaceuticals to Compton, other than through his work.'

Gheeta and Palmer took notice.

'Go on,' said Gheeta, sitting next to Claire and following the monitor screen.

'Well, European Pharmaceuticals is a pretty big concern – its headquarters and most of its factories are in Romania. It files its tax returns through Jersey to avoid company taxes, but its directors are filing in the UK so we have their details on the HMRC database, which as you know we have access to.'

Palmer gave Gheeta a questioning look, quite aware that many of the databases she had access to were not generally available unless by a warrant. He preferred not to question their legal availability, or how she had managed to gain entry, as her IT abilities had many times quickened up the solving of a case, and not always by legal means. So he always covered himself by asking the same question.

'Do we have legal access to the HMRC database, Sergeant?' He knew what the answer would be.

Gheeta gave him a shrug, 'I couldn't possibly comment, sir.'

Claire carried on. 'The company board is made up of one Romanian family who own the company, the Bogdan family. They control eighty percent of the shares. The interesting bit is the other twenty percent – they are held by a trust in Jersey, a family trust in the name Jameson, with its two principals being Mihaela Jameson and Horace Jameson.

Palmer squinted his eyes, 'That name rings a bell.'

'Sir Horace Jameson, MP and Chairman of the House of Commons Public Accounts Committee.'

'Well I'll be damned.'

'And his wife, Mihaela Jameson, née Mihaela Bogdan.' Claire sat back with a triumphant smile on her face.

Palmer widened his eyes. 'Now isn't that interesting? As far as I can remember the Public Accounts Committee audits and scrutinises government contracts.'

'They do, 'Claire agreed. 'So should somebody have a problem with a contract or not like how it's being handled, it would be referred to the Public Accounts Committee to take a look at.'

'So if Hart, Clive or Butwell thought there was a problem with European Pharmaceuticals that Compton refused to address, any of them could have pushed it up the line to Jameson's committee?' asked Gheeta.

'They could, and many civil servants have used that route in the past,' said Claire. 'And guess who has precedent in choosing which complaints are looked at by the Committee?'

'Jameson,' Palmer answered, with a touch of malice in his voice. 'Sir Horace Jameson, husband of Mihaela Jameson, née Bogdan, who together own twenty percent of European Pharmaceuticals.'

'Correct.' Claire was pleased with herself. 'Do I get a pat on the back for my diligent work?'

Gheeta laughed. 'This is the Met Police, Claire. The only pat on the back we get is when HR puts an arm round us to tell us the government cuts mean we haven't a job anymore.'

'That's very cynical, Sergeant,' said Palmer. 'But very true as well.'

They all laughed. Gheeta crossed to the progress board and added Jameson and M Bogdan to the growing crime family tree.

'Now we have a pattern emerging, guv.'

'We do indeed,' said Palmer, crossing to stand beside her. 'The one missing link is Compton – what has he got to do with the Bogdans and Jameson, and what is the main reason for three deaths? I can't believe they are the result of a dodgy consignment of Pestiment.'

He turned to Claire. 'Have a word with the NCB (National Central Bureau, each Interpol member country has one – they liaise on cross border crime) and ask them to send a request to the Romanian NCB for any details on this Bogdan family, or on European Pharmaceuticals – they may have some useful information. There has to be a good reason for murdering three people.''

'Money, sex and drugs, said Gheeta.

'What?'

'The three main reasons for murder, guv: money, sex, and drugs.'

Palmer laughed. 'Well, we've got the drug, Pestiment, but we haven't got the money and sex yet.'

CHAPTER 16

The money showed its hand the next morning when DS Atkins gave them his findings in the Team Room.

'A simple scam, really: the original price negotiated by NICE for the Pestiment drug was hiked up to twice that, without any new contract or so much as a reason for doing it. The new priced invoices were rubber stamped for payment by Compton – totally against the NICE protocols, but nobody seems to have noticed.'

'I bet Clive did, being the auditor of that account – and then he told Butwell and they told Compton, and he did what, nothing?'

'No,' said Gheeta. 'He must have told Jameson about it and probably took a backhander to keep quiet.'

'I don't think he told Jameson officially, sir, 'said Claire. 'Compton didn't refer it up to the Committee using the proper paperwork channel. There's nothing in their files referring to European Pharmaceuticals at all, no mention of them.' She shook her head.

'You bet there isn't.' Palmer was seeing a pattern emerging. 'Not with Jameson's involvement with the Bogdans and a twenty per cent share in the company. So Clive and Butwell would have questioned why nothing was being done, and at that point, and with Julie Hart on the warpath over quality issues as well, somebody decided it was time to silence them. Our man Compton has to be involved, or the issues with Pestiment would have gone up the chain in the correct way.'

The Team Room door opened and Reg Frome came in.

'Good morning all – ah, I see DS Atkins has beaten me in.' He addressed Atkins. 'Have you brought them up to speed?'

'Just on my findings, sir.'

'Okay, good. Right.' He sat on the edge of one of the trestle tables. 'Justin, I don't want to upset your investigation or get in the way, but what I'd like to do is put a team of Forensic Accountants into the Ministry NHS Accounts department and concentrate them on the European Pharmaceuticals accounts.'

Palmer had known Frome since their early Hendon College days, and having worked on quite a few cases with him knew there was a good reason for this action.

'Okay, explain.'

Frome nodded to Atkins, who gave the reason.

'European Pharmaceuticals provide seventeen drugs to the NHS – some are one-offs, ordered when needed, and some are automatic repeat orders, triggered when stocks reach a certain low point; and some are longer courses of treatment that cost thousands of pounds for each course. They were paid nine and a half million last year.'

Palmer, Gheeta and Claire were astonished.

'Nine and a half million?' Gheeta wanted confirmation she had heard right.

'Yes, nine and a half million.'

'Pounds?' Palmer was also amazed.

Frome nodded. 'Correct. So considering the amount, you can understand why I would like to check those drug accounts. Atkins has pulled out the Pestiment figures, and they alone account for two hundred thousand pounds of extra payment made since the price hike – the unauthorised price hike.'

'This is the old insurance company scam, isn't it.' Palmer had sussed it out. 'European Pharmaceuticals tender at an unbeatable low price, get the account, and then hike it up on the renewal date. Only this lot didn't wait for the renewal date, they hiked it as soon as they could – with the help of Compton and Jameson who blocked any whistleblowing.'

'And they also cut the quality to save costs and make even more. They had it both ways,' said Gheeta. 'Time to pull in Compton?'

Palmer thought for a few moments. 'No, hang on until we get the ATM CDs, and if they show Compton at Luigi's with our victims on the days they disappeared, then we can go and get him.'

'Those should be with us in the next hour, guv,' said Gheeta, checking her watch.

'Good.' Palmer turned to Frome. 'So, if you could hang on until we get that and pull in Compton I'd be obliged. If he's in as deep as we think he is, and your lads storm the accounts department, he could run.'

Frome acquiesced. 'No problem, Justin. Give us a call when it's clear to go. I've already got Bateman pulling a warrant for it.'

Palmer's face sank into gloom. 'Oh no, that means I'll have him ringing down for an update on the case, and have him peering over our shoulder from now on.'

CHAPTER 17

Horace Jameson MP was getting decidedly nervy. He didn't like that feeling – he wasn't used to it. Horace Jameson was used to being top dog, calling the shots, getting his own way; he had schemed and cajoled his way to his current prominent political position, and wasn't about to relinquish it because Compton was beginning to fold.

He was in Compton's office at the Ministry, taking stock of the information Compton had told him about a Forensic Accountant from the Met who had been allowed to look at the Pestiment files in the Accounts department's computers.

'Did he have a warrant?'

Compton didn't answer, just nodded.

'Did he take the computers away?'

'No, he was here all day.'

'Probably copied all the information he needed onto a disc or USB.'

'How do we cover our tracks?' Compton wasn't asking, he was pleading, visibly shaking. 'This could put us in jail for life.'

Jameson had no intention of going to jail for life, or any time at all. He had already worked out in his mind that Compton would be the one to take the fall if everything fell apart. He'd wiped all email communication between the two and changed his mobile number. Bogdan had been kept up to speed, and a plan had been hatched. The trail would end at Compton's door. The holiday villa, the expensive house and cars, the cruises – how could a middle management civil servant like Compton afford all those? He couldn't, unless he was on the fiddle – and a very large fiddle at that. The paperwork all ended with Compton, he had never sent a request to Jameson or the Public Accounts Committee to take a look at European Pharmaceuticals. All their conversations were just that, conversations – nothing written down, no emails, so if the police were following a paper trail it led to, and ended at, Compton.

But the worrying part was Compton's behaviour – he had already threatened to *'take you down with me'*. There was only one answer: Compton had to be shut up, and then a few pointers placed for the police to find that would put him firmly in the top spot as the organiser of the scam. There would be consequences, of course. European Pharmaceuticals would be implicated, as the money for Compton's lifestyle had to have come from them. He had spoken to Alexandru, and the Bogdans weren't worried. They had positioned themselves personally away from the actual payments, so a fall guy in the company's UK office would take the flack and be dismissed; the company would apologise profusely, negotiate a reimbursement to the NHS, and carry on quietly until it all died down, and then find another fall guy. Jameson didn't think the Ministry – and especially the Health Minister – would want the affair in the public domain. Incompetence of this nature where taxpayer money was involved was like manna from Heaven to the tabloid press. He stood and buttoned his overcoat.

'Okay then, we had better get a plan going. Can you be at Luigi's about six o'clock? I'll get Alexandru along and we can work something out.'

'I'll be there.'

CHAPTER 18

Assistant Commissioner Bateman read the report from Palmer as Palmer sat silently across the desk from him the next morning. He took a deep breath and put the paper down.

'I don't think I have ever come across a case with so much circumstantial evidence as this has.'

'There's a lot of it, sir, yes.' Palmer agreed.

'But all circumstantial, no factual or physical, you won't get a conviction on this evidence – I doubt whether the CPS (Crown Prosecution Service) will prosecute on this.'

'Stomach contents are physical, sir.'

'True… So how do you want to proceed, bearing in mind the status of Sir Horace Jameson?'

'Why should I worry about that, sir? Criminals come in all shapes, sizes and backgrounds. You only have to remember the MPs' expenses fiddles to know that – half of them would have gone inside if it wasn't for their buddies in the judiciary. Some poor bugger nicks a few clothes for his kids from a shop and gets a police record and community service, while Sir Blah-de-blah from Eton and Cambridge and member of the old boys' network steals twenty grand on false expenses, gets caught, pays some back, and that's it. No sir, I don't care much for the elite classes who think they can roll over the law as they please.'

AC Bateman was quite aware of Palmer's views on social class, the Royal Family, politicians, and businessmen who make their money in the UK paying staff minimum wage and live in a tax haven with their millions. He had heard it all before, and whilst he agreed with some of the points and secretly harboured a respect for Palmer in voicing them, he was pretty sure that had Palmer kept them a little more to himself, he could quite possibly be sitting in Bateman's chair, or an even one higher – a point that Mrs P. had often made to Palmer after he had had one of his *'have and have nots'* rants. Bateman asked the question again.

'So how do you want to proceed?'

'Well, depends on the result DS Singh gets from the ATM camera. If they show Compton going into the Italian restaurant with the three deceased on the days they died, then that, with the restaurant's bookings file showing he was there that day, is enough to pull him in for questioning on an arrest warrant. With that evidence Compton can't deny he was in the restaurant, can't deny he was with Hart, Clive and Butwell on the day they died, and if he does we have his Visa receipts for the meals they ate.'

'Okay, I agree with that. What about Jameson?'

'I'm hoping Compton will crack and spill the beans, he seems a pretty soft customer – got the shakes and sweats when we were just *talking* about Pestiment. If he doesn't then we have several avenues of attack to use on Jameson: he's married into the Bogdans, and together with his wife they have a twenty percent share in European Pharmaceuticals – which, by the way, he hasn't entered in the Parliamentary Record of Interests. But the main thing is for us to find out how and where the victims were killed, by who, and who knew. I would like to put tails on Jameson and the Bogdans once I get Compton in the cells – I think they'll panic a little, thinking that Compton will crack with three murder charges levelled at him and point a finger at them. They might try to scarper back to Romania – if they do that, we've lost them for good.'

'Romania's an EU country, we can extradite.'

'Romania is about the most corrupt and lawless country in the EU, sir. We can't even extradite to Romania because their prison cells are under the required size in EU law, so we have to house them here – seven hundred of them, costing the British tax payer millions each year. If the Bogdans get back there, money talks and we will never get them back here for a trial. I don't intend to let them have the chance to run. I've asked NCB to request any details on the Bogdans from their Romanian colleagues, so we will have to see if that throws up anything further.'

Bateman could see a future scenario where the Bogdans fled and the tabloids blamed the police for not putting enough manpower on the case. That buck stopped at his desk.

'How many officers do you need for the tails?'

'Just four.'

Bateman nodded, 'Okay. I know you have your preferred chaps, so as long as their superiors agree go ahead.'

'Thank you, sir.'

Palmer's squad basically consisted of himself, DS Singh, and Claire. Claire being a civilian could not be used on outside work, and so, when the need arose, Palmer had a list of tried and tested officers he had used on cases before that he called on. DS Singh would make the calls to find out which ones were available – that meant on leave, or catching up on days off they were owed. She never had much trouble in pulling in the required number – the detectives liked Palmer, he called a spade a spade, didn't suffer fools, and had a hundred per cent case solve rate. But most of all, he was a copper's copper – he didn't pull rank and if they had to make a split second decision he would back their choice to the hilt, even if he secretly thought they'd made the wrong one.

'One more thing,' Bateman added as Palmer rose to leave. 'Don't touch Jameson until you are one hundred per cent sure of a conviction. Interview him as a witness by all means, but not as a suspect under caution until you've a copper-bottomed case, understand?'

'Yes sir, understood.'

CHAPTER 19

'All present and correct.' Gheeta smiled at Palmer as he walked back into the Team Room. 'All three victims appear on the ATM CCTV files on the days Forensics estimate their deaths occurred, and all in the company of guess who?'

'Compton.' Palmer didn't need to guess – he would have put money on it.

'Correct, all go into Luigi's and after about thirty minutes they leave and a taxi picks them up outside. They don't hail it and there is another person inside it already, but I can't make him or her out. I've had it enhanced but still can't see who it is.'

'So in all three cases the last sighting of our victims is with Compton, leaving the restaurant and getting into a taxi?'

'Correct. Can I pull him in now, guv?'

'Yes, I think so – that's pretty conclusive, isn't it? Get an arrest warrant and bring him in as a suspect in three murders, that should loosen his tongue. If we can get a number plate for one of the taxis we can check their call roster and find out where they picked up the mystery person, and probably who he or she is and where they were dropped off.'

'Tried that, guv – can't get a clear shot of any of the plates. All sideways on.'

'Shame.'

He wasn't there. Compton wasn't at work at the Ministry, he hadn't signed in with his pass card that morning. Gheeta and the two uniformed officers she had taken with her checked his office – unopened internal mail sat in his in tray, nothing in the out tray. She felt the coffee machine – stone cold, the cups sparkling clean and unused.

Enquiries with his deputy Prior and in the main staff offices confirmed he had not been seen that day or phoned in sick. She checked his day diary: no appointments listed, so he wasn't working elsewhere.

She called Palmer with the news.

' Hmm...' He thought for a second or two. 'Okay. Could be nothing in it, or he could have gone on the trot.'

'On the *trot*, guv?'

'Done a runner, Sergeant, gone AWOL – old Cockney phrase. Don't suppose they use that kind of language around the Barbican executive apartment blocks like what where you lives in these days. The East End ain't what it used t' be.' He mimicked a Cockney accent, badly.

'Don't s'pose they use it much in the blingy toffs' suburbs of Dulwich Village like what where you lives in either, guv,' she replied in an equally bad Cockney accent.

Palmer smiled to himself. He enjoyed their occasional social-based banter. 'Okay, meet me at Compton's house. I'll get a squad car. Have you got the address?'

'Yes, it's on my laptop – Bromley somewhere, I think. Be about an hour from here with the blues on.'

'Okay, whoever gets there first park up a little distance away and wait for the other to arrive. Keep the uniform chaps with you.'

CHAPTER 20

Olive Compton opened the front door of the Comptons' detached 1930s house in a quiet back street of Bromley before Palmer and Singh had made it up the gravel drive to the large porch. She looked worried.

'You've found him, haven't you.' It was a statement, not a question. 'What's happened – where is he? Oh my God, he's had an accident hasn't he?'

Palmer realised they had dropped onto something not quite right in the Compton household. What it was he did not know, so safety first then.

'Perhaps we might go inside, Mrs Compton. I take it you are Mrs Compton?'

'Yes, yes of course.' She led them into a spacious hall and then into a spacious lounge, expensively furnished. 'Sit down, please,' she said, pointing at an obviously expensive button back leather sofa and armchairs. Palmer took a chair as Gheeta took the sofa and unpacked her laptop. Both had noticed a large framed photo on an antique burr walnut coffee table; it showed the Comptons and the Jamesons obviously enjoying each other's company and an al fresco meal on a balcony in a foreign country, with the blue sea as a backdrop behind them. Mrs Compton stood and darted her eyes between the two of them.

Palmer spoke. 'Mrs Compton, I'm Detective Chief Superintendent Palmer and this is Detective Sergeant Singh. We came here to have a chat with your husband, but by your words and action I take it something else has happened?'

'You don't know, do you?' she said.

'We don't know what, Mrs Compton?'

'He's missing, he didn't come home last night. His mobile is off. Something's happened – he's not like that, it's so out of character. I thought you might have news.'

'I'm afraid not. I take it you have reported him missing to the local police?'

'Yes, yes,' she fidgeted nervously. 'They didn't seem too worried.'

'Well, people do sometimes stray off their normal routine. I'm sure he will turn up soon with some normal explanation.'

Gheeta wasn't so sure; with three bodies so far it seemed to her a fourth could quite soon join them – either that or Compton had felt the heat mounting on him from Palmer and run. She quickly tapped a message on her laptop to Claire telling her to put out a *stop and hold* notice to the Border Force and airport departure terminals on Compton.

'Has he done this before?' Palmer made conversation, unsure of what tack to take.

'No, no, never. He's always phoned me, even when he's only going to be a little late. We are people of routine, Superintendent.' She smiled self-consciously, ' Boring I know, but there it is.'

'*Chief* Superintendent,' Palmer corrected her, as Gheeta knew he would. Palmer insisted that after working in the Met for forty-five years to get to that rank, people would damn well use it. 'Do you know of anything bothering your husband of late?'

'Bothering him?'

'Well, he does have a responsible position at the Ministry – could be stress?'

'No, no,' she laughed. 'Reginald is a supreme delegator.' A thought struck her. 'If you didn't come here about my call reporting him missing, what did you come here for? You said you wanted to talk to him – what about?' She looked worried.

Palmer gave her his killer smile, the one Mrs P. says could have turned the Krays into lovable babysitters. 'Just a few questions about one of the pharmaceutical companies the Ministry uses. We think he may be able to *help us with our enquiries*, as the phrase goes.'

'Oh, I'm sure he could. He prides himself on knowing everything about everything in that Ministry. It's his life, you know – been there since leaving university.'

Palmer rose – there wasn't any point in continuing the conversation. 'Well, let's hope he turns up soon. I'm sure you're worrying about nothing, Mrs Compton.'

He and Gheeta said their goodbyes and left.

'She's bloody good, isn't she?' Palmer said to Gheeta as they walked down the drive to the squad car.

'Glad you noticed, guv. I didn't believe one bit of the *worried wife* bit either.'

'I think we need to keep an eye on her. Did you notice the photo on the coffee table?'

'Oh yes, pride of place I'd say – make a lovely quartet, don't they? I sent a note to Claire to put a stop notice out and she is phoning round to get four officers into the team for surveillance. They'll be with us in the morning.'

'Good. I think we have to start surveillance on Mrs Compton and the Bogdans – the pace is hotting up. I think we ought to have Claire dig a bit into the Comptons, they seem to be living well beyond their means.' He directed Gheeta's gaze to the new Range Rover and BMW parked in the drive. 'One for him and one for the wife, over a hundred grand there.'

'They could be on personal lease, guv. Most of the brand new cars on the road these days are.'

'Could be, but that's still a grand a month.'

Back in the Compton house, Olive Compton watched the two detectives walk away as she speed-dialled on her mobile.

CHAPTER 21

'Oh I see we got the A Team!' Palmer said jovially as he walked into the Team Room the next morning and saw the four extra men that Bateman had sanctioned. He knew all four from old; they had all been with him on previous cases where extra bodies had been called for.

Detective Sergeants Harvard, Patel, Trent and Russell stood up as he entered.

'Sit down lads, sit down.'

Gheeta smiled to herself; she knew how Palmer hated all this rank deference in the force, how it was protocol to call his rank *boss, guv,* or *ma'am*, those above as *sir* or *ma'am*, sergeants as *sarge*, and constables by their surnames or nicknames. He would never use officer's first names, but usually just their surnames.

'Has Singh brought you up to date on the case?' He asked more of Gheeta than them as he removed his Crombie and slung it over a chair.

'I have guv, and Claire needs to bring you up to date on developments.'

Palmer stopped midway through removing his trilby and looked at Claire. She smiled a self-satisfied smile.

'You don't call me JCB for nothing, sir.'

It was Palmer's nickname for Claire, because she would dig and dig on the internet once she had the scent of something until it surfaced.

She carried on. 'Olive Compton, husband of Reginald Compton...' She paused for effect. 'Sister of Horace Jameson.'

Palmer couldn't believe it. 'Are you kidding? His sister?'

'I've got the birth certificates and the wedding certificates – absolutely cast iron solid, no doubts. Also, looking at Mrs Compton's social media posts on Facebook, they have a nice holiday villa in Cyprus. I checked with the Cypriot equivalent of our Land Registry and confirmed it's theirs – bought for two hundred and sixty grand a year ago, fully paid for, no mortgage or loan attached to it. Look.'

She passed a computer printout of the villa to Palmer who finished taking off his trilby, put it on the table with his Crombie and sat down with the picture.

'Very nice, very nice indeed, the money for that didn't come from Compton's salary, no way. Anything on his whereabouts overnight?'

Claire shook her head. 'No, 'fraid not. He hasn't attempted to leave the country, at least not by any legal route.'

'Right, I would think that he is in a state of panic by now. He obviously knows we are looking for him, so he would probably go to his cohorts to try and find a way out of the mess. So, Patel and Trent, you two catch up with Mr Bogdan and keep tabs on him – Claire has his address. Harvard and Russell, do the same with Jameson – he spends a lot of his time in the Commons, so we will need clearances for you both.'

He looked at Gheeta and raised his eyebrows.

Gheeta nodded. 'Okay, that's SO17 – part of the Diplomatic Protection Group, they cover the Commons. I'll give them a call.'

Palmer looked at the officers and spread his hands. 'She is a mine of information.'

Gheeta smiled. 'I'll get a P2P radio frequency for us from comms as well.' She opened a storage cupboard beneath the computer desks and pulled out six handheld radios.

'A what?' Palmer asked.

'A P2P radio frequency guv, Peer to Peer, one allocated only to us and nobody else as long as we want it. As soon as I have it I'll program our radios with it and we will have our own little network.'

Palmer was impressed, 'How long will that take to come through?'

'About thirty minutes, guv. Comms has unlimited access to frequencies on the Met's waveband. But remember,' she addressed the officers, 'all calls are recorded in comms' databases, so normal radio protocols exist.'

Palmer didn't need to explain that to these experienced detectives but he did, just in case. 'In other words, mind your language and don't say anything that a brief can use later to get a prosecution thrown out of court.' Some officers who had volunteered to help Palmer's cases in the past hadn't been invited back when the need arose, but these four had, more than once. 'Right then,' Palmer stood and rubbed his hands. 'Off you go, gentlemen. Keep Claire up to date with what's happening and let's see if we can't find Mr Compton, if he's still around. I would think that Jameson and the Bogdans would like to get to him before we do, so hopefully one of them will lead us to him.'

CHAPTER 22

'So what are you going to do then?' Compton sat in Jameson's Commons Office, flicking his gaze from Jameson to Bogdan, hoping for an answer. 'What, eh? Palmer's been to my office and now my house.'

'Well…' Jameson sat back in his chair and tapped his fingers on his desk in thought mode. 'Pretty obviously the police are after you. The three deaths circumstantially lead back to you...'

Compton interrupted. 'Circumstantially yes, but no actual proof that I killed anybody – and I didn't, did I?' He looked at Bogdan. 'You did.'

Bogdan feigned surprise. 'Me? Can you prove that? I have no recorded contact with you that can be traced. No emails, no paperwork.'

'No, but they know that Pestiment was used in the fraud, they know that. And that is your company's product.'

Bogdan laughed. 'Fraud? What fraud? Maybe a mistake was made at the factory with the ingredients? No, no fraud.'

'And the price increases that never went before the finance procurement committee?' Compton looked at Jameson. 'That's you implicated.'

Jameson shook his head. 'Why? If I never had the paperwork from you, how could I process it?'

'You did have the paperwork. I sent it through. You told me to send it.'

'I never got it. There's no mention of it or indication of its receipt in the committee's paperwork records. Nothing.'

Compton took a deep breath, realising he'd been played all along. 'You've set me up from the start, haven't you? Right from the start.'

Jameson gave a cynical smile. 'The start? The start of what? I don't have the faintest idea what you are talking about.'

'Or me,' added Bogdan.

Compton was annoyed – annoyed at himself for getting into such a vulnerable position. But more than annoyed he was scared – very scared; well out of his comfort zone and looking at three murder charges.

'I'll tell them everything. I'm not a killer, you two are. I never would have come into your scam if I'd known it would end like this. I'm going to see Palmer.' He stood to leave.

'You know what will happen if you do.' Jameson's tone was stone cold. 'They'll not find a shred of evidence to support your claims, but they will find your half a million pound Cyprus holiday home, paid for from your Swiss bank account, and then they might wonder how a middle management civil servant can pay for such a place. And then, when they convict you, they will seize it under the Proceeds of Crime Act, and they will take a look at the Swiss bank account and seize that too.'

'Fraud,' Compton spat the word out. 'That's just fraud, not murder, I'll take that. Probably get a few years in jail, whilst you two, you'll both get life. The police will piece together where the money came from, they'll put two and two together and see why three of my staff were killed. I'll tell them why they were killed – they were killed to keep you two in the luxury lifestyle you enjoy, that's why, and I was stupid enough to play along.'

He turned and left the room, slamming the door behind him.

Jameson looked at Bogdan. 'Well?'

'I'll handle it.' Bogdan rose and left the room, pulling his mobile from his pocket.

In the foyer of the House of Commons, Compton handed his pass into the desk and they marked him as 'left'. Behind him Bogdan did the same, keeping out of Compton's sight. He followed him out into the street and down Millbank. Compton turned into Great Peter Street, his mind being in such turmoil he was unaware of Bogdan following him at a discreet distance talking into his mobile phone. He turned into Lord North Street, heading for Smith Square and his solicitor's office. He had decided to take legal advice, admit everything to his solicitor under client privilege and see what his advice would be.

So engrossed in his thoughts was he that when the black Transit pulled up twenty yards in front of him and two men slid open the side door, he walked straight towards them. In a matter of a split second he was seized and bundled inside the Transit, the door slid shut and the vehicle moved away. Nobody had seen or heard anything except for Bogdan, who turned off his phone and put it back into his pocket as the Transit circled the square and returned to pick him up in the passenger seat.

CHAPTER 23

Olive Compton looked across the desk in Horace Jameson's Parliament office. She was angry. Jameson was adamant.

'I really don't know where Reginald is, Olive. I really do not.'

'Oh yes you do, you damn well know. You and your get rich quick scheme – you persuaded him to get involved, you've been working him like a puppet. You think he didn't tell me what was going on, eh? You think I don't know all about the price hikes, the Pestiment fraud, and the ones that came before? Where is he, Horace? Where have you taken him? The police came round, you know, they know all about it – of course they do, why else would they want to talk to him? Did he tell you they had an accountant in the Ministry going through the files for European Pharmaceuticals? '

'I really don't know what you are talking about, Olive.'

'That won't wash, Horace. You always were the sneaky one of the family. Do you think I believed Reginald when he said the thousands of pounds that appeared in his bank account were productivity bonuses? Of course I didn't – middle management in the civil service don't get tens of thousands of pounds in bonuses every three months. Middle management in the civil service don't need a Swiss bank account to hide money.

'No, he was trapped. He told me how you had trapped him into the scam in Romania and there was no way out. I told him it would end in tears, but somehow you had a hold over him, didn't you? Now the roof has fallen in and he's prime suspect. He would have come to you, I know he would. You do know where he is. Where is he, Horace?'

'Olive, if Reginald had a fraud going at the Ministry I can assure you I know nothing about it. We very rarely spoke about work.'

Olive Compton stared coldly at her brother. 'Perhaps you didn't hear me right, Horace. I said Reginald told me all about it. I know what was going on.' She stood, and putting both hands on the desk leant forward towards Jameson. 'If he's not home by nine tonight, I talk to Palmer. Understand? Nine.' And with that she left Jameson's office and made her way out of the Palace of Westminster.

Jameson dialled on his mobile. A terse 'Yes' was the answer from the other end.

'She's just leaving me.'

'Okay, we are just about finished here.'

He clicked the phone off, let out a long breath, and sat back into his chair deep in thought.

CHAPTER 24

In the Team Room Palmer and Gheeta were arranging photos of the victims and players with timelines on the white progress board on the far wall when the radio buzzed into action.

'Russell to base.'

Palmer and Singh turned towards it as Claire picked it up and answered. 'Go ahead Russell.'

'I'm at the public entrance to the House of Commons in case Jameson leaves this way, but Mrs Compton has just come out. Do I follow her? Harvard is watching the MPs' entrance for Jameson.'

'Hang on Russell, the boss is here.' She handed the radio to Palmer.

'Russell, it's Palmer here. Yes, you tail her and leave Harvard to watch for Jameson. Harvard, did you get that?'

'Yes, understood, Harvard.'

'Good man. And Russell, are you okay with that? Tail her.'

'Will do, Russell, over and out.'

The radio went dead. Palmer sat down.

'So she probably went to visit brother Horace then – we need to confirm that. Claire, give Commons reception a bell and confirm her visit, time in and time out. Don't mention Jameson, they'll probably tell you that with a bit of luck.'

Gheeta could already see an Olive Compton excuse for the visit. 'He is her brother, guv. If questioned she'd just say it was a normal family business visit whilst she was in town shopping.'

'I know, but it might all tie in with a timeline at some point.'

As Olive Compton's car turned into her quiet Bromley road, the black Transit had already left the Compton's drive and passed her going the other way. Then it passed Russell in a plain squad car two hundred yards behind her, before turning out onto the main London road.

CHAPTER 25

Olive Compton's screams could be heard all over
Bromley as they pierced the quiet suburban air. DS
Harvard was out of his car and sprinting towards the
Compton house in seconds. In the drive, Olive Compton
was standing transfixed in front of the automatic garage
door which had finished its journey to the top of its
runners and displayed the inside of the garage, where
Reginald Compton hung at the end of a rope tied to a
steel cross member, his dead eyes staring into nothing.

Harvard ran past the screaming figure of Mrs
Compton who was rooted to the spot in shock. He righted
the wooden garden chair that lay on its side beneath the
slightly swaying body, which would seem to be the way
Compton had planned his death, and standing on it
grabbed him round the thighs, lifting the body to ease the
noose. Other neighbours were arriving and also seemed
shocked into statues at the garage door.

Harvard shouted at the nearest man who had
obviously been gardening and held a pair of shears.
'Bring those over here and cut this rope!'

The man was not hearing. The sight of a body
hanging with a noose around its neck would shock
anybody into a static state.

'NOW!' yelled Harvard. Compton was heavy.
'Here, NOW! Cut the fucking rope NOW!!''

The ferocity of Harvard's command pulled the
man from his trance state and he quickly joined Harvard
on the chair and set about cutting the rope. The rope was
tough, the man was not, and he was shaking which
complicated things.

'Here, you hold him. I'll take those.' Harvard took the shears and the man grabbed Compton's legs. Half a dozen hard hacks at the rope and it parted. The released weight of Compton's body was too much for the man and he and the body tumbled to the floor, bringing Harvard down with them as the chair fell sideways. He knelt on the hard concrete floor and could see people around Mrs Compton who was now also her knees, hands over her face, sobbing loudly. 'Somebody call an ambulance,' Harvard shouted at them as he loosened the noose round Compton's neck and began CPR.

The road was blocked off fifty metres each way from the Compton's house. Police vehicles blocked it and officers turned people away unless they were neighbours of the Comptons, and if so they were listed for visiting later for a statement. An ambulance and forensic vehicle were parked by the drive. Palmer and Singh left the squad car that had brought them with its blues on and siren wailing after Harvard had called in the events, and they hurried to the garage where Compton's body had been covered with a blanket and a crime scene canopy closed off the garage to all but white paper-suited Forensics personnel. Palmer would have preferred to have seen Reg Frome and his team on site, but since Forensics had been outsourced by the Home Office in a cost-cutting exercise, the local force SIO (Senior Investigating Officer) had control of who attended and he was not aware of Compton's link to the other deaths so had no reason to call in Frome's Murder Squad Forensic officers. Palmer had the authority to call in Frome to oversee it, but seeing as this wasn't another drowning he decided to let the local team complete their examination.

Harvard joined them at the garage door and introduced the SIO, who was quite prepared to let Palmer take charge when he was brought up to speed on the case. But Palmer could see no benefit in that as everything seemed to be in order and progressing by the book. The SIO was basically the equivalent of the foreman on a building site; he kept control and saw the project through.

'You alright, Harvard? Bit of a shock this.' Palmer was genuinely concerned. He had been forced to attend senior officers' conferences on counselling for officers who had experienced such scenes.

'I'm fine, sir. Not my first dead body by a long way.'

'First one you've had to cut down though I bet.'

'Yes, that wasn't very pleasant. But the adrenalin bangs in and you go on autopilot.'

'Okay, but you know the rules – you'll have to endure half an hour with a counsellor within fourteen days, I'm afraid. Take me through the timescale.'

'Well, I followed Mrs Compton from the Commons to the NCP car park in Victoria Street and when she went in there I realised she would probably be going home. I radioed DS Russell to bring our car from the underground car park at the Commons and he pulled up just as she drove out of the car park, so I took over the motor and followed her whilst he walked back to keep an eye on Jameson. She came directly here, no stopping anywhere on the way – straight here. I parked up a little down the road as she turned into her drive, and next thing she's screaming her head off.'

'So we assume she got out of her car, pressed the garage door button and up it went, revealing hubby dancing on air.'

'It's a key lock, not a button,' said Gheeta, pointing at it. 'So we must assume he had the key, let himself in, closed it from the inside and set himself up for the jump. Takes some guts.'

Harvard agreed, 'His mind must have been in a real state.'

'Guilt can do that to a person,' said Palmer. 'If he'd been instrumental in the deaths of three of his staff and knew we'd got him in the frame, what could he do? He knew he'd be going down for life. Probably couldn't take the stigma and loss of respect, so this was an easy way out.'

Behind them a black morgue van pulled up and the occupants got out and slid a trolley coffin from the back which they wheeled towards the garage.

'They'll have to wait until Forensics have finished before the body is released,' commented Palmer. 'Where's Mrs Compton, have they whisked her off to hospital?'

'She's inside, sir. The ambulance chaps gave her a sedative, and as luck would have it her sister-in-law arrived as she was arguing against being taken to the hospital, and the sister-in-law offered to stay with her at home. The doctor authorised it, thought she'd be better that way as long as she had company to keep an eye on her.'

'Well, that's handy – at least we know where Mrs Jameson née Mihaela Bogdan is for tonight, so we have two suspects in the same place.'

'You've raised Mrs Compton to *suspect* level, guv?'

'I think so, I can't see how she couldn't be in on the scam with all this money around – the two cars, the big house, the Mediterranean holiday home. She's got to be in on it.'

'We will need a statement from Mrs Compton sometime, guv,' Gheeta pointed out. 'So that could be a good time to put some pressure on her.'

Palmer nodded. 'Better give her a day or so to calm down before we do that. Right then, nothing we can do here, Harvard, it might pay you to ask the medics for something to keep handy in case you get delayed shock – can't have you going all wobbly on us.' He gave Harvard a smile and a pat on the back. 'Good work son, well done. Not the easiest of scenes to stumble on but you handled it well. Good work.'

Gheeta feigned shock. 'Blimey Harvard, I think you might just have had some praise off Detective Chief Superintendent Palmer. I'd make a note in your diary if I was you – that only happens once in a decade.'

'Praise when praise is due, Sergeant,' said Palmer.

'I can't recall you ever praising me, guv,' Gheeta said accusingly with a glint in her eye.

'Well as I said, sergeant – praise when praise is due.' He gave Harvard a wink.

Gheeta smiled defeat. 'Touché.'

'Right then,' said Palmer. 'Nothing we can do here so we might as well call it a day. I've got Mrs P.'s steak and kidney pie waiting at home, and some things in life are too good to miss!'

CHAPTER 26

Olive Compton blinked to clear her fuzzy sight as she came out of the sedative's clutches. Somebody was sitting on the bed beside her. The day's events hit back into her memory and she raised her head, panting. Her hand was held by another.

'Olive, it's Mihaela. Lay back Olive, it's all right. You are at home, stay calm.'

The disjointed reminiscences of the day slipped into place in her brain. The garage, the body, then... then what? The meeting with Horace raced to the front of her mind – Horace, the brother she despised, the brother who had snared Reggie, and now his wife was next to her. She pulled her hand from Mihaela's as her vision cleared as quickly as her brain.

'You murdered Reggie, you and Horace – the pair of you, and that criminal brother of yours. You bastards, you killed him!' She spat the words out, her face creased with anger and hate. 'You pushed him too far and then killed him. Get out of my house!'

She made to get out of the bed, but Mihaela pushed her back down and held her there, their faces an inch apart.

'Listen to me, Olive.' The voice was cold and uncaring. 'And listen well. Everything you have got – the money, the villa, the house, the cars – it all came from Horace and Alexandru. Reggie knew what he was getting into, and went into it eyes wide open. He had no need to turn on us and threaten to go to the police, no need at all – we had it under control. He brought this on himself. Now, calm, down and carry on as the grieving wife, and it will all pass over. Make a fuss, and you'll lose everything. You want that? No house, no money, no villa, you want that? Just do as Horace says and it will be okay.' She relaxed her grip and sat back up. 'Understand?'

Olive gave a cold smile. 'Oh yes, I understand only too well. You think that if I keep quiet you can go on making your millions whilst I lie to the police and wrestle with my conscience for the rest of my life, after burying a murdered husband without taking revenge. Think again, you little shit. I don't care about you or Horace, or your scheme. Now get out of my house, I have an important phone call to make.'

She pulled herself up into a sitting position and turned to the phone on the bedside table. But as she reached for it a hand clutched round her neck and pulled her back down onto the bed.

Olive Compton struggled – she struggled like she had never struggled before, her arms and legs flailing at Mihaela; but in the end Mihaela's younger strength won, and the pillow she held down with force over Olive's face had its intended result, and Olive's body went limp.

Mihaela Jameson arranged Olive Compton to look to be in a sleeping position on her side to anybody checking from the bedroom door, then she made a call on her mobile and left the house, nodding to the uniformed officer at the gate.

'She's taken a sleeping pill. I'll be back before she wakes in the morning.'

CHAPTER 27

'I don't take sugar.' Palmer looked questioningly at Mrs P. as she shook a spoon of white powder over his bran flakes and walnut halves, which was his regular breakfast. 'You made me give up sugar five years ago. What's all this about? Don't tell me Benji says it's good for you so we are back on it?'

'It's not sugar, it's inulin powder. And I'm surprised you want any breakfast at all after three helpings of steak and kidney pie last night'

'That's for diabetics – I'm not diabetic.'

'That's insulin, this is inulin – dried and crushed chicory root. It's good for you, provides a lot of benefits and fibre. One spoonful a day on your cereal or in a drink.'

Palmer pointed to his two cod liver oil capsules and his two omega-3 capsules waiting beside his bowl. 'I won't need any food soon, I'll be full up with supplement pills. I'll rattle like an empty paint spray tin when I run.'

'Run? When do you ever run Justin Palmer, eh? I'll order you a tracksuit and you can come on the jog.'

'No chance.'

'Benji has sixteen capsules or tablets a day, organic food and pressed fruit juices – not that concentrated sugar rubbish – and look how healthy he is.'

'He should be healthy. I do a day's work which keeps me fit, while all he does is mince down to the shops and faff about all day.'

'He does a lot of charity work.'

'Only 'cause nobody will give him a proper paid job.'

'Justin Palmer, you know that is not true. He's retired.' She took two of the omega-3 capsules from the jar and broke them into Daisy's bowl.

'What are you doing? Don't tell me you've got Daisy on supplements too?'

'Dogs get rheumatic joints just like humans, and she's getting on a bit now so why not?'

'She's *getting on a bit*? She's only ten – and anyway, I haven't got rheumatic joints so why do I need them?'

'Prevention is better than cure. Won't do her any harm,' said Mrs P., breaking two cod liver oil capsules into the bowl.

'You'll have her going vegan next.'

'No, but I am thinking that *we* might.'

'I hope you are kidding.'

'Well, it would keep us slim and fit, and if everybody went vegan we wouldn't need so many cows, and global warming would slow down as less methane was produced.'

'If we all lived on vegetables, nuts and pulses *we'd* produce a lot more methane than the ruddy cows do.'

'You produce enough as it is, Justin Palmer. I'm thinking of getting twin beds.'

'I'm going to work, got a serial murder case to solve…'

CHAPTER 28

'Right then, put a call into the FLO at the Compton's place and see if Mrs Compton is in any condition to talk to us yet.'

Gheeta's mobile rang before she could make the call. Her face fell as she took the call. She clicked off, took a deep breath and spoke softly.

'Mrs Compton died in her sleep overnight, guv.'

Palmer was speechless for a few seconds. 'You are kidding.'

'No, the doctor's on his way. The FLO was there at eight this morning and hadn't worried about her sleeping in as she thought it was probably the sedation drugs. She took her a cup of tea about fifteen minutes ago and found her.'

'What time did her sister-in-law leave her last night?'

Gheeta pulled up the timeframe on her PC. 'Nine thirty.'

'We had better get hold of her for a statement, and inform Jameson – after all she was his sister.'

'Sir Horace Jameson does seem to be quite involved in this case, guv,' noted Gheeta. 'Three deaths in his brother-in-law's department at the Ministry, then his brother-in-law hangs himself, and then his sister dies within a few hours. '

'I take it that alarm bells are beginning to ring in your head the same as they are in mine, Sergeant.'

'Yes guv, quite loudly too.'

Claire spoke without stopping her work at the computer in front of her.

'I think they are about to ring louder after what I'm unearthing, sir. Take a look at Mihaela's Facebook page, sir.' Claire pointed to her monitor screen.

Palmer leant forward to look, as did Gheeta. The picture showing was of a wedding: the Jamesons' wedding. All were in attendance: the bride and groom, the Comptons and several other guests. But it was not the usual outside the church photo – this was quite different. They were all stood along the side deck rail of a rather large motor boat, holding their glasses of champagne up for a toast.

Claire continued. 'The boat is an eight berth motor cruiser, and you can see her name on the side: Copac Du Bani.'

'What's that mean?'

'Romanian for *'Money Tree'*. I've checked the UK Boat Register and she is legally registered with the Thames Environment Agency, so she uses the Thames as a base. According to the registration document her home berth is at the Imperial Wharf Marina.'

'Where's that?'

'On the Thames at Fulham. But that's not all, sir.'

'Go on.'

'The boat is the property of European Pharmaceuticals.'

'Why would they want a motor cruiser?'

'Tax dodge. They can claim it and its running expenses against tax.'

'I can't even claim my car.'

'It gets better, sir. Look at this.' She sat back as Palmer and Singh leant in to look at the screen.

'A Cessna Skyhawk , price half a million dollars. Owner: European Pharmaceuticals, kept at London City

Airport. Used by the company and piloted by Alexandru Bogdan.'

'Tax deductable?'

'Of course.'

'No wonder they pulled such a big scam on the NHS – that lifestyle takes a lot of financing.'

Gheeta walked over to the progress board. 'And no wonder they wanted to protect it. It's all coming together, guv: Hart, Clive and Butwell were getting too close to revealing what was going on with European Pharmaceuticals products; Compton was getting worried about the consequences for him, and Jameson was obviously involved in some way through his wife and her brother, Alexandru Bogdan. '

Palmer joined her. 'So then Hart, Clive and Butwell were wined and dined individually at Luigi's, sweet-talked and taken for a ride along the Thames in the Copac Du Bani, and disposed of over the side along the way?'

'Could well be, it fits. Compton had us and our Forensic Accountant all over him and knew we'd connect him into the scam and that that would bring murder charges – or accessory to murder charges – and he couldn't bear the disgrace so topped himself?'

'I don't go for that,' said Palmer. 'I think Jameson is involved big time – his wife's pedigree points to that. He's not going to be unaware of what's going on, he's a flipping shareholder isn't he? And as Chairman of the Public Accounts Committee he is in a position to choose what they examine and what they don't examine, so anything coming onto his desk about European Pharmaceuticals would get binned pretty quickly.'

Gheeta returned to her desk. 'I think there's probably some mileage we can get out of this motor cruiser, guv. If it was used to ferry the victims down the Thames and dump them, it had to pick them up somewhere local to Whitehall, somewhere along the embankment.'

Palmer shrugged. 'Maybe they went to the Fulham Wharf after their Luigi meal and boarded there.'

'No,' Gheeta didn't buy that. 'If that was the case they'd have been dumped in that part of the Thames – the killer wouldn't bring the boat all the way up here just to drop them overboard, would he?'

'Probably not,' Palmer agreed. 'Anyway, I've got an appointment with Professor Latin down at the morgue. He's got something to do with Compton that he wants to show me. You two work on that boat and its movements, dee if we can't place it this end of the Thames on the nights in question.'

CHAPTER 29

Palmer walked down the long corridor of the Met's morgue and pathology labs in Southwark, his nostrils taking in the smells of formaldehyde and disinfectant that permeated the air. He wasn't keen on such places – death was what this building worked on, its causes and the methods of assisting it to happen. He also wasn't too keen on Professor Latin, an old friend of the Squad who had helped nail some pretty bad villains in the past by discovering clues on bodies that the eye couldn't see. Trouble was, the Professor had a tendency to bad language as his natural method of communication; hence Palmer had opted to pop over the water himself when the call came that Pathology had something of interest to do with Compton's death, rather than send Gheeta or have her accompany him.

Palmer turned into Lab 4 where Compton's body lay spread on the steel slab, with the Professor leaning over. On the next table lay Jeremy Clive's body. Four other pathology technicians busied themselves around the lab. Professor Latin straightened up and threw Palmer a smile of recognition.

'Justin old friend, how the fuck are you?'

'I'm fine, and you?

'Soldiering on, keeping the fucking wheels of the Met turning.'

Palmer noted that the other occupants of the lab in their green theatre suits were accustomed to the language and batted not an eyelid. Latin went straight to business.

'Seems you're having some fun with wet corpses Justin. Reg Frome gave me a call and asked me to have a quick look, so I had sonny jim here sent over from West

End Central. Very interesting too.' He moved to beside Clive's body. 'When they came out of the river where did the two other bodies go?

'West End Central morgue, same as that one.'

'I thought so, lazy bastards. I bet they just assumed it was a suicide and that was that.'

'I'm assuming it was murder. We have quite a lot of evidence pointing that way.'

'And the other two bodies, what was the verdict on them?'

'They were a while ago. Coroner gave a death by misadventure on both.'

'Polite way of saying suicide without upsetting their nearest and dearest.'

Palmer nodded agreement, knowing full well that verdict was indeed the way coroners described suicide.

Latin carried on, 'Right, well, it wasn't suicide, Justin. No fucking way.' He pulled down the rubber sheet covering Clive to show a deep post mortem incision down the chest. Palmer winced. 'I had a look at the lungs, and guess what I found?'

'Water – he drowned.'

'Water yes, and he drowned yes, but he drowned before he went into the Thames, Justin. The fucking water in his lungs was common or garden tap water, not river water. This poor bastard was held under a bowl or bath of tap water 'til he croaked. He was brown bread before he entered the river – if he was still alive at that point he would have sucked in river water into his stomach and lungs. Fuck all river water in there Justin, fuck all – pasta in the stomach yes, but Reg said you knew about that. Seems it was the last meal of all three victims, so at least West End Central knobheads had a look there. Pity they didn't do a complete job. If you want to exhume the earlier victims I can have a look in their lungs.'

'Cremated.'

'Evidence destroyed then, pity. Anyway, onto this chap.' He moved to Compton's body. 'I bet the fucking coroner would go for misadventure on this too when it comes before him. Man found hanging in his own garage, looks a dead cert – pardon the expression – looks a dead cert for suicide, eh? Wrong.' He pointed to Compton. 'He was murdered too.' He smiled a wide smile at Palmer.

'Go on.'

'Well, look at the neck. Big red bruising round it where he snapped into the noose and hung in it. See it?'

Palmer peered close. 'Yes.'

'Now, take a fucking look at this.' He picked up a pair of photos from a nearby table. The first one showed the front and back of Compton's neck in black and white. The pale neck had a dark line round it. He pointed to the line. 'That's the bruising from the tightened rope.'

'Okay.'

'Now look at this one.' He pulled out the second photo which was a close up of the bruising section of the neck. 'See how the dark bruising has an even darker line running down the middle of it?'

Palmer could see it – it wasn't very pronounced but it was there, a thin darker line running along the middle of the rope bruising line.

'Yes. What is it, a metal core to the rope?'

'If the rope has a metal core it could well be, but it doesn't – just a plain jute fibre rope. No, your victim had been garrotted before he was hung up. He was already dead, Justin. Somebody or some persons wanted it to look like suicide, same as our poor drowned fucker, but he was fucking murdered and then hung.' He put the photos down and stood arms folded, with a big smile like the cat who got the cream. 'I'll get copies sent over to you at the Yard, exhibit one and two, and my full reports on both these stiffs. Now all you have to do, Justin old mate, is find the fucking killers.'

CHAPTER 30

'Thames Environment could teach you a thing or two about keeping records, guv,' said Gheeta as Palmer strode back into the Team Room the next morning.

He put his coat and trilby on a table. 'Nothing wrong with my record keeping, Sergeant. You know how much I enjoy doing the daily report so that Bateman can see what *real* policemen do all day, and then it can languish in some old filing cabinet in a basement forever. Such a great benefit to the Met.' He walked over to her. 'I take it you've found something on the Thames records?'

Gheeta pointed to her monitor and scrolled down a list of Thames boat movements.

'The motor vessel Copac Du Bani is recorded as visiting the Westminster Pier a few times guv, and every one of those times coincides with the evenings Clive, Butwell and Hart were seen leaving Luigi's, after which they were never seen alive again.'

'Jesus!' Palmer sat next to her.' So they weren't taken to Fulham then. Westminster Pier is the one this side of the bridge by Big Ben, isn't it?'

'It is, and the river cruises pick up and put down there so CCTV is operating twenty-four seven on Health and Safety regulations. We should be able to get CCTV footage of the boat and those who got on or off it. Claire is getting it now.' She nodded towards Claire who was on the phone to Thames Environment. She finished her call and put the phone down.

'They are emailing a file with the CCTV for the three evenings we are interested in. Thirty minutes.'

It seemed like the longest thirty minutes in Palmer's life. He filled Gheeta and Claire in with the information from Professor Latin as they waited for the files to arrive on the computer. Then impatiently he paced the room, checked his watch and paced the room again. He did this several times, and in the end Gheeta suggested he go and get coffees from the fifth floor machine before his incessant pacing drove her and Claire mad.

Palmer returned, having spilt most of the coffees on his shoes in his haste down the stairs.

'Anything yet?'

Claire nodded. 'Downloading it now, sir.'

The three of them watched the monitor as Claire opened the file and played the video. One after the other, the relevant files of the days Gheeta had asked for showed them come down the steps from the embankment to the Westminster Pier jetty. They were with Compton and Horace Jameson.

'So Jameson was the mystery man in the taxis,' Palmer commented.

Crossing the jetty, the three met with another man waiting beside the berthed Copac Du Bani.

'Who's that? Do we know him?'

'No guv, but I'll get an ID from running the pictures through our FRP (Facial Recognition Program). I'll lay odds it's Bogdan. It's his boat.'

They watched as each time all four went on board, and in a few minutes the boat left the pier and was out of shot.

Palmer stood and made for the door. 'Well that's a bit more than circumstantial, isn't it? Bateman can't refuse a warrant on that evidence.'

Bateman signed off the warrant once Palmer had relayed the pathology findings on Compton's neck, Clive's lungs and the Westminster Pier activity. He hurried back down to the Team Room to get things moving quickly now that positive evidence was in his possession.

'Claire, give Harvard and Russell a call and tell them I'm on my way with the warrant, just in case Jameson decides to leave the Commons. Follow and report if he does. You come along with me Sergeant, in case his wife is about and starts being awkward. '

'Hang on a minute, guv,' said Gheeta, who was tapping away at her keyboard. 'We've missed a trick here.'

'Go on.'

'According to the FLO report from the day Mrs Compton found her husband in the garage, her sister-in-law turned up pretty quickly and volunteered to stay with her all night – and we now know who the sister-in-law is don't we.'

'Jameson's wife, Bogdan's sister.'

'Correct, so don't you think it might be advisable to have Professor Latin take a look at the body? I mean, I'm not suggesting anything but…'

Palmer took a deep breath. 'Yes, in the light of other things happening in this investigation I think you are right. Claire, find out where Mrs Compton's body is, then get onto Professor Latin and tell him I'd like him to do a PM on it. Explain why – he'll understand, he's up to speed on the case.'

Claire nodded and reached for her phone.

'Sergeant, we had better get moving and get hold of Jameson, and then get a warrant on the Bogdans and bring them in.'

CHAPTER 31

In the main hall of the House of Commons Palmer and Singh met up with Harvard and Russell, who were making themselves blend in with the tourists and MPs' guests.

'He still here?' asked Palmer.

'Yes sir,' Harvard answered. 'We asked the clerk on the desk to give us the nod if he checked out. There's about ten different ways out of this place, including a tunnel under the road to Portcullis House. But MPs have to let the desk know if they are leaving.'

'Okay, let's go and get him. Russell, you stay here just in case we miss him.'

'You can't just waltz in, sir,' said Russell. 'You have to sign in at the desk and they ring up to the member and let him know you are coming. If he doesn't come down for you or send one of his staff, a clerk takes you up.'

'No way,' Palmer dismissed that option. 'The last thing we want is for Jameson to know we are here. Russell, you go to the desk – show your ID and keep the desk clerk occupied whilst we slip through. Tell them you need to see, I don't know… who's a name MP?'

'Boris Johnson?' offered Gheeta.

'No, too big a name. Who's your MP, Harvard?'

'No idea, sir.'

'No idea? Your own representative in this fortress of democracy and expense-fiddling and you don't know his or her name? Tut tut.'

'Who's yours, guv?' asked Gheeta.

'That's not the point.'

She smiled, 'Try Oliver Letwin, I saw him leaving as we came in so that should keep the clerk occupied trying to find him.'

'He will do. Okay, let's go.'

Harvard walked to the desk as Palmer and the others approached another clerk by the members' corridor. Palmer flashed his ID.

'Sir Horace Jameson is expecting us,' he pointed to Harvard at the desk. 'They are letting him know we are on our way. Lead on.' He indicated with his hand for the clerk to 'lead on'. Which he did.

Horace Jameson dried his hands under the blow drier in the second floor Commons male washroom, straightened his tie and brushed a hand across his thinning hair in the mirror before turning to the door. Walking out into the corridor he strode along and turned into his own corridor, where he came to an abrupt halt and quickly stepped back out of sight. He had seen the clerk with a uniformed female police officer, and two what he presumed to be plainclothes officers at his door.

Jameson quickened his gait as he made his way to the north staircase and down the floors to the lower ground, and along the tunnel under Whitehall to Portcullis House. He needed time to think. There was only one reason for the police to be knocking on his door, and that person was Olive Compton – she must have told them everything. He speed-dialled on his mobile.

'I don't think Sir Horace is in, sir.' The clerk looked at Palmer. He had knocked twice without any answer,

'Let's have a look, shall we?' Palmer reached past and opened the office door, stepping inside quickly. Harvard and Gheeta followed, leaving the clerk slightly bemused. It just wasn't done to enter an MP's office without him or her in attendance.

Palmer looked around. Jameson's briefcase was open beside his desk, his raincoat on the hook and his laptop fired up on the desk.

'Perhaps he has gone to the washroom,' offered the clerk.

'Perhaps,' agreed Palmer. 'Take my sergeant and show him where that is, would you?' He smiled the famous *'just do what I say or else your world will implode'* smile at the clerk, as Harvard gently took his arm and ushered him out.

'Do we wait, guv?' asked Gheeta.

'Yes, but not for long – he's obviously in the middle of doing something, so he should return pretty quickly.'

'And if he doesn't?'

'If he doesn't then he's got wind of our imminent arrival and scarpered.'

Gheeta radioed Russell at the entrance desk. 'Jameson's not in his office and might be on a runner, so keep your eyes peeled.'

'Will do, he's not signed out at the clerk's desk.'

'Okay.'

'I think we might take this – evidence.' Palmer closed Jameson's laptop and passed it to Gheeta.

'I can download it onto a USB, guv – save lugging it with us.'

'No, I'd rather have it physically – then its contents can't be altered and his prints will be all over the keys. Give it to that kid from Forensics, the accountant chap.'

'Pete Akins.'

'That's him – have him get Reg Frome to dust it for prints, and then he can look through it for anything relevant to the case. With a bit of luck he'll find something to tie Jameson into the killings once and for all.'

Harvard returned.

'Not in the washroom, sir. The clerk was called away, couldn't see any point in bringing him back'

'No, that's fine. So where has Jameson gone then? If he's guessed we are onto him where would he go?'

'Bogdan's?' suggested Gheeta.

'Might well do. Give Patel and Trent a heads up.'

Gheeta radioed them with instructions to arrest Jameson on sight.

'Got it,' Patel acknowledged. 'No movement here in or out.'

They gave it another five minutes, just in case Jameson appeared, and then collecting Russell from the foyer on the way, made their way out and back to the squad car in the underground Commons car park.

'Where to?' asked Russell as he put on the driver's seatbelt.

'Fulham, the Imperial Wharf Marina I think,' said Palmer. 'Time to take a closer look at that boat.'

CHAPTER 32

On board the Copac Du Bani moored at the Imperial Wharf Marina, Horace Jameson and Alexandru Bogdan sat in the wheelhouse.

'We have to go now, The police will have found Olive and they'll soon have every exit blocked, and we'll never get out.' Jameson was clearly agitated and panicking. 'You can carry on in Romania – set up a different company and go for contracts again.'

'And you?' Bogdan asked.

'The Caymans – no extradition treaty with the UK, and I've got enough money over there to see me out.'

'My sister might not want that. She might prefer to be with the family in Romania.'

'Romania has an extradition treaty with the UK, they'll have us all arrested and extradited.'

'Why? They have nothing on her.'

'Oh come on Alexandru – who was the last person with Olive Compton, eh? You think the pathologists won't discover suffocation as the reason for her death? You think in a case like this, with damn bodies turning up everywhere, that Palmer would just let her be cremated without a thorough post mortem? Don't be daft. And then Mihaela's in real trouble.'

The sound of an approaching siren made them turn round and look out to the road, where Palmer's squad car was pulling into the marina.

'See! They're here already,' Jameson could see the walls of a prison cell closing around him. 'Get going, get us out of here!'

Bogdan hit the starter motor and the waters aft started to churn as the twin propellers idled, ready for action. 'Slip the rope.'

Jameson ran to the rear of the boat, unhooked the mooring line and tossed it over the back. He could see figures running along the far end of the marina towards them, shouting for them to stop; one was in police uniform. A loud crack startled him from behind. He turned to see Bogdan holding a pistol.

'What the... Are you out of your mind?'

'It stopped them,' Bogdan laughed.

Jameson looked and saw that the figures were flat on the ground. God! He hoped Bogdan had missed.

Bogdan pushed the throttle forward and the Copac Du Bani's two powerful engines roared into action, the propellers gathered speed and bit into the Thames water and she quickly left the side of the marina and moved into the Thames, heading upstream gathering speed.

Palmer was angry with himself as they got up off the wooden jetty and stood and watched the launch power away into the distance.

'Shooting at a police officer raises this to a red alert. I should have had Patel and Trent watch the boat and not Bogdan's house, damn it.' He turned to Gheeta. 'Give Claire a call and have her contact the river police and ask them to stop that boat. But warn them that Bogdan's armed.'

Before she could, Gheeta's radio spoke.

'Patel here, come in.'

'Go ahead Patel, we can hear you,' Gheeta answered.

'We have movement at the Bogdan house. Mrs Jameson has just left in a bit of a hurry, over.'

Gheeta looked at Palmer for instructions. He reached for the radio and took it from her.

'Palmer here, Patel. Follow her, but keep a distance – we don't want her to clock you. Keep me informed where you are, and where you might be heading. Over and out.' He gave Gheeta the radio back. 'With a bit of luck she's on her way to meet the other two and will lead us to them, so we can nab all three at one go.'

'She's a murder suspect, guv,' said Gheeta. 'Shouldn't they stop her now?'

'And what if she's armed like her brother? No, just keep her in sight.'

Gheeta used her mobile to ask Claire to alert the Thames River Police.

'Guv, I think we ought to get a firearms unit join us now don't you?'

'Good idea, yes.' He turned to Harvard and Russell. 'You two okay?'

Russell nodded. 'Yes, bit of a close shave that one, sir.' He pointed to Harvard, who showed the tear in his jacket sleeve that the bullet had made as it zipped through.

Harvard smiled. 'Close, eh?'

Gheeta was concerned, 'Did it graze you?'

'No, but half an inch to the left and...' He shrugged.

'Well, it wasn't half an inch to the left, so all's well that ends well.' Palmer was, as usual, unsympathetic. 'And get two quotes for the invisible mending, not one – this department's budget is very tight.'

Gheeta shook her head in disbelief, 'I don't think a career as a FLO would suit you, guv. Can't see you comforting the bereaved somehow.'

The three of them laughed. Palmer had a wicked grin. 'Did I ever show you my scar, Sergeant?'

Gheeta cringed theatrically. 'No guv, and I don't think I want to see it either.'

Harvard was intrigued; had Palmer been shot in the line of duty? He'd not heard about that in the Yard's Team Room chatter. 'What happened, sir? Were you shot?'

'No, had my appendix out.' Palmer's smile was as wide as was their expressions of realising they'd been had. He licked the tip of his index finger and drew a figure one in the air. 'Gottcher, come on, back to the motor – we better try and liaise with Patel and Trent. I'm pretty sure Mihaela Jameson, née Bogdan, is on her way to meet up with those other two somewhere and it must be near to the river, so drive along the embankment and keep as near to the riverside as we can. Our best chance is that the River boys find the boat before it docks somewhere and the buggers disappear.'

'She seems to be heading towards the East End, sir.' DS Trent was on the radio as DS Patel drove the unmarked squad car in which they were following Mihaela Bogdan. 'Pretty slow as there's a lot of traffic.'

'Okay,' Palmer acknowledged the message. 'We are heading that way, keeping as near to the river as we can. Anything from the River Police, Claire?'

'No, nothing sir – all quiet.'

'She's clocked us!' There was annoyance in Trent's voice. 'She's clocked us, sir. She just went round a roundabout twice – we turned off it when we realised what she was doing, but then she sped off back the way we came. Shit!'

'Okay, try and pick her up again – this is an open radio link, so Claire can hear us. Give her the description and number of the car, and Claire, put out a '*stop and arrest*' on her as an accessory to murder, possibly armed.'

'Will do, sir. Go ahead with the car details, DS Trent.'

Palmer sat back in his seat as Trent relayed the information to Claire. 'Damn.'

'One thing though, guv,' Gheeta said. 'Her doing a runner like that leaves no doubt that she's involved.'

'That's true. Do you think she's going to jump on the boat and they'll make off on it?'

'Won't get far. Whether they go north or south on the Thames guv, they can't hide; and with the River Police on the lookout it's only a matter of time. I think they'll dump that boat as soon as they can. Mihaela is probably on her way to a rendezvous point to pick them up.'

Palmer agreed, 'And then where will they go?'

'Well, I don't think they'd be foolish enough to go to either Jameson or the Bogdans' houses. They'll assume we have both places under surveillance.'

They drove on in silence, waiting for something to break. Nothing did. The boat seemed to have disappeared.

Palmer changed his mind about surveillance and decided to have Harvard and Russell drop him and Gheet at the Yard, and then continue on to cover the Bogdans' house just in case they went there to pick up belongings . As Mihaela had clocked Patel and Trent's car following her earlier there was no point in them going back there, and they were sent to cover Jameson's flat in Hyde Park Gardens.

'Has Jameson got family there?' Palmer asked Claire over the radio, before they parted company with Harvard and Russell.

'Hang on and I'll check, sir.'

Two minutes later she came back to him. 'No, no current family except Mihaela. He was previously married to an American lady, but they got divorced six years ago and she went back to the States. No children listed.'

'Good, no complications then. Right,' he addressed them all. 'Listen up, everybody. Could be a long night, gentlemen, so I suggest you pick up a sandwich and drink and do four hour shifts of watching and sleeping. DS Singh will notify the local chaps that you're there, just in case a neighbour gets jumpy and rings them about two shifty looking characters parked up in a car.' He laughed at his own comment. 'Stay alert – and remember, Bogdan has a gun, so no heroics please.'

He and Gheeta walked into the Yard as Harvard and Russell drove off. Palmer checked his watch.

'Blimey, is that the time?'

'Goes quickly when you're enjoying yourself, guv.'

They both smiled.

'I think we've done quite enough for today, Sergeant . I'd better list the day's happenings for Bateman's damn report, but you get off home. I'll send

Claire off as well when I get up to the office. I've a
feeling we could be in for a busy day tomorrow,'

'I'm going back to the office, guv. I asked for
Olive Compton's mobile to be sent over from the house –
I want to have a look through it and see who she was
talking to on the day she found her husband and
afterwards. I want to know if she knew about the scam.'

'Okay, up to you Sergeant.' Palmer knew better
than to argue with Gheeta on technical evidence matters;
after all, that was why he'd brought her into the team. 'If
that's the case then you send Claire home and Bateman's
report can wait until tomorrow. I'm off for another slice
of Mrs P.'s steak and kidney pie.'

CHAPTER 33

Mihaela Bogdan was sure she had lost the car that had followed her from the house, but she took no chances. She pulled into the Kings Cross multi-storey car park, took a ticket from the machine, and drove right to the top floor before parking up. She sat for ten minutes, watching the ramp; a few other cars came up and parked, but she was certain none were the police. Getting out of the car, she made sure she was not being followed by taking the stairs down two floors and then up again. No, she was clear.

She left the car park and walked down to Russell Square, where she rented a Fiesta from Hertz car rental; a Fiesta would blend in with traffic. She made her way towards the City Airport, skirting it and pulling up alongside the Royal Victoria Gardens on the Riverside. Alexandru and Jameson walked individually out of the gardens and got into the car.

'Are you so stupid, eh?' She spat the words at Alexandru. 'You shoot at the police?'

'They would have got to the boat before we had time to cast off if I hadn't. I didn't hit anybody.'

'Are you sure?'

'Yes, and anyway that's not as stupid as what you did.'

'I had no choice.'

'No choice in what?' Jameson asked.

'Nothing.' Mihaela gave him a false smile.

Jameson was still in shock. He had tried to figure out a way for himself to come out of this mess clean, and with alibis to distance himself from the whole thing, but he couldn't. His privileged world was falling down around him – the only way out was to run, run fast and far. His overseas money stashes would underpin a new identity; he'd be okay if he could just get out of the country to somewhere with no extradition treaty – that meant South America, and Panama was favourite as he had money there lodged with Mossac Fonseca, the company that handled most of the major money laundering for dodgy banks and individuals the world over. Even since the Panama Papers had revealed Mossac Fonseca's true business model it had continued its business, and he had assurances that his investment was safe and growing. Yes, Panama was his best destination. He speed-dialled on his mobile.

'Who are you calling?' asked Mihaela.

'Olive, I haven't been able to get a reply all day. She came to see me the other day and said she knew what was going on. I want to tell her to keep quiet, or she'll lose her house and everything else.'

The Bogdans exchanged furtive glances.

'She may be under sedation,' suggested Mihaela. 'She had one hell of a shock.'

'Yes, probably.' He put the phone away. 'From what she said to me I don't think she knows how big the operation is.'

'Are you joking? Where does she think the money for the holiday home, the cars and the big house came from?'

'Reggie told her it was productivity bonus payments'

Mihaela started the car and they moved off.

'Where are we going?' Jameson had no idea what was going on.

'The boss wants to see us.'

'The boss? So, I am going to meet the big boss at last, am I? I thought he was in Romania?'

'He's here now.'

'Can he get us out of the country?'

'Yes.'

Jameson relaxed a little. He had never met 'the boss' – didn't need to as everything went through Alexandru from day one – but he was glad to know that somebody was in control of the situation. He tried Olive's number again. No answer.

CHAPTER 34

'This tastes different from last night.' Palmer examined the portion of steak and kidney pie on his plate. 'Looks different too.'

'It is, I made it separately from the pie you had yesterday. It's a *healthy* steak and kidney, made from tofu.' Mrs P. was prepared for Palmer to comment, so she picked up the empty packet and read from it. 'A soya-based food supplement with flavouring. No fat, pure vegetarian, good for the heart.'

'Not so good for the taste buds,' Palmer mumbled, pulling a face.

'Tastes like meat to me. Anyway, the amount of brown sauce you splash on I'm surprised you can taste anything.'

'And what about these, are they the same as I had this morning?' Palmer pointed his knife at three capsules set beside his plate.

'No, they are supplements. They replace the protein and other good things that your body got from meat .'

'So we don't eat meat, but we eat tofu which is flavoured to taste like meat, and swallow capsules to replace the good bits in the meat that the tofu hasn't got.'

'Yes.'

'Daft – easier to eat the meat.'

'And the fat?'

'I work it off.'

'Doing what, riding around in squad cars and sitting in the office? Actually I might get you a bike.'

'A bike, what for? I can't chase around London after a serial killer on a bike! I don't think ringing a bell would clear a way through traffic like a blues siren does.'

'You could leave the car at home and cycle to Herne Hill station, get the Victoria train in and walk the rest of the way. Do you good.'

'If I left a bike at Herne Hill it would probably get nicked, and the walk from Victoria to the Yard would take an age so I'd be knackered before I started! No, wait a minute, I have an idea – I could have my work suit in a rucksack, wear a tracksuit and jog from Victoria, and then collapse with heart failure when I got to the Yard. How's that?'

Mrs P. sighed. 'I am only trying to help you, Justin. At our age it's important to take care of our health.'

'I take Daisy out when I'm home in time.' He leant down and stroked Daisy, who was lying beside his kitchen chair; she had been given a leftover from Mrs P.'s tofu steak and kidney before Palmer had got home, and was hoping no more was coming her way. She knew that if Palmer took her out for an evening walk round Dulwich Park, she'd do all right on the treats he secretly kept in his jacket pocket for her.

Palmer managed to finish the pie – in fact he quite enjoyed it, and the raspberry non-dairy cheesecake for afters, but he wouldn't admit it. 'Right then,' he said. 'Washing up and then I'll take the dog round the park.'

If dogs could smile, there would be a wide one on Daisy. She knew she wouldn't come home hungry!

'I'll do the washing-up, you take Daisy – and walk faster, or jog. And go round twice.'

Daisy knew that wasn't going to happen.

CHAPTER 35

In the morning Gheeta was first in, just before Claire, and had quite a bit of news for Palmer when he arrived.

'River boys found the boat, guv.'

'Good.' He took off his coat and trilby and slung them across a table. 'Where was it?'

'Canary Wharf, nobody inside.'

Palmer wanted clarification. 'Do you mean there was no one on board, or that they didn't find a body inside?' He smiled.

'Bot,h guv. I notified Mr Frome and he's putting a Forensics team inside to see if they can come up with anything that shows our deceased had been onboard at some time.'

'That would be nice evidence if anything shows up, very nice.'

'Olive Compton's mobile has yielded a bit of light. She has phoned Jameson at the House of Commons on a few occasions, latest was four days ago – lucky for us she also texted him about calling in to see him at the House as well.'

'Lucky for us why?'

'Because she used his name in the text so we know it's for him, and it gives us the mobile number she sent the text to, which must be his, so we can trace his whereabouts.'

'We can?'

'Easy peasy.'

Palmer had long been amazed, and sometimes totally bemused by Gheeta's IT knowledge. He had given her carte blanche to input various apps and algorithms into the

Squad's computer systems if she thought they would enhance the prospect of solving a case. He knew full well some were illegal and hacked from other encrypted systems of the law enforcement agencies worldwide, and others from the cyber jungle of the dark web – although he had no idea what the dark web was until Gheeta had explained it. So he turned a blind eye, and the Squad benefitted from her expertise.

'Easy peasy it may be for you Sergeant, but for mere mortals like myself I'll bet it's an unfathomable miracle how this works.'

'It's not, guv. Look.' She turned in her chair and explained. 'The phone works by emitting radio signals; these radio signals are emitted not only when a call is made, but all the time when the device is switched on. The signals which the mobile telephone emits are picked up by radio towers and masts, which are part of the respective mobile network. These masts are typically referred to as transmission towers, or transmission masts – this is because they not only pick up the signal, but they enable the exchange of signals between two mobile phones during a call. Similarly, the signal emitted from a transmission tower or mast can be picked up by another device, such as a computer.

'The mobile phone communicates wirelessly by radio signal with the nearest transmission mast at any time it is switched on; as the location of each mast is fixed, the phone's location can be identified with the use of the appropriate technology. This is what phone tracking is all about. This phone tracker technology is quite complex, but it is fairly easy to get an idea of how it works.'

'Fairly easy?' Palmer's head was beginning to ache.

'Yes guv, the technology measures the power level of the signal coming from the phone and the antenna patterns of the mobile phone. Based on this data, the system can determine which transmission mast is closest to the phone, because each mast has a sector in which it works, so the sector will show on the map of mast sectors. The technology works to determine the distance from the respective transmission tower to the mobile phone; if the system uses interpolation of the signals from two or more towers located close to one another, it can produce the phone's exact location with a very small allowance for error. This is possible because all masts that are in a certain area will pick up the signal coming from the device. To them, the signal will come at different strengths, so with effective computation precise location is perfectly possible. Understand, guv?'

Palmer nodded. 'Just about. So basically it means that if Jameson's phone is on, we can track where he is by the signal coming from it.'

'Correct. Well done, guv.'

Both Claire and Gheeta sarcastically applauded. Palmer took a long sweeping bow. 'All right, enough of that. So now we need to give the mobile companies his phone number so they can pin-point him for us.'

'No, no need for them to be involved.'

Palmer knew exactly what the implication of that remark meant. He and Gheeta held eye contact for a few moments, his eyes saying: *you've hacked it haven't you*, and hers saying: *damn right I have.*

She turned back to her keyboard and started tapping. 'I haven't put his number in yet, so let's try it and see shall we? If it's turned off we won't get a flag. Give me a few minutes as I have to combine the mast reception IPAs of the main mobile networks, so whatever one he's on it will register a hit when he switches his phone on.'

'Do you want me to put the mobile network map on the screen?' asked Claire.

'Yes, put one up for inside the M25 circle – that should cover enough ground to start with. Leave the access open.' She looked briefly at Palmer before continuing. 'The network map is the map of all the masts in London that the mobile networks use to monitor use – if you remember we used it in the case of that naval scientist who went AWOL with a WMD?'

Palmer remembered the case. 'Yes, I remember. That was eighteen months ago, so why have we still got their network map? Don't they need it back?'

'We've got a copy of it, guv.'

Palmer shrugged. 'Silly question really, wasn't it.'

'Yes, guv.'

CHAPTER 36

The Quality Hotel in Kings Cross didn't exactly live up to its name – a bit like Premier Inns. Room 208 that Horace Jameson woke up in on the fifth floor certainly wasn't 'quality': pretty basic, with a sink and shower, no bath, a TV that had a picture that faded and returned, a kettle, three tea bags, two coffee bags, two sugar bags, two powdered milk sachets, and two cups, no saucers. It was a twin bedroom, and Bogdan's snoring from the second bed hadn't helped Jameson get a good night's sleep, or anywhere near that. Add to that the all-night noise from certain females bringing their clients up to rooms paid for by the hour and slamming doors and arguing over money and he was quite glad it was time to get up.

He washed – at least the soap was new and the towels clean – he dressed quickly and sat in a leather chair that had seen God knows what happening in that room as Bogdan stirred, mumbled some sort of morning greeting, used the toilet loudly, washed and dressed.

'Not exactly the Savoy, is it?' Jameson said as the kettle boiled and he made two cups of coffee.

'No, and not the sort of place the police would even think of looking for us,' said Bogdan.

'I hate to think what breakfast will be like.' Jameson hadn't any high hopes of a five-star breakfast if the two star room was the standard.

'We won't eat here.'

'What's the plan?' He sipped the coffee. 'God that's awful.'

'The plan is to sit tight until we are told otherwise.'

Jameson was taken aback by this.

'Told otherwise by whom?'

'I told you before, the boss – he is arranging to get us out of the country. Drink your coffee and put the TV on, we could be here a while.'

A knock on the door had Bogdan reaching under his pillow and dragging out the gun. Jameson felt his heart jump into his mouth.

'It's me.' Mihaela was outside.

Bogdan slipped the security chain off and opened the door. Mihaela came in and sat on a bed.

'Sleep well?' she asked Jameson.

'Not a wink.' He took a gulp of coffee. 'You?'

'No, I was expecting the police to crash through the door at any time.'

Alexandru smirked. 'They'll be back at the boat, taking it apart.'

'We should have sunk it or set it alight,' Mihaela said. She noticed Jameson take out his mobile. 'What are you doing?'

'Ringing Olive, I'd have thought she would have rung me by now. Very strange.'

The Bogdans exchanged looks.

CHAPTER 37

'Bingo!' Gheeta could hardly disguise her excitement. Just half a minute after loading the networks mast pattern overlay onto the London street map on the big screen, and there it was: a pulsating red dot.

'Jameson's mobile is on, and that is where it is and hopefully he is too. Zoom in a bit, Claire.'

Claire tapped her keyboard and the map zoomed in, making the area around the red dot larger and the road names visible.

'Kings Cross, he's somewhere in the Collier Street and Killick Street area.'

'Can we get more precise?' Palmer was thinking it would take an army of officers to check that area,'

'Sorry sir,' said Claire. 'That's the best we can do – hope he moves, then it makes it easier.'

'Okay, give our four detectives a call and send them to the area and ask the local SCO19 unit (The Met's Specialist Operations Unit) to assist with an ARV(Armed Response Vehicle) wagon of Firearms officers, in case we stumble on Bogdan and he starts shooting again. They are to stay out of sight in their vehicle unless needed. Tell our chaps to show mugshots to all the hotel and shop staff in the area and advise them that they have recourse to a Firearms unit if needed. Best bet is that Bogdan and the Jamesons are in a hotel sorting out an escape route and we can surprise them.'

'Will do. Shall I put Bateman in the loop?'

Palmer picked up his coat and trilby. 'Better had, but let me get clear of the building first in case he wants to play it strictly by the book and hand control over to

Firearms. Right then Sergeant, off we go to Kings Cross and join the hunt. Claire, you keep us up to date if that dot moves.'

Claire was talking to DS Patel and waved a hand in acknowledgement of the instruction. Gheeta grabbed her laptop shoulder bag and followed Palmer out of the Team Room as she slipped the laptop inside it.

CHAPTER 38

Jameson was startled. He had fallen asleep after three hours of watching daytime television and now somebody was shaking his shoulder roughly.

'Up, up – come on Horace, we have to go. Come on.'

'Whaaa... what?' He opened his eyes and could see Alexandru and a hotel porter.

'We have to go, come on.' Alexandru pulled him up. 'The police are checking the hotels further down the street. They'll be here soon.'

Jameson pulled himself together at the news. 'How do they know we are here?'

'They don't, but they know we are in the area. They could have had a tip off, they might have traced the car – they have cameras everywhere these days.'

'Where are we going?' asked Jameson as he struggled with his jacket.

'It's all arranged, we'll be out of the country in a couple of hours. We are going down the back fire escape, and Mihaela's gone to get a hire car. Come on, quick – shoes on!'

Jameson stumbled out of the room as he jammed his shoes on and hurried after Bogdan and the porter along the corridor to the staff stairway, glancing behind and hoping that they were ahead of the police and could clear the hotel without being seen. They raced down the flights of stairs, and at the bottom their friendly porter pushed down the bar to the exit door and held it open as Jameson and Bogdan ran outside into a wide alleyway between the back of the hotel and the next tall building. Bogdan pulled a wad of bank notes from his pocket and peeled off some for the porter, who nodded in thanks and disappeared back inside, pulling the door shut after him.

'Which way?' asked Jameson.

'We wait,' replied Bogdan.

They didn't have to wait long, as almost immediately Mihaela drove down the alleyway in a Fiesta and they jumped in.

'The whole area is buzzing with police, and there's an armed unit parked up at the corner of the street.'

'An armed unit?' Jameson looked behind them, a sense of fear in his voice. He prodded Bogdan with his finger accusingly. 'That's you taking a pot at them at Fulham. Bloody fool.'

Bogdan pushed him away and snarled. 'We got away didn't we? Wouldn't have if they'd reached the boat.'

Jameson turned to Mihaela. 'Where are we going?

'The airport.' Mihaela looked at her husband in the mirror. 'Calm down, Horace. Everything is under control.'

'Heathrow?' Jameson was worried. 'They'll be on the lookout for us there, and I don't have my passport with me.'

'No not Heathrow – London City Airport. It's only ten minutes away and you won't need a passport.'

Bogdan turned in the passenger seat. 'Our company jet is kept there. The boss has gone ahead to file a flight plan and get it all set to take off – everything is fine.'

CHAPTER 39

On the fifth floor at the Quality Hotel Palmer edged slowly along the corridor behind three fully suited and booted AROs (Armed Response Officers), their SIG5G516 carbines held ready with safety catches off. Behind them, Gheeta, Patel and Trent and the hotel manager followed, hugging the wall. As they approached room 208, the lead ARO motioned Palmer's people to squat down, and then signalled his men who had positioned themselves either side of the door to go in. It only took one strong kick of a steel toe-capped officer's boot on the lock for the wooden frame to splinter and the door to swing open at speed, allowing both officers to rush in shouting 'POLICE!', followed by their sergeant.

Palmer waited with bated breath, expecting the sound of rapid gun fire. All was quiet, and after a few moments the sergeant leant out of the door and beckoned him in. The room was empty.

'The place is clear, sir,'

One look around at the state of the room was enough to tell Palmer that it had been vacated in a hurry. He took the three mugshots of the Bogdans and Jameson out of his pocket and showed them to the manager.

'You're sure that these are the people who rented this room?'

The manager looked at the pictures. 'Yes, I told your man at reception – they are the people who had this room. I took more notice than usual of them, not our usual type of customer.'

'Your usual type being slappers and joes, eh?'

The manager was clearly embarrassed. He ran a finger to loosen his collar. 'Businesspeople.'

Palmer gave a sarcastic smile. 'Of course.' He turned to Patel and Trent. 'You two give the room a once-over, see if they left any clue as to where they are off to now.'

Gheeta's radio buzzed. She opened the comms speaker. 'Go ahead, Claire.'

Claire's slightly distorted voice came from the speaker. 'Jameson is on the move. His phone signal is going east on the A501.'

'Right.' Palmer was making for the door. 'Come along Sergeant, and you and your men too,' he said to the ARO's Sergeant. 'What's your name?'

'DS Lee, sir.'

'Okay Lee, we need to stop this now – can't have Bogdan driving around London with a gun. Patel, Trent, I don't think they'll have left any clue as to where they are going in this room, so as soon as you've had a good look around close it off for Forensics to comb later, and then come after us. Keep the radio open.'

They hurried down the corridor to the stairs, which Palmer foolishly took two at a time until his sciatica stabbed his right thigh, reminding him of his age and his dodgy discs; the remaining stairs were taken singly. At reception, Harvard and Russell were stopping guests from going further than the ground floor lounge.

'They've done a runner,' Palmer shouted to them. 'Leave your motor here and come with us.'

CHAPTER 40

They all piled into the ARV Transit, squashing into the rear side seats with 6 AROs. They reminded Gheeta of Star Wars bad guys, all in black and their helmet visors hiding a human face. She pulled up a street map on her laptop and gave the driver directions to the A501. They relaxed a bit. Palmer rubbed his thigh.

'Slappers and joes, guv?' Gheeta raised her eyebrows with the question.

Palmer carried on rubbing his thigh. 'An old biblical expression, Sergeant.'

Claire's voice on the radio interrupted. 'Base to Palmer, he's gone on the A13, over.'

'A13, got it,' answered Gheeta and acknowledged the driver's nod that he'd heard too.'

'Where the hell are they going? This is the Essex road, they've ditched the boat so they aren't going for that.'

'The airport, guv!' exclaimed Gheeta. 'London City Airport, it's where they keep that company plane. They're going to make a dash for it on the plane.'

Palmer leant forward to the driver. 'Step on it, blues on – London City Airport. Do you know the way?'

'Yes sir, we do air hostage rehearsals there.'

'Good, this time it might be for real.'

Claire came back on the radio. 'Message for the boss from Professor Latin on Olive Compton's cause of death, over.'

'Go ahead Claire, he's listening.' Gheeta held the radio nearer Palmer.

'She was suffocated, over.'

'Thanks Claire, out.' Gheeta slipped the radio back into her tunic pocket and looked at Palmer. 'Murdered then, guv. Got to be Mihaela, she was the only one at the Compton house other than uniformed officers.'

'Turning out to be a nice family these Bogdans aren't they, eh?'

'How does a chap like Jameson get involved in this, guv? Well-respected MP, he had it made surely – why get mixed up in this scam?'

Palmer gave a wry smile; politicians were not his favourite people. 'Politicians, Sergeant, have only two things on their minds: ego and wealth. Why do you think so many of them are ex-lawyers?'

'I don't know, why are so many of them ex-lawyers?'

'Because they can earn more and have all their living expenses and mortgage payments paid by you and me, and on top of that they get their own little fiefdom, known as a constituency, where their ego knows no bounds.'

'You ever tempted to enter the Commons, guv? Sounds right up your street?' she said with a twinkle in her eye.

'The only way I'd want to enter Parliament, Sergeant, is holding a damn great bomb with the fuse lit. Anyway, enough of that – get onto this airport and make sure they hold our fugitives up at Passport Control. I take it London City is on the list when *'stop and detain'* orders go out?'

Gheeta pulled out her laptop and tapped the keyboard for a few moments. 'They are sir, but they have their own security – doesn't come under the Met. No Met officers in attendance'

'Really, why not?'

'Privately owned and operated, owned by a Canadian investment company – have their own security people.'

'Oh brilliant, just what we need! Bogdan doing a runner with a gun, and a load of amateur security bods to stop him – sounds like a recipe for disaster. Get on the phone Sergeant, and try and find who's in charge of security at the airport, and tell him or her what's happening. Tell them not to engage Bogdan and his party, just watch.' He had a thought. 'Tell them to get the control tower to delay any take-off of the Bogdan plane – use any excuse, but that plane is not to take off.'

It took some time for Gheeta to find the right person at the airport to talk to; she had to jump through hoops to get to him. The switchboard thought it was a hoax call – how could she prove who she was? In the end she had Claire get AC Bateman to make a call to the nearest police commander in the area who knew the airport manager, and things then moved fast. But it took time and the ARV was fast approaching the airport by the time it was all in place.

'Front or back, sir?' the driver asked Palmer.

DS Lee made an observation. 'If we go in the front sir, dressed like this we could create panic amongst the public, and there's every chance the suspects will see us and it could all go off. We generally use a back entrance when training – better chance of getting in unnoticed.'

Palmer agreed. 'Back entrance. Do you know where this private plane might be kept?'

Lee nodded. 'Private hangars are over on the far side, away from the public areas. Far side of the runway on a concrete apron.'

'Okay, get us as near to them as you can. Be nice if we can take this lot down without anybody noticing,'

'Bit of a tall order that, guv, 'said Gheeta, looking at the AROs sitting in their black combat gear, full head helmets, tunics housing CS gas grenades, Glock pistol, taser and holding their carbines. 'They sort of stand out a bit in a crowd.'

The ARV turned off the road, drove down a short delivery road and halted at a steel bar barrier at the back of the airport. The driver spoke to the private security company guard who approached from a small gatehouse. He gave an instruction into his radio and the bar rose, and the ARV moved through and swung towards the large hangars at the far side of the airport. They stopped behind the first hangar where they couldn't be seen from the runway or terminal buildings, and where the Airport Security Chief was waiting. He greeted them and introduced himself.

'Creber, Tony Creber, Chief of Security. Your AC put us in the picture. Anything we can do to help, just ask.'

Palmer introduced himself, Gheeta and DS Lee.

'Busy, aren't you?' Palmer had been surprised how big the airport was and by the activity going on around the runway, with several international flights taxiing to take-off positions and another landing.

'Just under five million passengers last year, and as you can see there's a lot of development going on.' Creber waved in the direction of a large amount of building work and construction that was underway.

Palmer was impressed. 'I would never have known. Anyway, down to business – the best thing, Mr Creber, would be for your staff to stay out of the way. The people we are after are armed and have already used a firearm against us. Best to let DS Lee and his chaps round them up. If you could give us a layout of the place that would help. Where's the European Pharmaceuticals plane kept?'

Creber pointed down the line of hangars; all had their giant roller shutter doors up except the last one 'They have a place in the last hangar, share it with six other company planes. I checked and they have lodged a flight plan for an hour's time.'

'Where to?'

'Romania, that's their usual route – there and back a couple of times a week. I've not alerted the control tower or the security personnel to what's happening, thought it best if the people you are after saw everything as normal.'

'That's good, well done. So they haven't checked in yet?'

'No.'

'Really? That's a bit worrying, as they were ahead of us on the road.'

Gheeta spoke. 'I'd better give Mr Frome a call guv, in case this is a red herring and they've doubled back to the boat at Canary Wharf. Wouldn't want him surprised by Bogdan waving a gun at him.' She moved away to make the call.

'Right then, I think we might get into that hangar and arrange a nice surprise for when they arrive.'

'You should be alright for getting in,' Creber said. 'There's a back door and the front is a roller shutter, there's a small judas entry door in it. We never lock them – these company planes are in and out all hours of the day and night.'

Gheeta closed her phone and joined them. 'All quiet at the boat, guv. Mr Frome has taken the ignition switch out of the engine so it's not going anywhere, and he's calling for a couple of AROs to attend just in case.'

'Good, I'll put money on them going for the plane, they…'

Gheeta interrupted him, pointing down the hangars. 'Guv, we've got action.'

He turned to follow her pointing finger. The big roller door of the last hangar was slowly rising.

'What's happening, Creber?' Palmer dispensed with the formalities and wanted an answer, quick.

Creber was flustered. 'I don't know. Nobody is due out, control would have let me know if they were.'

The nose of a plane edged out of the hangar; its number became visible on its side as it emerged and stopped half in and half out.

'GL142, guv,' said Gheeta. 'That's our plane.'

'How the hell have they done that then? How have they got in?' Palmer looked coldly at Creber.

Creber was stumped. 'I don't know, there's only this supplies gate and the main terminal and they haven't...' His voice tailed off. 'Oh Christ!'

'What?'

'The construction site, they must have come in through there – it's fairly open during working hours for the cement lorries and construction deliveries. They must have come in through there.'

DS Lee had his binoculars focused on the plane.

'There's only the pilot on board, sir. No passengers.'

He handed the binoculars to Palmer, who took a look. 'Well I'll be damned...' He turned to Gheeta. 'Giuseppe.'

'You are kidding, guv.'

'No, our restaurant manager Giuseppe is flying that plane. No wonder Compton took the victims to that restaurant, he's part of this whole scam.'

Another part of the jigsaw fell into place in Gheeta's mind. 'I wondered why he didn't recognise Compton from the mugshot I showed him when he'd been there so often and was on the booking app. I put it down to the restaurant being such a busy place he didn't really have time to take any notice of the customers.'

'Well, the good news is that our little band of brigands haven't arrived yet, so Giuseppe, or whatever his real name is, won't be taking off until they do. Lee, can you take out the tyres from this distance?'

DS Lee raised his carbine, taking off the bolt lock. Palmer quickly raised an arm and pushed it down again.

'No, no I don't want you shoot them out yet – just wanted to know if we are in range.'

DS Lee clicked the bolt lock back on. 'Yes, but I'd rather get behind the plane and shoot from there, as these bullets can travel a mile and if I missed I could accidentally take out a passenger over in the terminal on the other side of the runway. If we can get behind it there's only open space and water if we miss.'

'Oh no, no way can we put the public in danger. Okay...' He thought for a moment. 'Sergeant, you circle round to the construction site and have them close that

entrance off – we don't want anybody escaping out that
way. Radio Patel and Trent, they should be long
finished at the hotel room and be nearing us by now –
get them to circle round and meet you at the site. If you
see Bogdan driving in that way, let us know. And stay
out of their sight. Harvard and Russell, you stay at this
gate with Creber and make sure nobody comes in or
goes out. Lee, you and your men will come with me and
use the cover of these hangars to get up close and
personal. Mr Creber, make sure your control tower does
not give permission for take-off, understand me? That
plane must not take off.'

Creber nodded. His heart was thumping and his
legs shaking a little. He wasn't sure what was causing it:
the fear of a major firearms episode at his airport, or the
fear of Palmer's wrath if the plane took off.

'And if it does take off, guv?' asked Gheeta.

'I'll have the RAF shoot the bugger down over
the ocean.' He gave her a look that said *and don't think
I wouldn't'*

Gheeta gave a resigned shrug and smile. 'You do
realise the amount of paperwork that would produce,
don't you guv – as well as a minor heart attack for your
favourite AC.'

'Then we'd better make sure it doesn't get off
the ground, hadn't we Sergeant? Off you go, secure that
building site.'

They all went their separate ways as Palmer had
ordered. He tagged onto the end of the line of AROs as
they moved towards the plane, keeping out of sight
against the hangars, ducking inside each one as they got
nearer. At the last one before the plane they moved
quickly to the back and out of the rear door before

moving to the back of Bogdan's hangar, and just as Creber had said, the back door was unlocked. Lee pushed it gently open and waved Palmer forward. Looking into the hangar he could see several other small aircraft.

'I can hit the tyres from here, sir,' said Lee.

Palmer had a thought. 'No, let's try and get to the plane and pull Giuseppe out before his mates appear. Much better if we can do it all without any fuss, if that fails you can shoot them out.'

They crept and eased slowly from plane to plane two AROs along the right wall of the hangar, two along the left, Palmer and Lee in the centre.

Once at the rear of the plane they edged along the fuselage to the open door, Palmer could see inside where Giuseppe was checking instruments and looking out of the cockpit window every now and again, probably expecting the Bogdans to show up at any moment.

DS Lee passed his carbine to Palmer and signalled he was going into the plane. In the space of a few seconds he had entered it, pulled Giuseppe from his seat to the floor and out of the door spread-eagled face down on the ground with a hard knee in his back holding him there. One ARO from each side quickly joined them and put Giuseppe's hands together behind his back, held there by zip tie hand restraints. Lee took his carbine back from Palmer.

With their attention on Giuseppe nobody had noticed the figures making their way silently from the back door towards them, using the parked planes for cover until a command was shouted.

'Step away from him, NOW!'

All eyes turned towards the inside of the hangar where Alexandru Bogdan stood beside DS Singh, holding his gun to the side of her head. Behind him Mihaela and Jameson waited anxiously.

'NOW I said,' he repeated the order. 'I have nothing to lose.' He looked at the remaining AROs at the side walls, who had levelled their carbines towards him. 'Put your guns down and join the others.'

'Sorry guv,' shouted Gheeta. 'They saw me before I saw them.'

Bogdan prodded the gun into the side of her head. 'Shut up! Do as I say, Palmer.'

The AROs who had their carbines trained on Bogdan looked to DS Lee for a command.

Lee mumbled to Palmer between pursed lips. 'We could take him out, sir. Six of us, one of him.'

Palmer took the initiative; Gheeta's welfare was the most important factor, and Bogdan's gun was right against her head. 'No. Call your men in, Lee. Do as he says,' he ordered.

DS Lee beckoned them in and they lowered their weapons to the floor and joined him, as he did the same.

'You're making it worse for yourself, Jameson,' Palmer spoke loudly to the MP. 'At the moment you are facing a fraud charge. Carry on and you'll be on a charge of assisting in multiple murders.'

'Shut up, Palmer.' Bogdan could see how Palmer was trying to drive a wedge between him and Jameson. 'Another word and your Sergeant will get a bullet in her leg, understand?'

Palmer nodded that he did.

'Good. Move out of the way, move to the side of the hangar.'

Palmer and the AROs did as they were told. Mihaela stepped into the plane and was quickly back out with a knife, which she used to cut Giuseppe's hand restraints.

Jameson had been trying to place Giuseppe's face – he knew he'd seen the man before, but where? Then it came to him.

'You're from Luigi's, aren't you? The manager.'

Giuseppe didn't answer; he just got back into the plane, followed by Mihaela. Jameson asked Bogdan, 'Is he one of your people?'

Bogdan kept his eyes on Palmer as he answered. 'I told you my boss was here.'

'Luigi is your boss? He is running this whole thing?'

'His name is Stefan, he is my older brother – and when we get to Romania you will see just how big my family's operation is. You'll be amazed, our business here is just a small part of it. Now get into the plane.'

The plane's engine spluttered into action and the propeller turned.

Jameson stopped in the doorway and shouted above the engine noise to Palmer. 'Mr Palmer, I am sorry it all got a bit out of hand – it was never meant to involve murder, but I promise you that my sister Olive is not involved. She has nothing to do with it – nothing.'

Gheeta looked at Palmer. 'He doesn't know, guv.'

Bogdan pushed his gun hard into her head. 'Shut up!'

Palmer nodded. 'Well, this should make things interesting.' He shouted back to Jameson. 'Your sister is dead, Mr Jameson. Your wife Mihaela killed her – suffocated her in her own bed.'

Jameson looked down from the doorway to Bogdan. 'What's he on about, Olive dead?'

'An accident.' Bogdan kept the gun against Gheeta's head.

Anger was welling up inside Jameson as he realised what had happened. He stepped out of the plane. 'An accident? Suffocated at home in bed, an accident?' He grabbed Bogdan's shoulder wanting answers.'What accident?'

Mihaela appeared at the door. 'I killed her, you stupid man. You think I was going to let her ruin everything? We worked hard to set this up, and she was going to ruin it.' She laughed at Jameson. 'You idiot, you think I ever loved you, an old fool like you? You think any girl would want you around, eh? You were just part of the jigsaw, you fool – part of the plan and you fell for it, you and your ego. Now piss off, before we kill you too.'

Jameson's mounting fury had overtaken the shock at what he'd heard. He made a lunge towards her, but Bogdan swung the gun and pistol-whipped him across the back of the head and he fell to the ground unconscious, with blood seeping from a wound.

Bogdan kicked Gheeta in the back of her knee, sending her sprawling.

'Don't! Not a step further, or else,' he ordered Palmer and Lee, who had started towards him. They stopped as he turned the gun towards them, as he backed away and carefully stepped up into the plane, keeping the door open enough to show the gun pointing at them as it revved up and taxied slowly across the apron onto the main runway. The door closed as it gathered speed, and the AROs ran for their weapons.

Suddenly a BMW 5 series with blues flashing and its siren screaming sped into sight from behind the righthand side of the hangar; Patel and Trent had arrived. It raced across the apron towards the plane.

Palmer held his hands up towards the AROs, who were taking aim at the Cessna. 'Hold it, don't fire – that's one of our cars.'

The BMW was catching the plane; shots were fired at it by Bogdan from a sliding side window. Patel was at the wheel and pulled to the opposite side of the plane out of view of the window; he and the plane were now doing sixty plus and the nose was starting to lift for take-off. Patel floored the accelerator and came at it from the side, hitting the tail wing which bent and shed some pieces. The plane wobbled into the air as Stefan Bogdan fought to control it and keep it steady.

'That's not going to get very far!' Palmer snatched Lee's binoculars and focused on the plane.

Gheeta had scrambled to her feet and joined him. 'If he makes it past the end of the runway he's going to ditch in the Thames, guv. And if he makes it across the water then it's going to come down on houses. That could be awful.'

From the other side of the runway sirens announced the arrival of the airport fire tenders that were speeding along, expecting the doomed plane to crash back onto the runway and explode into a fireball.

They weren't needed. Stefan Bogdan cleared the runway and the end of the airport, keeping a steady but wobbling height over the old St James dockyard; and then his luck ran out as the damaged tail wing's bolts, weakened by the uncontrolled swinging, gave out and the wing plummeted down, splashing into the dockyard waters.

'He's had it now.' Palmer could see panic movement inside the plane as it fought to maintain height, figures moving frantically around inside, and then having lost the air thrust of the tail, it stalled and hung in the air for a moment before nose-diving into the Thames.

CHAPTER 41

'This is where we came in, wasn't it guv?' Gheeta said as she looked down from the concrete embankment of the Thames northside towards the activity going on in the middle of the river, where police launches were keeping the passing boat traffic away from the area where the plane had hit the water and sunk; a large crane salvage barge was on its way to lift it out. Around them the local force was making sure the press was kept at a distance. It always amazed Palmer just how soon the press and TV managed to get to crime scenes; somebody had made a phone call and would get a brown paper envelope at a later time. The SIO (Senior Investigating Officer) had taken over the scene, and Palmer had relaxed once the first responders had patched Jameson up and taken him off to the local hospital for a scan. He was accompanied by two officers, and had been arrested for conspiracy to murder and read his rights by Gheeta as soon as he had regained consciousness. He hadn't said anything; the thought that the future was a long time in a prison cell was not an appealing one to an MP.

'A bit *deja vu*, I'll give you that Sergeant,' replied Palmer from beside her.

It had been half an hour since the plane had ditched and disappeared below the water surface. River police had arrived within minutes of Gheeta calling them and divers soon followed. They had pulled the bodies of the Bogdans from the plane – all were dead. As is usual with people falling into the river, it's not a matter of whether you can swim or not; it's the cold that kills – hits you like a heart attack, causing loss of control of the limbs, and that's it, the end.

The bodies were bagged, loaded into a mortuary van and taken away for post mortems. For once in this case the cause of death would indeed be drowning and not murder.

Palmer turned to where his other four detectives stood in conversation with DS Lee and his team, who appeared quite human now having removed most of their ARO clothing. Palmer looked at them with a certain pride in his heart. If the future of policing had men like these amongst its number it looked pretty safe to him.

'Well, gentlemen,' he said. 'I'm afraid I'm going to have to ask for daily reports ASAP – AC Bateman will be on my back for them pretty quick in this case, with seven deaths and an MP involved, I should think he's having palpitations already. And thank you all for your help – not a nice ending, but at least we got an ending.' He addressed Patel and Trent. 'One thing, gentlemen, how did you two know what was going on? You must have known or you wouldn't have come round the corner like a bat out of hell after that plane.'

Patel smiled. 'DS Singh, sir. She was asking us where we were over the radio when they jumped her; we were about a mile away, but she left her radio open so we could hear every word of what was going on in the hangar, and so we stood back out of sight waiting for a moment to act.'

Palmer raised his eyebrows and looked at Singh. 'You left the radio open on purpose?'

'Of course, guv.'

He gave a sanguine nod. 'You know, I don't know whether to believe you, Sergeant, or was it just an accident?'

Gheeta's radio crackled into action as Claire's voice came through. 'She's not just a pretty face, sir.'

They all laughed. Palmer smiled.

'It's still open then?'

Gheeta nodded. 'Yes guv, the button's stuck. Been open all day.'

Gheeta and the four detectives acted in unison as they licked the tip of their index fingers and drew figure ones in the air accompanied by a chorus of 'Gottcher.'

Across the river on the south side a lone figure in a dark green overcoat detached himself from the crowd watching the Skyhawk being lifted from the murky depths and made a mobile call to Romania as he walked away.

CHAPTER 42

Palmer's mind was turning over the case in his mind as he drove home. He wasn't looking forward to all the paperwork, but no doubt Sergeant Singh would handle it in her usual competent way. Yes, she was a real diamond.

Driving past Dulwich Park main gate an apparition came into view. A colourful snake of WI ladies and a few attached husbands were jogging into the park; a miscellany of shapes, sizes and ages, some bouncing energetically along, some staggering and a few stopped to ease their panting lungs. At the front were Benji and Mrs P., she dressed conservatively for the occasion in grey tracksuit and cap as were most of the ladies. Benji, on the other hand, looked like a human version of an angry artist's pallet, his Lycra shorts and vest a mixed colour tie-dyed disaster accentuated by bright crimson trainers and a pink headband. Benji being a portly figure didn't lessen the initial shock visual impact.

Palmer smiled to himself. He wouldn't mention he'd seen them when Mrs P. got home. Or maybe he would? Perhaps he might drive into the park at the back gate and get it all on his dash cam. Nah, that wouldn't be fair. Be fun though! He swung the steering wheel.

CHAPTER 43

Alastair Prior had been quite surprised to have been offered promotion to Head of Procurement and Finance Monitoring at the Ministry a short while after the unexpected and awful death of Reginald Compton.

The full circumstances had been kept very low key by the Ministry and the Met. with few particulars reaching the public other than a fraud had been uncovered. Those of the staff who were even mildly interested had made a guess that it involved Compton making false expense claims, a pretty regular occurrence in Civil Service dismissals, he had probably been caught and the ignominy and disgrace of it had led to his suicide. Murder had not been mentioned, just death. The press had been fed a line that the three other deaths were just coincidental and that story had died too. The plane crash into the Thames was an unfortunate accident which the AAIB, Air Accidents Investigation Branch of the Department of Transport were looking into. First results hinted at pilot error.

Prior walked out from Luigi's Restaurant and waited whilst his meal provider paid the bill and joined him buttoning up a dark green overcoat against the autumn chill. Well, if one of the perks of being the Head of Procurement was being dined by the suppliers Alastair Prior couldn't complain.

'That was a very nice meal Andrei, very nice, thank you.'

Andrei Bogdan smiled and patted Prior on the back. 'My pleasure Alastair, I think it is very important for our customers to know who they are dealing with and we as a supply company also like to get to know our customers. As I told you, my brother Alexandru used to run the UK office but he has now gone overseas to the New York operation and like you I have recently been promoted here. European Pharmaceuticals thinks that customer supplier relationships are very important in these digital times when everything can be done at arm's length on a keyboard. Not the way we like to do business. The more you know about us the more confidence you have in us, which is why I am so glad you have accepted our offer of a quick trip to Romania to see our operations for yourself.'

Prior smiled. 'I'm really looking forward to it Andrei, 'I really am.'

' ********************

THE
BODYBUILDER

CHAPTER 1

'My word, it's a big place isn't it?' Palmer stepped out of the squad car and looked around him as he put his trilby on and buttoned up his Crombie coat. It was a trifle chilly standing inside the giant waste transfer centre in Brentford on a late September afternoon. It was shaped like a cathedral-sized tunnel with council waste collection lorries queued in a long line waiting to disgorge their morning's collection into one of the numerous large bays of household and business rubbish, with discarded paper swirling around in the small tornadoes the wind blowing through made.

DS Gheeta Singh came around from the other side of the car and joined him as she wafted her hands under her nose, trying to dispel the smell that permeated the air.

'I don't think I could work in this all day, guv. What a stink!' She nodded towards the black Transit from the Murder Pathology Department parked nearby. 'Looks like Professor Latin is still here.'

The rear door of the Transit opened and a figure clothed in the green Pathology Unit rubber suit and boots emerged and crossed towards them. Professor Latin, known to all and sundry as 'Prof', was a tall thin man, with a balding head beneath the department's protective white paper cap and his thick black-rimmed spectacles. In his late fifties, he was the key man in the Metropolitan Police Murder Case Pathology Department, a specialist department that dealt with the victims of murder or suspected murder referred to them from the various CID units of the Met, plus the Organised Crime Unit and

Palmer's Serial Murder Squad. Professor Latin had a bad habit: foul language. He stripped off one of his rubber gloves and shook Palmer's hand.

'How the fuck are you, Justin?

Palmer cringed and looked apologetically at DS Singh. She shrugged; having worked with Latin on many cases she was quite accustomed to it. It was said in the team rooms at the Yard that Latin's wife was just as bad if not worse, which was why, on an occasion many years before, Palmer had politely turned down an invite to a Met event where the Latins were listed to be on the same table as the Palmers.

Latin acknowledged DS Singh. 'Hello my dear, still keeping this old reprobate in order I see. About time they gave him a pension and told him to fuck off, and gave you the department, Give the young their head I say.'

'Yes, yes, yes,' Palmer had heard it all from Latin before. 'Why have you dragged us out here to some heap of rotting garbage, Prof? No doubt you have a good reason?' He knew there would be a good reason – Latin was not in any way a time waster.

The earlier text to Palmer from him had said: 'Get over here quick Justin, I think I have something that is right up your fucking street.'

'Put some overshoes on and I'll show you.' He opened the rear door of the Path van and pulled out two pairs of tie-up rubber shoe protectors that Palmer and Singh slipped on over their shoes.

'Right this way then,' he said when they were ready, pointing to a bay that was sealed off with crime scene blue-and-white tape and had large crime scene tarpaulin screens blocking any view of the inside. A uniformed detective inspector stood with two constables and a civilian in a hi-vis jacket outside the screens. Palmer and Singh made their way towards them. The DI noticed them and came to meet them.

'DCS Palmer?' he asked with an outstretched hand.

'That's me,' replied Palmer. 'And this is my detective, DS Singh.'

They shook hands.

'I'm DI Lucan, Brent Uniform Division,' he introduced himself as they walked to the bay. 'It's not a very pleasant sight I'm afraid.'

'Not a very pleasant smell either,' said Palmer as they approached.

The hi-vis jacketed civilian turned as they reached the tape. Lucan introduced them to each other. 'This is Mr Weatherby, he's the site controller. This is Detective Chief Superintendent Palmer from the Serial Murder Squad.'

The niceties over, Palmer was keen to get on with the job. He turned to Latin.

'Right then, what have we got?'

He followed Latin around the end of the screens into the bay with Gheeta behind them. It was huge – a gigantic heap of mixed waste, split refuse bags, unfinished takeaways, wipes, nappies, plastic bottles, and great lumps of God knows what. And there was the reason for Latin's call – a naked female body lying on the top of the rubbish where it had fallen when dumped out of the back end of a waste tipper lorry as it emptied the morning's collection. The body was nude, and the body was incomplete – her left arm was missing.

'Jesus!' Gheeta exclaimed from beside him as she pulled her laptop from its shoulder bag and started taking pictures, moving carefully around the dumped rubbish.

'Jesus can't help her, not now,' said Latin. 'Careful, Sergeant, don't move anything.' He knew she wouldn't – she was too experienced to touch evidence before Forensics had been over it – but he made the point anyway in case the horror of the scene had jarred her brain.

Palmer looked carefully at the body.

'What am I missing, Prof? You haven't brought me out here to look at a body with one arm unless there is something else about it.'

Latin laughed. 'Indeed not. Two things, Justin – firstly, I've got another young female body in the morgue, also with an arm missing; and secondly, the missing arm in both cases has been removed with a certain amount of fucking skill. The knuckle joints joining the arms to the shoulder have been separated surgically and correctly, not just hacked through.'

Palmer's interest grew. 'Somebody collecting female arms then?'

Latin laughed out loud. 'That's your fucking job, Justin. All I'm saying is that I think both amputations were possibly by the same skilled individual – too much of a coincidence. There's a few other similarities that I can test for at the lab and then I'll be absolutely sure, but I'm ninety-nine percent sure already that it's the same person doing the amputation in both cases. Pop over to the lab in the morning and I'll be able to tell you for certain, as there's a couple of other things I want to look at which should confirm it.'

Ninety-nine per cent was enough for Palmer.

'All right, what's next?'

'Next I get the body bagged and back to the lab for a full PM.'

Gheeta asked a question. 'Wouldn't Forensics want to have a look before we move it?'

Latin shook his head. 'No, I had a chat with Reg Frome at Murder Squad Forensics on the phone and he said there was no point in them going over it. If the body had been shoved around in the back of a waste lorry on its round and then dumped here, there wouldn't be anything for them to look for, and the victim's DNA and prints could be taken later in the morgue.'

Palmer didn't totally agree with that, but saw the point.

'All right, take the body to your unit in Deptford.' He turned to DI Lucan. 'This bay is to be kept shut and I would be grateful if you could spare one of your officers to stay and make sure nobody goes near it, especially the press. They'd love this story if they got hold of it, so let's try and keep a lid on it for as long as we can.'

He turned back to Latin. 'I know you said Reg said there was no point in Forensics having a look, but I'm going to ask him to reconsider. I notice the girl hasn't any jewellery or rings, which is unusual for young ladies of that age. So just in case one might have come off in the jostling of the body in the back of the lorry, I'll have them do a metal detection sweep on the heap.'

Weatherby could see a problem in that. 'There may be tins and bottle tops in the heap. Shouldn't be, as it's waste from commercial premises not household so they have separate bins for tin and plastic, but...' he shrugged. 'People are lazy when it comes to recycling properly.'

Palmer nodded. 'That's okay, Forensics will sort that out.' He looked down the row of bays and the lorries backing in to tip their contents. 'What happens to all this stuff?'

Weatherby feigned shock, 'Stuff! How dare you, Detective Chief Superintendent! This *stuff* is the fuel to heat your house and keep the lights on.'

'It is?'

'Too right it is. This is a Waste Transfer Station – there are a few of us around the country and that's what we do, we transfer waste. When the bays are full up we lift the contents into steel containers where it is pressed down to a quarter of the original size, and then when full those containers in turn are taken round to the railway yard at the back of this building and lifted onto bogeys, which are then hauled by rail to various incinerators nationwide. Most of ours goes to the Energy Recovery Centre in Avonmouth, where it's burnt to provide the steam to turn the turbines that send electricity to the national grid that provides you with a hot bath.'

Palmer was impressed. 'I'll need one to get rid of the smell. I shall view our kitchen waste bin with reverence from now on, Mr Weatherby. And please congratulate your staff on spotting that body – if it had gone to the incinerator the poor girl would have gone unnoticed.'

'Oh, we get a dozen or so bodies a year turn up inside waste bins emptied here. Sadly, most are newborn babies, and I've no doubt we miss a few too.'

Gheeta was interested. 'What happens to ones you find?'

'They are taken away by social services and the police.' He nodded towards DI Lucan. Gheeta looked at Lucan for an explanation.

'DNA,' he said. 'We get the DNA and hopefully can match it on the national database and find the mother, in the case of babies, then social services take over. I don't know what happens then – our part is done. If the body is adult then we check missing persons, and if we get a match send round the FLO to break the news.

Gheeta turned back to Weatherby. 'How come your chaps doing the collecting didn't notice the body when they wheeled the bin to the lorry and tipped it in?'

'It's commercial waste, not household waste. Big bins on wheels, not your standard household size ones. Our men push them to back of the lorry, click on the grips, and the hydraulics do the rest: lifting it and turning out the contents. The men never see what's inside.'

'So this lorry was on a commercial premises only route?'

'Yes.'

'I'll need that route map and a list of the premises that it picked up from.'

'No problem, I'll have a copy made for you.'

Gheeta took a contact card from her tunic pocket and passed it to him. 'If you could email it over to me as soon as possible please.'

'I'll have it sent later this afternoon.'

Palmer was happy with that. 'Right then, I think that's all we can do for now, Forensics have had a sift through – oh, and keep the lorry here too if you would, Mr Weatherby. They'll need to check the inside of that as well.'

CHAPTER 2

Palmer didn't hurry on his way to Professor Latin's laboratories the next morning. He wanted to give Latin time to complete the post mortem tests on the victims; and anyway, visits to the Murder Morgue – as it was known in the Met – to view opened up bodies and parts of bodies whilst breathing the acrid smell of dead flesh and formaldehyde was not an enjoyable experience, and certainly not the best way to start the day

He left his Crombie and trilby at the reception area and donned the necessary light plastic overalls, cap and rubber boots. At least by changing out of them on leaving the premises later the smell could be left behind too.

'Ah, good morning Justin,' Latin greeted him as he walked into the operations lab. 'Come in, come in, this will interest you.'

Palmer nodded to the other pathologists working at other parts of the lab that he knew by sight and joined Latin at the side of a stainless steel worktop, where the body from the waste centre lay discreetly covered by a green rubber sheet. Green seemed to be the favourite colour of pathologists.

Once a human body has been through a post mortem, it resembles the carcass of a pig or cow at the butchers – the inner organs having been removed to be weighed and saved in large glass containers of formaldehyde, and any blood and bodily fluids cleaned away. The long cut from the chest to the groin that had been made to gain access to the various organs within was then closed and held shut by medical clips. The only difference with this body from others displayed on various worktops in the lab was that the left arm was missing.

    'Right.' Latin pointed his rubber gloved hand to the left shoulder. 'As you can see Justin, no arm. The humerus has been separated from the scapula by a pretty skilful incision and cutting of the glenoid cavity.' He stood back and smiled at Palmer. 'You don't know what the fuck I'm talking about, do you?'

    'The arm has been cut off.'

    'Basically yes, the humerus being the top bone of the arm, the scapula being the shoulder blade, and the glenoid cavity being the soft tissue holding the two together within the joint. Somebody with a knowledge of human joints has severed the two. This isn't your usual hacking job of a common or garden killer, Justin – it's quite professional, just a single incision to expose the joint at exactly the place where it should be made. Whoever did this had at least a rudimentary knowledge of how joints work, but I'd say a much better knowledge than that'

    'A surgeon?'

    'Could be, or a doctor, a vet, a butcher – somebody working in an abattoir, a medical student. It's a big list.'

    Palmer couldn't resist. 'A pathologist?'

    Latin smiled. 'I'll check I have a fucking alibi.'

    'What about the other corpse? You said you had another female one with a missing arm.'

    'Yes indeed, over here.'

    He led the way across the polished concrete lab floor to the far end where a block of steel cold storage units three high and ten across stood. Each unit was coffin size and slid out on rollers. Latin pulled one half out and lifted the covering rubber sheet off the occupant.

She was white, attractive, late twenties, with close-cropped dark hair, and her right arm was missing. The body had that pale blue-grey hue that takes over from the natural pink as the blood inside congeals and loses colour. She looked almost ghostly to Palmer.

Latin pointed to the shoulder. 'Same MO. I would go so far as to say the same or similar knife or scalpel was used as on the other body. But there's more.'

Palmer raised his eyebrows. 'More?'

'She was dragged out of the Thames near Putney. River police thought she might have been a suicide who got tangled up in the propellers of a launch or one of those tourist trip boats.'

'A *nude* suicide?'

'She was clothed. After yesterday's find I've taken the liberty of sending her clothes across to Reg Frome.'

'Good idea.'

'There is more, as I said. We had to pump her stomach which was full of Thames water – which contains microbes that would hasten the deterioration of the flesh, which we needed to arrest so we could do further tests and analysis of that water – and guess what? It showed rohypnol.'

'The date rape drug?'

'The very same. It was still there because the stomach was intact. The shock of being plunged into the cold water of the river had basically closed all her human orifices and nothing had left the body.'

Palmer wasn't keen on the image that came into his mind, 'Too much information.'

'You can never have too much information when dealing with bodies, Justin. Anyway, I checked our new body from the waste tip this morning, and bingo – rohypnol in the stomach contents of that one too.'

'Had there been a sexual assault?'

'We can't tell on this one, it's been bumped about in the river for a couple of weeks, but on the other one, no – we've done a semen test and nothing shows.'

'So it would seem the drug was used to tranquillise the victim.'

'Yes.'

'And then she was killed.'

'Yes.'

'How?'

'This one I can't tell, except to say no marks of any violence taking place. Yesterday's corpse was suffocated.'

'Suffocated whilst under the influence of rohypnol? How can you tell?'

'High level of carbon dioxide in the blood, caused by the lack of oxygen getting to the lungs – and her eyes are very bloodshot, something that stays after death in cases of suffocation.'

'Anything else?'

'Time of deaths: the body in the river had been there about a fortnight judging by the water permeation of the skin, and yesterday's body had been dead a maximum forty-eight hours.'

'Why would somebody want two human arms in a fortnight? Very strange.'

Latin shrugged. 'Murderers sometimes like a memento of their crime.'

'Could be, but I would think a finger or ear would be more apt – and certainly a damn sight easier than an arm. Put an ear or finger in a fridge, but two arms? You'd need a freezer.'

CHAPTER 3

Doctor Martine Hawk smiled across the table at the young lady sitting opposite her.

'Don't be so nervous, I don't bite!'

They both laughed.

'I know, but any job interview is a bit daunting,' the young lady said, trying to calm her inner nervousness. She needed this job.

Doctor Hawke nodded, 'Yes I know, I've done a few in my time. That's why I thought it best to have a chat here, in a cosy pub. It's a bit busy, but still better than the formal office type interview don't you think? More relaxing, especially as you've come all the way from Manchester by train for it.'

'It was very kind of you to pick me up at the station, Doctor Hawke. Very kind.'

'Not at all – I did think of having our chat in the station buffet, but the thought of British Rail coffee and sandwiches vetoed that idea.' They both laughed. 'This is much better.'

The Doctor looked at her notepad on the table in front of her. 'You've had experience of being a PA before, and your references are very good I must say. But you've always worked in Manchester, so why a sudden change to London?'

'Divorce. It came through a fortnight ago, and I really just want to forget the past and start afresh. I couldn't do that in Manchester – too many old friends and people from the past that I really want to airbrush out of my life.'

'An acrimonious divorce?'

'Very.'

'What do your family think about you moving away?'

'Oh, they don't know that's my plan. I want everything in place so I can tell them and go – don't want time for them to argue and cajole me into staying. My mind is made up.'

Hawke looked at the application form with the paperwork. 'So are you still Julie Fenstone?'

'No, sorry – I was still married when I filled in your form online, but now I'm Julie Bury. Maiden name.'

'All a bit cloak and dagger, eh? Do the family know about the job application, do they know you're here today?'

'Good God no. As I said, I want everything in place before I say a word back home.'

'Well, you have all the qualifications for the job and your experience is a great addition, which will help you slip into it quickly.' Hawke sat back in her seat and smiled warmly at Julie. 'Well, Miss Julie Bury, I think you've just landed your first job as a single woman again. I am sure it will suit us both admirably and help you adjust to your new life in London.' She held her hand out for Julie to shake, which she did.

'Oh thank you, thank you so much, Doctor Hawke. You won't regret it.'

'I am sure I won't. Now, I think we should celebrate with a glass of champagne and then I will drive you back to the station.'

'I'll get a later train, I think. I want to register with a couple of estate agents for a bedsit or similar.'

Hawke thought for a moment. 'No need. I have a granny annexe at the bottom of my garden and no granny to go in it – just a small bungalow I had built for my mother's retirement. But alas, she developed dementia and had to go into a home. It's never been used and sits behind a tall leylandi hedge, so it is completely private from the house. You can have that until you find a place.'

'Are you sure?'

'Of course I am, and I promise to leave you alone and keep my nose out of it. I won't be *popping in,* it will be just like your own place until you find something. It's fully furnished, so no great expense.'

'But you could let it out and take a rent for it.'

'No, no I don't want any strangers in it. I don't see myself as a landlady. No, as I said, it's yours until you find something. Now…' She stood up. 'I'll get that champagne and we can toast your future. '

As Doctor Martine Hawke moved through the people in the bar, her right-hand felt in her trouser suit pocket for a small glass phial.

CHAPTER 4

Palmer's Team Room at Scotland Yard is opposite his office on the third floor. His office is small and has his and DS Singh's desks, two filing cabinets, and a coat and hat stand – all standard government issue from a good decade ago – crammed into it. The Team Room across the corridor is a fairly large rectangular space, with one side being large windows overlooking the Embankment and the Thames, and along the other side of the room are computers, servers and keyboards on benches, all of which DS Singh brought in and set up. She also brought in – and still brings in – various programmes that could assist in their work; many of these programmes are not supposed to be there and have been added by DS Singh using her IT expertise to copy them from other encrypted sites and worldwide law enforcement agencies' hardware – all being very useful in cracking a case quickly, which is why Palmer turns a blind eye and doesn't ask too many direct questions as to their provenance.

Gheeta is ably assisted by Claire, a civilian computer clerk that she had Palmer get transferred from the Yard's computer pool, an updated version of the old 'typing pool'. They had met at lunch in the staff cafeteria one day, and Claire had impressed Gheeta with her IT knowledge that was obviously being unused and wasted in the 'pool'.

Both were at work on PCs when Palmer walked in after his visit to the path labs. He noticed that Gheeta had wiped clean the large white progress board that was screwed to the far end wall, and had neatly pinned up a picture of the waste tip victim to it. This board acted as an aide memoire to Palmer, who often studied it when a case was moving along and the evidence threads began to link the pictures and writing on it like spaghetti.

They exchanged greetings and the ladies sat back and listened as Palmer took them through Latin's results, and gave Gheeta a picture of the first victim's face to add to the board.

'Right then,' he said when he'd finished. 'What's happening? Usual procedures getting into place?'

Gheeta nodded. 'Yes guv, we've got the route map for the waste lorry so we can pinpoint where the body was picked up from – well, not exactly *where* but somewhere along that route.'

'Okay, but we have to consider that she may have been brought there from somewhere else and put into that waste bin. But it's a start.'

'And Claire's getting a list of missing persons – female and under forty – for that area.'

'Right, the Prof will have DNA soon so that should help.'

'Only if it's on the database guv, and neither of the victims look to be of the criminal kind.'

'You never can tell, Sergeant. One of them might have been done for shoplifting, drunk and disorderly, on the game, you can't tell these days – and even if they're both clean we might get a match for a family member who's fallen foul of the law at some time.'

A perfunctory tap at the door announced the arrival of Reg Frome as he walked in. Frome was head of the Murder Squad Forensics Department and handled all the forensic investigations for Palmer's Squad, Organised Crime and CID when murder was involved. He was the spitting image of Doc from the *Back to The Future* films, even down to the shock of bushy white hair.

'Good day, Serial Murder Squad.' He smiled at them as they returned the greeting. 'And may I say how nice it was of you to send me and my team to wallow knee-deep into a pile of sloppy, evil-smelling waste material on a fool's errand with metal detectors – a million thanks.' He sat down and gave them a false glare. 'It will not be forgotten.'

Having worked with Frome ever since their days long ago when both had started their police careers after induction at the Hendon Police College, Palmer knew Frome wouldn't have come in if the search had proved negative.

'What have you got, Reg? What did you find in the heap?'

'Nothing of consequence, Justin – a few tin lids, some industrial metal shavings and other commercial and industrial rubbish.'

'Nothing?'

'Not in the heap, no.' He pulled out a small transparent evidence bag from his jacket pocket. 'But in the back of the tipper lorry – voila!'

Palmer reached across and took it. 'What have we here then?'

Gheeta could tell. 'Ear stud, it's an ear stud.'

Frome nodded. 'Yes, it is. A silver ear stud – not the sort of thing you'd expect to find in industrial and commercial waste so who knows, it may have been the victims.'

'Just the one?' asked Claire. 'I wear them off-duty but they usually come in pairs, one for each ear.'

'Yes, just the one – we found it in the edge ruts of the tipper truck. Had a good look round but there wasn't another. Interesting thing though – it's foreign. We had a look through the magnifying lens and found a French essay mark and importer number.'

Palmer shrugged. 'Can't see how that helps identify our body, it could have been imported in the thousands.'

Frome agreed. 'Probably still is, but that's all we could find, Justin.'

'It could help, guv,' Gheeta said. 'If we identify the body and one of her relatives or friends identify the stud as belonging to her, it could be a major piece of evidence if we track the killer and find the other stud.'

'Lots of *ifs* Sergeant, but you never know. Okay, thanks Reg, great job done – appreciate it as always.'

Frome nodded and made for the door. 'You're welcome, just make sure you don't lose it. Three of my people waded through stinking rubbish for three hours to find that.'

The two victims' DNA codes came through from Latin's lab and Gheeta emailed them down to the Crime Data Department for running through the computers – a long job, and one that has to be checked twice just to make sure the readings are correct.

Palmer looked at the waste truck's work route on the big screen on the wall above the computers that Gheeta had brought it up on, whilst Claire pulled up details of the businesses on that route that were business rate registered with the local council. Many were owned and registered to landlords who divided them and then rented them out in smaller units, which meant the occupiers would not be listed so the landlords would have to be contacted for details. It might well turn out that the body in the bin had been brought in from elsewhere and dumped in it as Palmer had said, but each and every business had to be talked to and asked if any female member of staff fitting the girl's description had left suddenly or just not turned up for work in the last fortnight. This was going to be a long job, and help was needed; time to twist Assistant Commissioner Bateman's arm.

CHAPTER 5

Assistant Commissioner Bateman gave a false smile across his desk to Palmer sitting opposite. Bateman was forty-seven years old, slightly built and the epitome of a social climber in society, but his climbing was in the police force; he sucked up to anybody in authority he thought might assist in his career path towards his goal of being Commissioner. He was always immaculately turned out, in a uniform with ironed creases that could cut bread. His nemesis was his head, in that it was bald, totally bald. It didn't worry anybody except AC Bateman. It was hereditary: his father had been bald, his brother was bald, and he wasn't sure but he had a suspicion that his sister had started to infuse false hair pieces into her receding locks. He had once tried wearing a wig, but the silence from all quarters of the Yard on the day he wore it, and the number of staff who kept their hand in front of their faces as he walked past put paid to that idea.

There had always been a distrustful undercurrent to Palmer and Bateman's relationship; nothing you could pin down, but Palmer didn't like or agree with fast-tracking of university graduates to management positions in the force. He'd have them do the two years on the beat first, see how they handled a Rastafarian drug dealer with a ten-inch knife who just did not want to be arrested. Bateman, on the other hand, would like to be surrounded with graduates with '*Firsts*' in various '*ologies*', and was very pleased when the government brought in the minimum recruitment requirement of having to have a degree in order to apply to join the force. He believed the old school coppers like Palmer were outdated dinosaurs, and that crime could be solved by elimination and computer programmes, which is why he had tried unsuccessfully to transfer DS Singh away from Palmer into a Cyber Crime Unit. Bateman had no time for an experienced detective's knowledge and nose for a criminal being an asset, and the sooner he could shut down the Serial Murder Squad and combine it with the Organised Crime Unit, CID and Cyber Crime the better.

The trouble was that Palmer's team, the Organised Crime Team, CID and Cyber Crime were producing good 'case solved' figures which the political masters at the Home Office liked, and they therefore insisted the units carried on as they were. But what really irked Bateman most of all was that they really liked Palmer too. The press also liked Palmer, and the rank and file loved him. So Bateman managed to keep the false smile on his face as he looked across his highly polished desk at Palmer. He put down the case report.

'Nasty, very nasty… How many men do you need?'

'Four should do it.'

'Four?!'

'Well, the quicker we can get around to talking to the businesses on the tipper truck's route the better. I don't want any trail we might have a chance of picking up from there going cold.'

Palmer augmented his team when the need arose by pulling in detectives from other squads who were on leave, or were due days off. Gheeta had a list of tried and trusted officers who always responded to the call if they were available; working with Palmer was a career wish of most of the Yard's officers.

'Very well, but be aware of the overtime payments mounting up.' Bateman could see the good reason for Palmer's need of extra officers, but he also fought an ongoing battle with Home Office cuts in funding and the requirement to extend officers' hours in the fight against the epidemic of knife crime in London which was eating into his budget substantially. But he couldn't take the risk of more dismembered bodies turning up, and Palmer taking a press briefing and complaining about the lack of support. Being between a rock and a hard place was the experience of every force with the austerity cuts still in play.

Gheeta soon had four detectives from her list who were on leave and only too pleased to take the call to arms, and she arranged for them to come into the Team Room the next morning for a briefing.

Nothing else could be done until the DNA reports came through and hopefully threw up a name or two. Palmer's brain was in overdrive as he drove home to Dulwich. This was what policing was all about, the start of a case; his excitement was bubbling inside. Each time a new case started, he felt reborn. He'd had that feeling for nearly fifty years in the force – the chase was on, somewhere out there a killer was free, and it was Palmer's job to bring him or her in. He loved his job. He also loved Mrs P.'s toad-in-the-hole, which was waiting for him in the oven. Bliss.

'Are you kidding me?' Palmer held a sausage skewered onto his fork in front of him at the kitchen table and turned it slowly. 'It's *good* for me?'

'Of course it's good for you,' said Mrs P., sat opposite eating her dinner.

'It doesn't taste like it's good for me, it tastes like it's made of hedge clippings!'

'I told you we are going vegetarian – look at your stomach. You need to lose a couple of stone, Justin Palmer, or you'll have a heart attack.'

'Nothing wrong with my stomach, it's an adult six pack.'

'More like a firkin. Anyway, it will do us both good to eat less meat and more vegetables at our age.'

'You could have warned me, I've been looking forward to your toad-in-the-hole all afternoon.'

'Wouldn't make any difference if I'd warned you, be the same sausage.'

'Yes, but I'd have had a Big Mac on the way home. Am I ever going to see a real sausage or a piece of steak on my plate again?'

'Yes, of course you are, just not so much. Mark my words, you'll feel fitter and healthier in a couple of weeks.'

There was a tapping on the kitchen door that led to the side entrance of the house.

'That'll be Benji,' said Mrs P. 'He's bringing a crate of his home-made wine.'

Benji was Palmer's nemesis: real name Benjamin Courtney-Smith, he was a portly, single, ex-advertising executive in his late fifties, who had taken early retirement and now had, in Palmer's estimation, too much time on his hands and too much money in his pocket. A new car every year, plus at least two cruise holidays to exotic parts; he wore designer label clothes befitting a much younger man, a fake tan, enough gold jewellery to interest the Hatton Garden Safe Deposit Heist detectives, and all topped off with his thinning hair scooped into a ponytail, also befitting a much younger man. Palmer was unsure about Benji's sexuality, as his mincing walk and the waving of his hands to illustrate every word cast doubts in Palmer's mind; not that that worried Palmer, who was quite at ease in the multi-gender world of today. Of course he would never admit it, but the main grudge he held against Benji was that before his arrival in the quiet suburb of Dulwich village, Palmer had been the favourite amongst the ladies of the Women's Institute, the bridge club and the various other clubs catering for ladies of a certain age, but now Benji had usurped Palmer's fan club; and when he stood for and was elected to the local council on a mandate to re-open the library and bring back the free bus pass for pensioners, his popularity soared and their fluttering eyelids had turned in his direction.

Mrs P. left the table to open the door. Palmer gave Daisy the dog, who was prone on the floor, a light nudge with his foot and whispered towards her: *'see him off.'* Daisy looked towards the door and growled. Mrs P. waved a finger at her and she settled back down, job done.

'Hello, Justin.' Benji gave Palmer a big smile as he manoeuvred a wooden crate of wine bottles through the door, banging one side.

'Mind the paintwork,' was Palmer's greeting, which got a cold look from Mrs P.

Benji lowered the crate onto the kitchen worktop and stood back, puffing. 'There! Phew, that was heavy.'

'Would you like a vegetarian sausage? Palmer waved the sausage on his fork at him.

'What?' Benji was confused.

'Take no notice of him, Benji.' She looked into the crate. 'My word, what have we got here then?'

Benji's face lit up. 'Oh, you'll enjoy these – homemade elderflower wine! Natural flavoured wine, Justin – no chemical additives, just yeast and sugar, made by yours truly. I picked the flowers and made the wine.' He took an exaggerated bow. 'Can I pour you a glass?'

'You could if it was a bottle of Chilean Malbec in that crate – you wouldn't happen to have one of those, would you?'

Mrs P. gave him another cold look. 'Take no notice of him, Benji. We will have a glass of your wine please.' She pulled three wine glasses from the cupboard and a corkscrew from the drawer.

Benji pulled out a bottle and wound in the corkscrew. 'I gave the ladies at the WI a few bottles earlier. I read that elderflower wine is very popular with vegetarians, they swear blind a glass a day provides the antitoxins the body needs – keeps your energy levels up, and keeps you on the move.'

About an hour after their glass, Benji's elderflower wine started to keep the Palmers on the move too.

'I'll murder him. So help me, I'll murder him and his elderflower wine,' Palmer promised himself at two in the morning, after his fifth visit to the bathroom.

CHAPTER 6

The four seconded detectives were in the Team Room with Gheeta and Claire the next morning waiting for Palmer, who was busy in his office signing off the paperwork raised by Bateman's staff to allow the overtime payments. They chatted amongst themselves. Claire's investigation into the ear stud had paid dividends; it had indeed been imported into the UK from France, but not in thousands, just a hundred pairs, and all to just one English retailer who only sold online.

Gheeta received the news thoughtfully.

'But they could have been bought in France by a tourist or somebody on holiday couldn't they, and come into the country that way?'

Claire agreed. 'Yes, or bought in any of five other countries the maker exports to.'

'Okay, a bit of a long shot, but get the importer to give us the names and addresses of the buyers in the UK.'

Claire's face dropped. 'And, let me guess, contact every one of them looking for a missing wife or daughter?'

'Yes, and do it subtly.'

'Like, hello we've got a body in the morgue that we think could be your wife or daughter?'

'Yes, that should do it.'

Palmer walked in and a smile lit up his face as he saw the assembled team of three men and one lady, DS Sarah Lewis. He recognised them all from previous cases.

'Aah, familiar faces all. Good to see you again.'

Gheeta ran through their names, just in case Palmer had forgotten one; he was thankful for that, as he couldn't put names to two of them, although the faces were familiar. 'DS Lewis from Ruislip CID, DS Patel and Trent from Organised Crime, and DS Langham from West End Central CID. I've brought them up to speed guv, and issued a folder of victim mugshots, and they all have radios on a limited HF waveband from comms.' The Met has a broad band of high frequency wavebands allocated to them for use by radio, and issues a temporary high frequency waveband to various teams as and when a secure network is required for operational purposes.

'Well done, Sergeant. Right then, the first step is to follow the waste lorry's route and check on all the businesses it picks up from. Any female staff missing, any left in suspicious circumstances, all the usual questions. But don't show the victim's mugshot unless you feel it necessary – not everybody likes to look at a picture of a dead person.'

Claire stood up and passed a paper to each of them. 'This is a current council listing of all the registered businesses on the route – probably not up-to-date, but it's the best I can get. And this -' She gave each detective a colour photo. 'This is a blow-up photo of an ear stud found near the body.'

Palmer clapped his hands together. 'Right then, off you go – sort yourselves into two pairs, and remember this killer is a nasty bastard, so stick in your pairs and stay alert. No heroics.'

The team left.

'Claire got some info through on the ear stud, guv.'

Palmer raised his eyebrows and looked at Claire. 'Go on.'

'Import from France, only sold through one internet retailer in the UK. I'm contacting them for a list of clients who bought a set from them, and then seeing if any of those names are on the reported missing list. If no result there, I'll use their details from the retailer's sales list, give them a call, and hopefully find them all happily at home.'

Palmer nodded. 'Let's hope so.'

CHAPTER 7

DS Lewis turned to DS Patel with a resigned look on her face.

'I suppose we must, but I'm not going to enjoy this one.'

It had been a fruitless morning so far. Both teams had visited the premises on the waste tipper's route one after the other – Lewis and Patel on the right side of the roads, Langham and Trent on the left. Most were quite quick to clear: small commercial businesses, printers, gift warehouses, car sprayers and the like. None of the bosses or staff could shed any light on the two victims' identities. Now Lewis and Patel stood outside their next port of call, West London Abattoir – a large slaughterhouse behind a large wall with a security gate and small gatehouse pod manned by uniformed security staff.

Patel smiled, 'You a vegetarian then, Lewis?'

'No, but I really should be. I hate it when I see those lorries full of sheep or cows off to be killed.'

'Yes, it's not good, I'll admit that. But then if they weren't bred to be killed for food, they wouldn't get born at all. I suppose three months on a rich grass meadow is better than no life at all for a lamb.'

'Is it? Oh well, let's get it over with. Could well be that one of the butchers in here is taking his skills home at night and slicing off people's limbs.'

'They'd have the tools for the job.'

The security officers at the gatehouse checked their warrant cards and led them to wait in the large arrivals yard, where cattle pens stood empty waiting their next delivery, whilst a management person was summoned. A large white-coated individual in rubber boots and a hair net under his white cloth cap soon appeared.

'Harry Johnson,' he introduced himself. 'I'm the line manager. How can we help you?'

DS Lewis explained that they were looking for information on two murder victims, one of whom had been found in the area. She left out the gruesome details and showed Harry Johnson the pictures of the two victims' faces and the ear stud.

'No, can't say I recognise either of them, and if one of them had worked here she wouldn't have been allowed to wear the stud – no jewellery in the works. You can't have anything on you that might fall off, Health and Safety rules. Pretty young things, weren't they – why would anybody want to murder them?'

'That's what we are trying to find out,' said Patel. 'Would you mind showing these photos to the staff for us?'

Johnson wasn't too keen. 'Well, we've got an automatic production line going in the butchery, keeps moving the carcasses along as each butcher takes off his particular cut. I can't stop that line – time is money.'

Patel nodded sympathetically and then delivered the low punch. 'OK, then I just radio our boss and get a warrant to take over an office inside the building and have the staff in one by one to take a look.' He took out his radio.

Johnson quickly changed his mind. 'All right, I'll take them in and show them round.'

Patel smiled; he knew Johnson wouldn't want to lose his production bonus by stopping the line, and that he would take the photos in and dump them on a table for ten minutes before bringing them back with a negative answer. 'And I'll come with you,' he said. 'We don't want to miss anybody, do we?'

Johnson grunted. 'You'll have to get an overall and boots.'

'Size eleven.'

Lewis stifled a smile. 'I'll hang on here.'

Johnson led Patel away and Lewis wandered round the yard. The thought of the never-ending procession of animals resident in the pens for a short time before going off to meet their maker was not a pleasant one. A large wagon of sheep pulled up outside the gates. One security man hurried out to the driver and had a quick conversation before returning to the gatehouse instead of opening the gates. The driver seemed to have changed his mind and a short reverse was followed by the truck pulling away from the entrance and off up the road. Lewis turned away to shield her hands from the security pod and noted the number plate in her notebook.

Thirty minutes later Lewis and Patel sat in window seats in a cafe fifty metres up the road from the abattoir sipping coffees. Patel's tour of the butchers had not yielded any information, or any recognition of the victims' faces or the stud.

'So why are we sitting here watching the abattoir when we ought to be moving on to the next building?'

Lewis grimaced at the taste of the coffee. 'Just a hunch. Why would a truck full of sheep turn away from the gates after a word with the security man?'

'No room for them? The place was very busy inside.'

'The pens in the yard are empty.' Lewis shrugged. 'I don't know – you know when you get a feeling that something's not right but can't put your finger on it? It just felt... suspicious.'

'Is that it?' Patel nodded towards a cattle truck pulling up at the gates.

Lewis checked the number plate in her notebook. 'That's the one.'

'Well, he's getting access now.'

The tall gates swung open and the security man waved the truck through before closing them.

'And the only difference between now and earlier is that when he arrived before, there were a couple of coppers on the premises.'

'Might be worth letting Claire have a dig down on that truck and its load – sheep rustling is big business.'

'In West London?'

'The truck was from Cumbria, or at least that's what was written on the side: Cumbria Livestock Haulage Company.'

'Could be our killer is a regular visitor to London and not a resident – a long distance lorry driver who comes down, does a murder and takes a body part back with him.'

Patel feigned concern and patted Lewis gently on the arm. 'You need counselling.'

'It's possible.'

'Possible yes, likely no. Come on, only about two hundred other businesses to check out.'

CHAPTER 8

Being called out at three o'clock in the morning from a nice warm bed into a cold late September night was not pleasing to Palmer. It had been all right in his younger days as a CID detective, doing a 4am hit on the home of some lowlife criminal or drug dealer, but now his body was less receptive to that part of police work. The mind was still alert and when his phone beside the bed had rung and Gheeta's voice said: 'We've got another one guv,' his brain clicked into top gear. But as he swung his legs out of bed, his sciatica also clicked into top gear and reminded him of his age with a sharp stab to his right thigh. The duvet he'd taken with him was quickly pulled back over the bed by Mrs P., who was used to his late nights and having her sleep disturbed as he tried to get into bed without waking her; he never could, although she pretended to stay asleep. Each time she made a mental promise to get twin beds, but never had; there was something secure in having one of London's top policemen next to you at night.

The squad car had arrived as he left the house in the pale white moonlight and whisked him off to Praed Street Paddington, where a diversion was in place keeping what little traffic there was at that time in the morning well away from an all-night laundromat protected by crime scene tape stretched across the road. Several police cars and an ambulance were at the scene; the blue lights and activity had woken the occupants of the flats above the shops and other businesses along the road, and a small crowd was beginning to form at the barriers where uniformed officers told them there was 'nothing to see, so go on home please.' Of course none did, and their phones flashed continuously taking pictures of the scene.

Palmer got out of the squad car gingerly, having settled his sciatica down with continuous rubbing of the affected thigh on the journey. Gheeta emerged from the laundromat and met him.

'Well…' Palmer raised his eyebrows. 'What have we got here then?'

'All-night laundromat, guv – a useful place for homeless people or addicts to slip into for a kip or to shoot up, so the local lads keep an eye on it. The local patrol noticed a person slumped on one of the chairs at the back as they checked the place about an hour ago, and when they took a close look they saw it was a young lady who appeared to be asleep with a blanket over her legs. When they shook her, she toppled off the chair sideways and the blanket slid off – and guess what?'

'One arm missing.'

'One leg missing.'

'You're joking.'

'No, seems our killer is assembling a body, guv – limb by limb.'

They walked into the laundromat where Forensics had taped off much of it and were hard at work, dusting for fingerprints and using powerful hand held infrared lights to search for any small physical clues left by the killer. A photographer was hard at work, his flashes bouncing off the tiled walls; near the door the ambulance crew stood, not sure of their part to play. The local force SIO (Senior Investigating Officer), who had charge of the scene, came over.

Gheeta did the introductions. 'This is DCI Hardy sir, Paddington Green.'

Palmer shook his hand. 'Good to meet you, Hardy. What have we here then?'

Hardy was mid-forties: slim build, tight number two haircut, and regulation unbreakable glass spectacles.

'Single white female, sir – left leg missing, no other immediately visible wounds, and no ID'

'Was she dead when they arrived?' Palmer nodded towards the ambulance crew.

'Yes sir, the officers first on the scene checked for a pulse but nothing doing, so they called in the medics; first responder was here in four minutes and did what he could to try and revive her – adrenalin injected to the heart and defibrillator attacks – but he says he thinks she was dead a good five hours or so before they found her.'

'Right.'

'I asked him about the missing leg and he said it looks like a professional amputation job, not the result of an accident; so we checked the Paddington Hospital over the road in case she was an amputee from there.'

'Really?' Palmer's expression asked the question why? He couldn't see a recent amputee leaving a hospital on her own, no matter how bad the food was.

'Well, she may have been confused by the drugs – you know, morphine, pain killers and the rest – and somehow wandered out.' Hardy didn't sound very convinced himself.

'Hardly do a runner, could she.' Palmer couldn't resist that one.

Gheeta rolled her eyes. Hardy didn't get the joke.

'Okay, get the body over to Professor Latin's morgue in Deptford once the Forensics have finished here, if you would – he's doing the pathologies in this case.'

Hardy was surprised. 'You mean there's more like this?'

'Two without an arm ,and now one without a leg. Seems somebody has taken the sport of bodybuilding to another level. Right, Sergeant,' he turned to Gheeta, 'nothing more we can do here at present.' He checked his watch. 'In the morning, like in three hours time, get Trent and Langham off the waste truck route and over here to do house-to-house, and check any CCTV that may have picked up anything. I take it this place has a system?'

Gheeta pointed to a camera in a far corner. 'Its light is blinking so I assume it's on, guv. I've got a car picking up the owner and bringing him in.'

'I would have thought he'd live in the flat upstairs.'

'Manageress does, but she's in a bit of a state. She was there when the blanket fell off.'

'Oh dear.'

'Medics gave her something and I sent her back up to her flat with a WPC. I'll get a statement tomorrow.'

'Good. Well, nothing we can do here. Hardy, I'd like all forensic reports copied to Reg Frome at the Murder Squad Forensics, and anything else that turns up to come to us at the Yard please.'

'Will do.'

'Right, home for a couple of hours' kip and then back to the office, eh?'

'I'll hang on for the owner guv, get the CCTV disc.'

'Okay, if there's anything on it that needs immediate action call me back in.' He turned to go, but remembered one thing. 'By the way, how come Central ops rang you before me?'

'What do you mean?'

'Well, *you* rang me at home, so they must have rung you *before* me.'

Gheeta saw an opportunity. 'They don't like to disturb your sleep, guv. It's an age thing, and you're a grumpy bugger when woken up.'

Palmer kept his smile to himself. 'That's very considerate of them, but also untrue.'

'To give them their due guv, they did call you on your radio – it was on, but no answer.'

Palmer thought for a moment. 'It was in my coat, that's why.' He fished it out of his Crombie pocket. 'I left in my damn coat pocket – wouldn't have heard it from the bedroom.'

'And Central ops apparently haven't got your home number. Can't think why not.' Gheeta raised her eyebrows and gave him an old-fashioned look. 'I'll let them have it.'

'You will not, not unless you wish to go back on the East End beat as WPC Singh. I changed my number after getting three callouts on the trot in the early hours: one to a domestic, one to a minor road collision, and one to a drunk urinating in a local parish councillor's front garden who had asked specifically for me to attend.'

'The urinating drunk asked specifically for *you*, guv? Does Mrs P. know you keep such elite company?'

'I'll see you later, Sergeant.'

CHAPTER 9

Palmer was hopeful of a CCTV result from the laundromat when he came into the Team Room later that morning after very little sleep. Claire and Gheeta were already there.

'Well, what about the CCTV from the laundromat – did you get it from the owner? Anything on it?'

'Wasn't on.'

'Wasn't on?'

'It's a dummy camera.' Gheeta sounded as disappointed as he was. 'The owner just has it as a deterrent – said he hasn't anything worth nicking and nobody is likely to make off with an industrial washing machine, and when he had real cameras in the past they were stolen.'

'Bloody marvellous.

The laundromat victim's face photo was circulated that afternoon to all the MPBs (Missing Person Bureau) in the UK and brought an immediate response from the Manchester force. FRT (Facial Recognition Technology) can scan and check a thousand faces in seconds, and a match with full details was soon emailed down to Palmer's office where Claire, Gheeta and Palmer took a look at it.

'Julie Bury, 26 – divorced, no children, reported missing by her mother yesterday. Hasn't been seen for three days!' Palmer was amazed and pleased. 'That's good – I mean, not that it's good she's turned up dead, but good that we are onto it so quickly before any leads go cold. Right, get everything we can on her: address, work history, relationships, associates, club memberships, credit cards held, social life, the lot. Find out why she was in London – was she visiting somebody, business or social.' He looked at Gheeta. 'Off you go.'

'What, to Manchester?'

'Of course – I'll get a car to take you and let the Manchester force know you are on the way, and to afford you any help you need. Stay over if needed.'

'Really?'

'Of course. Bound to be a homeless hostel they can fit you into.'

'Can't wait.'

'Actually I think it's the Midland Hotel that keeps a suite for the Manchester force on short notice. Good hotel.'

Gheeta didn't stay over; no need to. Julie Bury had her own bedsit; it was tidy and clean, she had obviously been an organised person. Having that bedsit and not living at home negated the need for Gheeta to visit the parents; they had been told the bad news, although not the full gruesome details, and had a FLO (Family Liaison Officer) with them. Nothing out of the ordinary came to light in a physical search of the bedsit and Gheeta placed all the paperwork, bank statements, bills paid and unpaid into an evidence bag for a good sort out back at the Team Room in London. Photos on the wall showed Julie in better times: on holiday with various girl friends, and several with one male who Gheeta took to be her now-divorced husband. Checks would be made on him too.

By ten o'clock that night she had done all she thought necessary and called for a car to take her home – better to get home and get a good night's sleep in her own bed and start fresh in the morning than start the day with a long Manchester to London car ride in the rush hour. She sealed the bedsit as a crime scene, which meant that nobody would be allowed in until Palmer had decided that it didn't need an in-depth forensic investigation first.

CHAPTER 10

Palmer was surprised to see Gheeta was already in the Team Room the next morning when he arrived.

'You must have left early.'

'Came back last night guv, the search didn't take long. She lived in a small bedsit and was a very tidy person.' She pointed to Julie Bury's paperwork spread across a bench table. 'All in order and dated. Seems she was job hunting: five copies of application forms she sent off to various companies looking for secretaries or Pas, and her full CV sent to some national employment and recruitment agencies. Some with replies, all negative.'

Palmer walked to the case progress board. Claire had pasted the other two victims' photos up, including Julie Bury.

'Attractive ladies, weren't they.'

Gheeta joined him. 'Could that be a motive – jealousy?'

'Could be, but killing people just because they are attractive doesn't make a good reason, does it?'

'Other than war and somebody threatening to demote you to WPC on the East End beat, is there ever a good reason for killing somebody, guv?'

Palmer smiled. 'Let's get a profiler in and see if we can get some idea of who we are looking for. Give support a call and see if we can arrange that. Anything else on Julie Bury?'

'She had a Facebook page, sir.' Claire had been digging into social media for any sign of Julie Bury on the various platforms. Palmer and Gheeta crossed over to stand behind Claire who had pulled up the Facebook page. 'Just the usual stuff – she wasn't a regular poster, but it shows the other sites she was interested in. They are mostly recruitment agency sites that list jobs available, or ones where an individual can post their CV and hope for an interest from somewhere.'

'That ties in with the paperwork from the bedsit,' said Palmer.

'What about Twitter?' asked Gheeta. 'People on Facebook usually have a Twitter or WhatsApp account as well for chatting.'

'No, I checked them – if she was on them she didn't use her own name.'

'Okay.' Palmer wanted to know something. 'If she posted a CV and hoped for a reply, where would that reply come to – direct to her or to the platform admin?'

'Wherever she asked for it to be sent to on her original advert if she had one,' said Gheeta.

'I've trawled all those advert sites and she hasn't an advert on any of them – at least not in her own name,' said Claire.

'She could have got answers and then deleted the advert,' said Gheeta. 'We would have to get the site owners to check their deleted postings.'

Palmer shook his head. 'No point, it's the *replies* to her advert, if there were any, that we need to look at, or her contact with any other adverts if she was looking for a job. She lives in Manchester and is found dead in a London laundromat. Why did she travel to London, and when? We know she may have come down for a job, or a job interview, but we don't know when or how she got here.'

'Hang on a second.' Gheeta crossed to the table of Julie Bury's papers and sorted through a small box, pulling out a chequebook. 'This is her latest chequebook and no cheques have been issued for a month. Mind you, that's not surprising because most people and the vast majority of younger people use cards these days. If Julie came by coach or train, I bet she paid by card.' She passed the chequebook to Claire. 'Ring her bank and get a credit or debit card statement emailed through.'

The internal wall phone rang and Gheeta answered it. 'DS Singh... Yes... I know what you are talking about, yes... Has he?... Okay, be down in a minute.' She replaced the receiver. 'That's interesting, guv. The press department put out a short story about the body in the waste bin and the ear stud being the only clue to her identity. Lots of nutters ringing in as usual, you know the type – *'it's my mother's stud, haven't seen her for forty years,'* et cetera – but there's a chap in reception who says he knows her and can prove it. He's shown them a work visa with her picture and it looks genuine, and very like our mug shot.'

'Really? Things are moving along if he's genuine – only one way to find out. Come along, Sergeant.'

In the foyer to the Yard a duty officer pointed out a young man to Gheeta and Palmer. He was late twenties, casually dressed in T-shirt, jeans and a smart jacket – a well-groomed appearance overall. Palmer introduced himself and DS Singh.

'I believe you may be able to help us in identifying the body of a young lady, sir.' Palmer gave a reassuring smile.' Mr...?'

'Roberts, Gary Roberts.'

'Well Gary, what do you know?'

Gary Roberts was quite self-assured – not at all nervous or agitated, which was the usual body language with informers – and he hadn't asked if there was a reward, so Palmer felt he probably was just a genuine friend of the deceased.

'She is the sister of my girlfriend. Her name is Zerin Awad – my girlfriend's name is Mirah Awad.'

'Are they English?'

'No, Turkish. This is Zerin.' Roberts pulled the work permit from his pocket and passed it to Palmer, who looked at it before passing it on to Gheeta who scanned a copy into her laptop. 'Certainly looks like her. Will her sister identify the body and give us more information so we can contact the family? Why hasn't she come in herself, where is she?'

'She's outside. We have a problem – she's an illegal immigrant.'

'Really, why?' Palmer gave the work permit another look. 'Zerin seems to have had the right papers/'

'Yes she has – *had* – that work permit; she was a nurse, so didn't have much trouble in getting it. The NHS advertise a lot in Turkey for qualified nurses and doctors to come and work here. She worked in the NHS at Guy's Hospital in Southwark for the past six years.'

'Why didn't her sister apply for a permit through the British Embassy in Turkey? Is she a nurse?'

'No, she hasn't the qualifications – she's five years younger than Zerin, and the terms of access have got much tighter.'

'How long has she been over here then?'

'Only a year.'

'Only a year? So how long have you and her been together?'

'I work for an oil company and I was in Istanbul for six years; we became an item over there. I was transferred back to the UK last year and we tried every way we could to get a permit for her, but the answer was always no.'

'You could have married her? Wives are allowed in,' Gheeta pointed out.

'Only if you've been married a number of years. Too many people used fake quick marriages to gain access, so the authorities put a time limit on it.'

'How did she get in then?' asked Palmer.

'She travelled to Paris and I went over on the ferry with Zerin's passport on a one-way ticket; they are very similar in looks so we hoped immigration wouldn't look too hard at the passport, and we travelled back together on one-way Calais to Dover tickets.'

'No checks?'

'No, we just walked through the green channel. Took the chance and it worked.'

'So where does the ear stud feature in being able to identify her?'

'Mirah bought a pair of them in Paris as a present for Zerin. She bought herself the same, so when we saw the picture in the paper it was easy to compare.'

'Okay...' Palmer thought for a moment. 'I have no wish to add to your girlfriend's grief by creating an immigration problem for her, or for you as you're technically a people trafficker now by virtue of bringing her into the UK the way you did.' He smiled to ease the obvious worry that had quickly spread across Gary Roberts's face – he hadn't thought of that angle. Palmer continued. 'No Mr Roberts, you've saved us a lot of work and time by coming forward and I'm very grateful for that. So I think the best thing for all is that *you* identify the body and give us all the family information we need. No need for Mirah to be involved at all. How does that sound?'

Roberts's face broke into a smile of relief. 'Sounds very good, thank you.' He shook Palmer's hand.

'Right then, let's get it done. Pop out and bring Mirah in and my sergeant will arrange for a car to take you to the morgue. The sergeant will travel with you to witness your identification and then drop you off wherever is convenient for you. One proviso: you both must keep this to yourselves – we haven't caught the killer yet, so I don't want him or her tipped off that we are investigating the death as murder, understand? Of course you can talk to the family in Turkey, but hold fire on that for a couple of days until we tell you it's okay to do so. I think it is preferable to have their local police give them the bad news and support them, rather than a distraught daughter on the phone a thousand miles away, don't you? We will let you know when it's done.'

Roberts agreed. 'Of course.'

'Good, okay then. We will contact the Turkish Embassy and keep them up-to-date and have them get things moving in Turkey. Right, go and fetch Mirah while we get a car round.'

Roberts left the foyer to fetch Mirah. Palmer turned to Gheeta.

'No need for a full body ident, Sergeant – just show him the face. Keep the missing arm out of the equation at the moment; if they see that and talk about it then before long the press will get wind of it, and all hell will break loose in the media.'

Palmer went back up to his Team Room and updated Claire on what had happened.

'Poor kid, just helping out her family and some bastard does that to her.'

'And to two other girls as well, sir. What can possess a person to do that?'

'I don't know Claire, I really don't know.' At one stage in his career Palmer thought he had a good understanding of the criminal mind; nine times out of ten he could spot a *bad one* pretty quickly, and most came from criminal families. But these days, with so many knife killings and the huge amounts of money made from drug and human trafficking ,almost anybody could have their head turned.

'We might get a clue in the morning,' said Claire. 'The profiler is coming in at about ten, I sent all the case details over to her just now.'

'Her? I wouldn't have thought that was the kind of job for a woman?'

'Why not? WPCs, women in the army, women in space, women PMs – watch your back sir, we women are starting to rule.' She laughed.

'You already do in my house.'

The printer whirled and started to push out printed papers into the tray. Claire walked over and pulled them out.

'That was quick.'

'What was?'

'Sergeant Singh emailed me the work permit for Zerin Awad, so I asked Guy's Hospital for a copy of her application and anything else they may have on her so I can load it up with the information on Julie Bury and see if we get any matches – they've sent through their Awad file for us. I'll copy it all in, and hopefully we might get some info on the girl in the river that can be added as well. You never know, there might be a thread tying all the victims together.'

Palmer agreed. 'That would be very nice.'

A good half the programmes loaded onto the Squad computers were bespoke ones written by Gheeta to help progress a case faster, or ones that she had noted could be of interest to the Squad's efforts in case-solving and had copied in. Many were not for public use, and not even for the Squad's use really; but hacking into programmes was one of Gheeta's special gifts, and Palmer turned a blind eye as long as it helped the Squad. One of the most useful was her 'Match App': a programme which took the victim data from many European Law Enforcement Agencies' programmes – plus the FBI Match Analysis Programme – and combined them all into one programme which would flag up the most tenuous of matches between cases; if two victims had the same hairdresser or used the same credit card company, it would flag it up. Of course, that information had to be uploaded in the first place, so Claire spent many hours tapping in the most seemingly innocuous victim information, and every now and again – bingo! the results led the team towards an arrest. But, so far, not this time.

CHAPTER 11

Palmer had brought all the team in for the profiler's results and they sat around the Team Room tables the next morning with coffees supplied by Gheeta, paid for by Palmer, as Gail Preston, Forensic Psychologist from the Jill Dando Institute of Crime Science at University College took them through her profile of the killer they were seeking.

'From the information we have so far, 'she started, 'This killer could be of either sex.'

Palmer sarcastically thought that if that observation was the product of six years' degree study it wasn't giving him much confidence. But he didn't say anything as Preston continued.

'We know the expertise involved in the amputations must point to a current or past career or work in the medical field, or one of those linked to it. He or she is very precise, which points to a high degree of expertise in that field. The mindset of somebody who has committed this crime three times tells me that they are angry. This is not normal anger, not a flare up, but a sustained anger that has built up and is not being satisfied permanently by a single murder. The person has a problem similar to an addict; he or she has built up this anger and is probably saying to us, *look at me, see what I can do? I'll show you what I can do again and again and again.* He or she is a wounded animal; something or someone has pressed the start button for these actions. It may be they are a revenge for something, or maybe they are a demonstration of the person's power; but whichever it is, he or she has a plan. A person doesn't just remove human limbs one by one without a plan. Each limb is a different one, so we must ask ourselves what is the purpose? It can't be to get attention, or one limb would do the job – *did* do the job. No, this person is not interested in attention from you the police – he or she is showing off, but why and to whom is the question.

'I would say, with a high degree of certainty, that he or she is showing off to somebody who doubted them; somebody who has pulled the rug from under them in some way. The taking of three different limbs is a pointer. It points to one thing: those limbs are being used; the bodies were discarded, the limbs have been kept. This killer is building something – probably a body – and that body is the article that says *this is what I can do.*' She finished with a wide smile to the team. 'Over to you.'

Palmer thanked her for her input, and she left the team mulling over what she had said.

'Got to be a medical person sir,' said Lewis. 'The skill factor points to that, and if what the profiler said is right in this case, the medic is showing off to somebody.'

'Agreed.' Gheeta thought the same. 'But showing off to who, and why?'

'It's back to front, isn't it,' said Trent. 'If we find out the reason for the killer to do this to the three ladies, then we can backtrack to him, or her. It doesn't look like it's a relative, or just one killing would be the order of the day. If you've a grudge against one of your relatives or mates you kill them, not a bunch of other non-related people as well.'

Gheeta thought for a moment. 'You're right. For a killer to kill three unrelated people, he or she is either a complete mental case or is executing a carefully conceived plan aimed to impress, or maybe scare one person. Like the profiler said, it's saying '*look what I can do*'.

Palmer stood up. He had let them have their head and was pleased with the deductions that had surfaced. 'Good, very well done. I think you are correct in that assumption. This bastard is showing off, so if we can find the person they are showing off to, then we backtrack to the killer. The big problem is, how do we find that person, because they probably don't know they are being targeted in this peculiar way. Let's face it, if somebody kept bringing home human limbs to impress you, you'd be dialling 999 straight away, wouldn't you.'

'So the killer is building a body like the profiler said. And then what?' asked Gheeta.

Palmer took a deep breath. 'Well, once the body is complete, the job is done; and the killer would then present to whoever it is that he or she is building it to impress.'

Langham had taken all this in and worked something out. 'So if we accept that the killer is building a body, then he or she still has to get another leg, a torso, and a head to complete the job.'

They sat in silence, turning that awful thought over in their heads.

Palmer broke the silence. 'So we had better get stuck in and find him or her pretty quickly, hadn't we. I take it nothing came from the house-to-house on the waste lorry route?' The team shook their heads. 'Okay, no point in pursuing that now, as we now know who the lady in the garbage was. So all four of you down to Paddington and widen the house-to-house around the laundromat, see if we can't find some CCTV – she must have been brought there by car and then somehow carried inside.'

He checked his watch. 'Okay, go and have your lunch in the restaurant and then back to Paddington.'

The team left. Palmer walked to the progress board and studied the victims' faces. 'Shit! That CCTV at the laundromat would have been a real bonus.'

'We might have a bonus here, sir,' said Claire, who was working her terminal.

Palmer and Gheeta closed in behind her. 'What have you got?'

'I'm just going through and uploading all the information on Zerin Awad that Guy's Hospital sent through. She was a really well-qualified senior nurse, and guess what her speciality was?'

'Go on.' Palmer hated it when you had to ask unnecessary questions to get an answer.

'She was the senior nurse in the Amputee Rehabilitation Unit.' Claire sat back with a self-satisfied smile on her face.

'Well that ties in somewhere, but I'm not sure where,' said Gheeta. 'So we have somebody amputating the limb off an amputee nurse.'

Palmer was a bit confused as well. 'Hardly going to be a patient with a grudge, is it?'

'Could be another nurse, one who was passed over for promotion and Wada got the job?'

'It's a possibility, but we won't get that information from her paperwork, will we? We need to get to Guys and have a few chats with people in the department. Do those nurses have the skills to do amputations? I wouldn't have thought so, or they'd be surgeons. Catch DS Lewis in the restaurant and get her down to Guys instead of Paddington – ask her to chat around a bit and see if she can dig up anything; see if there was a bit of a problem between Awad and anybody else there.'

'I could go, guv?' Gheeta felt a bit overlooked.

Palmer sensed her feelings might have been hurt a little and gave her one of his killer smiles that could melt an iceberg. 'DS Singh, you are my deputy – to use you to poke around and ask questions that may bring nothing of use to this investigation would be a misuse of your talents. Send DS Lewis to Guys and then you can concentrate your undoubted investigative talent on the social media and other leads, which I am sure will lead us to knowing why Julie Bury came to London and what she was here for. That's important – *you* are important.'

A hardly audible whispering of the word '*creep*' came from Claire's position. Broad smiles appeared on all their faces.

'I'll go and get some more coffees,' said Palmer, as Gheeta sat at her workstation and began to delve into Julie Bury's social media.

CHAPTER 12

'I'll swear it's the same fucking person. No doubt about it, Justin.'

Professor Latin had popped into Palmer's office opposite the Team Room late that afternoon with his post-mortem report on Julie Bury, and taken a seat whilst Palmer had been laboriously writing up the day's report for AC Bateman.

Palmer stopped his one finger typing of the report and sat back as Latin continued.

'It's too precise, a proper job. The femoral artery has been tied off professionally with a suture to prevent blood squirting out – your common or garden butcher or abattoir worker wouldn't be able to do that. Our killer is too neat and tidy; he's separated the thigh bone from the femur by cutting delicately into the acetabulum to pull the femur from the pelvis.'

Palmer looked blank. Latin cupped his left hand, and using his right as a fist pushed them together.

'The fist is the top rounded joint of the thigh bone, the femur,' he explained. 'And the left is the acetabulum, or the dented receptive bit of the pelvis which it fits into to make the joint. That's where your killer has separated one from t'other. And he's done it expertly. A butcher or the like would probably use a saw, but not this killer – he's a pro, Justin. Top of the range job.'

'Why do you say 'he'? Why not she?'

'No reason, could just as well be a lady – either way they are a fucking expert. If I was you Justin, I'd start by checking the backgrounds of all the orthopaedic surgeons in London. Whoever this is, they'd be a fucking asset to clear the NHS waiting list for hip replacements!'

'The profiler reckons the killer is building a body as a revenge for something.'

'Really? And what is he or she going to do with the body once it is complete – send it by parcel post to whoever they are targeting their revenge on? I can't see DHL being too happy delivering that.'

A thought had struck Palmer. 'Now that's a point – no, they can't send it anywhere. So how do they get their revenge, if revenge is the point of this?'

'Well, they'd have to bring the person to the body, wouldn't they? So it would have to be complete by then.'

'Not necessarily.' Palmer's brain was in overdrive. 'Jesus! What if there was one piece missing and the whole plan was that the last piece comes from the revenge target, eh?'

'Well, with the way he or she is working, that final piece will either be the torso or the head; there's only one limb left to fit the jigsaw – that's the right leg – and then it's torso or head. But as you say, they can't send the body by post, so maybe the endgame is to bring the last victim – the one this is all being done to impress – to the body, which means it's being kept somewhere whilst it's being built and the limbs added; and that means formaldehyde, and a fucking lot of formaldehyde at that.'

'What do you mean?'

'I mean that the body parts and the partly-built body, if that's what is going on, would have to be preserved; or, to put it simply, they'd go off. So they must be being kept in formaldehyde, which preserves flesh – we use loads of it in the laboratory. Your killer must have a tank of the fucking stuff.'

'Christ, what on earth is going on in this killer's mind, eh?'

Latin rose to leave. 'No idea, Justin. But I'll look forward to another one-legged body arriving soon. Take care, old son – oh, and by the way, the congealment of the blood gave death at about six hours before she was found.' And he left as Palmer's outside line rang. It was Mrs P.

'Will you be home usual time tonight, or are you working late?'

'No, should be usual time. Why, what's happening?'

'Nothing, just that I've got a leg of lamb for tea and wanted to know so that I can put it in the oven at the right time.'

'I could bring home fish and chips to save you cooking?'

CHAPTER 13

'This is Julie Bury's twitter account, guv.'

Palmer was stood in the Team Room watching the big wall screen above the computers as Gheeta pulled up the account on her monitor and copied it to the screen.

'Mostly chat amongst her friends, but this is the interesting bit.' She imposed an arrow on one post. 'She tweets, '*yes Thursday is fine, will tweet when I have the train times.*'

'So she's arranging a meeting with somebody.'

'Yes, and two hours later she tweeted that she was getting the 11.10 from Manchester to Euston; and we know that was the day before yesterday and she was dead by the early hours of the next morning.'

'She must have had somebody meeting her at Euston, otherwise why tweet the train time?'

'Exactly, but the question is who?'

'Who did she send the tweet to?'

'A deleted account.'

'It couldn't have been deleted when she tweeted to it.'

'It wasn't, and if the person whose account it was is the killer, he or she is a pretty careful person; they deleted their account after that tweet so that even the recipient is deleted off Bury's tweet. This person is a very careful person and is dotting all the 'i's and crossing all the 't's to keep off the grid,'

'Get onto the Twitter people, they must be able to backtrack with all their millions of pounds of software.'

'Data protection, guv – they wouldn't do it, no way.'

'Have a word with the legal people downstairs and get a subpoena then.'

'Twitter would contest it and we'd be in and out of various courts all the way up to the Supreme Court – they've done it before and won in the end. They say they are a 'platform', and therefore not in any way responsible for the content and must adhere to the data protection laws. Takes months and they always win.' She let out a long breath. 'However, there is another way.'

Claire turned from working on her keyboard and rolled her eyes at Palmer. 'Oh ye of little faith.'

Palmer turned from the big screen and met Gheeta's gaze. He held it for a few seconds.

'You've hacked it, haven't you.'

Gheeta shrugged. 'I couldn't possibly comment, guv.'

The depth of Gheeta Singh's IT knowledge and ability never ceased to amaze Palmer, although he was quite used to it by now. How she managed to get some information was best not questioned.

Gheeta carried on. 'When Julie sent her tweets, the recipient's account held them and posted them visually when the recipient logged on via an algorithm. Don't ask.' Gheeta had seen Palmer's eyes glaze over and knew that explaining what an algorithm is to Palmer could be a lengthy task. 'That algorithm then disappears into the background when the account is deleted, but like everything on the internet it remains somewhere in the cyber-ether forever. It's just a matter of finding it.'

'And you have.'

'Of course, guv. It's what I do, isn't it?' She smiled at him.

'What have we got then?'

'Hawkeye.'

'Hawkeye? Isn't that something they use in tennis to see if the ball's in or out?'

'That's correct, but it's also the Twitter handle – the name – of the person Julie was tweeting with. Their real name I can't get, sorry – that's triple password protected by Twitter and is nigh on impossible to hack.'

Palmer sat down and rubbed his chin. 'So who is Hawkeye? We've nailed Julie's journey down, we know she travelled from Manchester Piccadilly to Euston on the 11.10 train.' Gheeta revisited the trail. 'She used her debit card to buy a Virgin train ticket for the journey and the purchase shows on her bank statement for that day. Virgin trains have confirmed it and also that it was a return ticket, but the return was not used.'

'So she had every intention of going back the same day, but something or someone prevented her doing that,'

'The killer, this 'Hawkeye' person?' said Gheeta.

'Could well be. Euston must have lots of CCTV cameras, so they might have pictures of her leaving the train and meeting this Hawkeye character. Looks like our next move is off to Euston then; and let's keep our fingers crossed we get a positive sighting from the station cameras.'

'Hold your horses!' Claire was tapping furiously on her keyboard. 'Hawkeye is the name on one of the job adverts on a Facebook Recruitment page that Julie Bury was monitoring. I'll push it up to the screen.'

Palmer and Gheeta watched as Claire uploaded the page to the big screen and scrolled it down to an advert.

London. Personal Assistant 18 to 32 required by executive in large city company. Previous experience in similar position an advantage. 148596

'What's the number at the end?' Palmer wanted to know.

'The advertiser's code number – if you are interested in the job, you click it for contact information.' Claire clicked on the number and up came the Hawkeye name with 'deleted' after it.' 'I bet that's the same Hawkeye as the Twitter handle, got to be.'

Palmer agreed. 'So Julie found the advert, fancied the job, clicked through to Hawkeye's Twitter account which would have been working at that time, and from the posts on her own Twitter account we know she made an appointment to meet Hawkeye in London. Fingers crossed Euston's cameras give us an ID.'

Palmer was getting that excited feeling in his brain that released the endorphin every time a case moved along at an increased pace, and things began to fall into place. He knew this case was at that point. The cross referencing had been done, the backgrounds had been checked, the doors were being knocked on, and the leads were gradually dwindling through. The next stage would be the killer's identification, and then the chase was really on – or hopefully not a chase but a straightforward arrest. That would make a nice change.

CHAPTER 14

'How many cameras?'

'Sixty-two'

Palmer was astonished. 'Sixty two!'

Palmer and Singh were in the Control Suite at Euston station with a DSM (Deputy Station Master) – one of ten at the station, this one had been assigned to help them. One large wall of the Control Suite was a bank of CCTV screens with six people monitoring them. Next to it was a large map of the station with the cameras highlighted.

The DSM explained. 'Many are statics – that means they cover the odds and ends of the station, back entrances, staff corridors, parcel stores and the like; mostly non-public areas. I'm told you want to take a look at a certain train arrival?'

Gheeta nodded. 'Yes please, the 11.10 from Manchester Piccadilly the day before yesterday.'

'Okay, give me a couple of minutes and I'll get it uploaded onto that screen.' He pointed to a solitary sixty-inch plasma flat-screen fastened at head-height to the wall away from the others. 'We get quite a lot of requests from various police forces, so we keep a separate viewing screen.'

Palmer and Singh wandered over to the screen and a couple of minutes later the DSM rejoined them.

'Right, all keyed up with all the footage from the day. That train came in at 14.20 on platform seven and it's one of our busiest, as you can imagine with trains coming in from Manchester and Birmingham, so we have several cameras on it. Still, it is going to be like looking for a needle in a haystack, but let's see what we can do.'

Gheeta opened her laptop and pulled up a picture of Julie Bury that she had scanned from a photo in the Manchester bedsit. 'That's the lady we are interested in. You don't have facial recognition software on this computer do you?' she asked, knowing the answer would be negative. Which it was.

The DSM was impressed by Julie's picture. 'Pretty lady – drug mule is she? Your Organised Crime chaps are in here quite a lot identifying mules.'

Palmer gave him an old-fashioned look. 'We are not Organised Crime. We are the Murder Squad.'

The DSM's face dropped. 'Oh… oh dear – is she…?'

'Dead, yes.'

'Oh, right. Then let's take a look. We have three cameras along platform seven, each covering a third of it, plus another at the barrier.' He pushed a button. 'This is the train arriving, and the back third passengers alighting. I'll run it slowly.'

The screen showed that the camera was at the far end of the platform so passengers alighting would be walking away from it, their faces unseen. The train stopped and the doors opened to release a throng of arrivals onto the platform; some rushed away out of the picture towards the barrier, others walked away at normal pace, and some obviously decided to go slow and let the crowd disperse.

'Unfortunately,' said Palmer, 'we have no idea what she was wearing, so it's all down to recognising her face. And that won't be easy from this angle.'

They looked intently at the screen as the passenger numbers dwindled away along the platform.

Gheeta was disappointed. 'Needle in haystack is right – she might have been one of those whose faces we can't see. No telling is there.'

'Well, we've the middle and front carriages to go yet,' pointed out the DSM. 'I'll switch to the second camera that covers the middle of the train.'

The screen blinked and again showed the train coming to a halt at the platform and passengers alighting at various speeds. The camera angle this time was better, as it was sideways on to the carriages and faces could be seen as they stepped down from the doors; but again, no recognisable face.

'Last one then please,' said Palmer, his initial optimism a bit deflated.

The DSM altered the camera. 'This might be better as this camera is pointing towards the train from the ticket barrier, so all the passengers are walking towards it – full frontal.'

Gheeta wondered to herself why he hadn't told them that at the beginning and they might not have wasted their time with the other two cameras, as after all, this barrier camera would show all the passengers faces. She put it down to the DSM having nervous tension brought on by the presence of Palmer; his persona often had that effect on people.

They settled in front of the screen.

'Can you slow it down?' asked Palmer.

'Yes.' The DSM twiddled a knob and the passengers went into slow motion. Gheeta again wondered why he hadn't told them he could do that at the very beginning. She put it down to the 'Palmer' effect once again.

'That's her!' Palmer pushed his finger onto the screen. 'Stop it there.'

It was indeed Julie Bury; she was towards the back of the arrivals, amongst the last of the passengers to leave the train. She had a satchel-like bag over one shoulder and wore a grey trouser-suit under a fawn-coloured light raincoat.

'She's looking for someone.' Gheeta noted the way Bury was trying to peer round those passengers in front of her towards the barrier.

They followed her to the barrier. As she came through it and was about to be lost to the camera's view at the bottom of the screen, her face was blanked out by the back of somebody's head approaching her from the barrier. The two heads became static for a short time.

'That's got to be her killer meeting her off the train.' Gheeta was sure – who else could it be?

'Yes, must be – the other passengers are walking by. Can you freeze frame and zoom in?' Palmer asked the DSM.

He could, and the enlarged picture showed the unknown head blocking out three quarters of Julie Bury's face.

'Slowly forward,' instructed Palmer.

Frame by frame, the DSM forwarded the CCTV images. Julie and the person with her were obviously talking, but it was impossible to tell from the hair if the other person was male or female.

'Turn round, you bastard,' Palmer said slowly at the head. 'Turn round.'

It did, but as it did so the pair were walking off beneath the CCTV coverage and no face was shown.

'You must have concourse cameras where we can pick them up again.' Gheeta looked at the DSM, daring him to say 'no'.

'Hold on, I'll get the camera up.' He crossed over to the large wall map and checked the number of the concourse camera covering the exit to platform seven. Coming back to their screen, he tapped the keyboard and as the correct camera came up, he input the time as 14.20 and stood back.

'Ready when you are.'

'Okay, let's go – zoom in to the barrier and stop when we get them at the barrier,' said Palmer

'Well, she was towards the last to leave, so let's speed up a bit.' The DSM was getting the message of what they were after and was beginning to lose that nervous tension and become one of the team; wait 'til he told his kids what happened at the office today! Dad helped catch a murderer! He pulled the focus up to zoom into the area around the barrier, and as they picked out Bury coming towards it he slowed it down. They watched as a person stepped out from the small crowd that was awaiting friends and relatives from the train and moved forward to meet Julie Bury. Julie shook hands and after a short conversation which was probably the introduction by the person meeting her, they turned and made off towards the station exit together.

'That's a woman, guv.' Gheeta was sure.

They followed the couple as they walked across the concourse towards the Underground station entrance.

Palmer prayed out loud. 'Please take the tube – please, *please* take the tube.'

The DSM looked at Gheeta. 'Why the tube?'

'Full-frontal cameras on the escalators. We'll get a great shot of the other person.'

'Shit!' The minor expletive from Palmer signified that the couple had passed by the Underground station entrance and carried on walking out of shot through the main exit to the busy Euston Road. 'Oh well, now we know she definitely came to London on the day she was killed and was met off the train; but who by?'

Gheeta shrugged. 'Hawkeye.'

Palmer took a deep breath. 'Could be, but it's all damn circumstantial so far.'

CHAPTER 15

It had been a long day and the last thing Palmer wanted as he turned his car into his drive was for the headlights to show a life-size stuffed dummy propped up against his porch; an incomplete life size stuffed dummy – its left leg was missing. The body and arms were a stuffed jacket, the head a small cushion with a face drawn on it, the right leg a rolled rug, but no left leg.

What the hell was going on? The killer couldn't possibly be aware of Palmer's interest in the case, or could he – or she? Could they have seen the Squad's interest in the Facebook and Twitter accounts of Julie Bury? Gheeta wasn't the only expert in IT after all; was this dummy a warning, or something much more? Was he the target? Was somebody from his past targeting him? His fifty odd years in the Met had filled quite a few prison cells with people who would love to get back at him.

It didn't make any sense, but this wasn't the time to sit and try and figure it out; he feared for what he might find inside his house. Palmer clicked the car's door locks on; he hadn't done that since the bad old days of chasing gangs round the West End and suddenly finding yourself outnumbered by large gentlemen wielding baseball bats.

He sat still and checked his mirror: all clear. He switched off the headlights and got out of the car, slowly getting his eyes accustomed to the darkness, and stood looking for any movement in the wide beds of shrubs and roses Mrs P. had planted and grown around the edge of their front garden over the years. Their leaves had mostly fallen by now, leaving a skeleton of branches, and no dark shapes were apparent amongst them. He made his way slowly to the porch on the lawn, avoiding the gravel path. Opening his front door slowly he crept into the dark hall, keeping tight against the wall. At the far end, light was streaming out of the open kitchen door; by now Daisy the dog would normally have wandered out from her rug and said hello. Nothing.

He stealthily made it to the kitchen – nobody was inside. There was a noise from upstairs, movement along the landing; he pressed himself against the wall beside a large hall stand that shielded him from view. Two people were coming down the stairs. He had the element of surprise on his side; he took the calculated chance that the first person would be Mrs P. and behind her the intruder. In the gloom Mrs P. passed him carrying something; it could be Daisy – had she gone for the intruder and been killed? Anger swelled in Palmer; he loved that dog.

As soon as Mrs P. had passed he rushed out from the hiding place and went full force into the intruder, knocking him or her against the wall. He pushed his left forearm across the intruder's throat and brought his right knee up, hard and fast, as Mrs P. switched on the hall light.

'JUSTIN! What the hell are you doing?'

Palmer stood back and saw she was carrying not a dead Daisy, who was at the bottom of the stairs looking at him with a *what have you done now?* expression, but an old double bed bolster pillow that had been in the loft for decades – one of Mrs P.'s *you never know when it might come in useful* items that clogged up the loft. In front of him, the back of his head pressed hard against the wall by the force of Palmer's arm over his throat, Benji's face showed a look of total fear.

It took a little time for each side to explain their actions. The dummy by the porch was the parish council's guy for the November 5th Guy Fawkes bonfire night celebrations; the bolster had been promised by Mrs P. for its left leg to complete it. Benji was in charge of the celebrations and had brought the guy round for Mrs P. to sew on the bolster before storing it in the council's lock up. Palmer explained the case he was involved in, using as little of the gruesome details as he could as Benji looked quite green already.

A little later Mrs P. had a face on like an evil stone gargoyle as she sat opposite Palmer in the kitchen, having just helped Benji back to his home next door after sewing on the *bolster* leg to complete the council's guy; he was all right, and a couple of G &Ts had helped recoup him. Palmer was tucking into his steak and kidney pie – real steak and real kidney.

'You are lucky he doesn't press assault charges,' Mrs P. spat out. 'What got into you? I think Bateman might be right about you, it's time to retire – maybe you're losing your marbles. You could have seriously hurt him, you know.'

Palmer nodded and reached down to pat Daisy, who had taken up her usual position beside his chair in the hope of some food scraps being surreptitiously passed down.

Mrs P. took a deep breath. 'Stupid man. Haven't you anything to say?'

'Is there any more pie?'

CHAPTER 16

It was the next day in the Team Room, and Gheeta and Claire's probing into Julie Bury's social media platforms and finances was yielding a few soft leads. Palmer had completed his daily report and sent it upstairs, DS Lewis was due in soon with her report on Zerin Awad's friends at Guys, and the other three detectives were still knocking on doors around the laundromat in Paddington.

Palmer was standing in front of the progress board which Gheeta had updated with the time frame from Euston Station to the laundromat. He was looking at Julie Bury's picture.

'Where had you been between the time you were met at Euston and the time you were found in the laundromat – twelve hours?' Palmer spoke out loud to himself. 'Latin's post mortem report says you had been dead a mere six hours before we found you in the laundromat, so where were you for the six?'

Gheeta overheard him and turned in her chair. 'Working? We know she came down for a job or job interview, so perhaps whoever met her had already offered her the job, and she was getting herself organised in an office somewhere and then the killer struck later?'

'So whoever it was we saw meet her at Euston wasn't the killer?'

'Not necessarily – could have been she'd got a job to go to, all signed and sealed, and that was just the bona fide employer meeting her to show her round the work place, and then she was going to take a later train back to Manchester to get her things and come back.'

'No, if it was all signed and sealed why not bring everything with her? It would save a double journey, and she could have arranged accommodation beforehand. No, the absence of any luggage says she came down just for the interview and intended to travel back – plus she had a return ticket.'

Gheeta could see the reasoning in that argument. 'Yes, and she bought that four days before she travelled, probably to make sure she could reserve a seat. The interview scenario makes sense.'

DS Lewis came into the room and flopped onto a chair, feigning exhaustion. 'I must have done a hundred miles yesterday up and down hospital corridors.'

Sympathy was not one of Palmer's strong points. 'Did you get anything that looks useful on Miss Awad? A disgruntled patient who threatened to kill her would be useful.'

'Sorry, sir.' Lewis opened her notebook. 'Quite the opposite; seems everybody liked her. She worked her way up to a supervisory role; wedded to the job by all accounts – no men friends of any consequence, kept her private life to herself, was the first port of call if any of her staff had a problem. Respected and highly thought of by her bosses.'

Palmer was impressed. 'Florence Nightingale of the amputee world then.'

'Yes, she was even called up before the General Medical Council a couple of months ago. Nobody knows what for exactly, but she was back at work the next day so not serious.'

'Interesting…' Palmer looked to Gheeta. 'Have a dig around and see what that was about.'

Lucy Ross from Press and Media interrupted their discussion as she came into the room. Palmer's face fell as he saw her.

'Oh no.'

'Oh yes,' Lucy shrugged, 'I'm afraid so.' She waved a newspaper at him and pointed to the headline: 'PART BODY IN TIP'. 'I had a call from the Metro about an hour ago about a rumour of a killer cutting up bodies in West London. Bateman said to deny it, so I did. But the Metro published and has quoted statements from several workers at the Brentford Waste Transfer Centre who say they saw a young woman's body with one arm missing in one of the bays, and it's still sealed off with a uniformed officer in keeping people away. Since this edition hit the streets our phone hasn't stopped with media enquiries and speculation. Apparently there could be up to ten mutilated bodies around London, so we need to put a lid on it now, Justin.'

Palmer knew what was required of him. 'A press conference?' He hated them.

'Two o'clock in the media suite – I'll see you down there twenty minutes before hand and we can sketch out how to handle it so as not to cause widespread panic amongst the female population of London. Now, would you like to bring me up to speed on what is actually happening?'

Palmer was resigned to his fate. 'Yes, of course. Over here.' He led her over to the progress board and talked her through it.

Lucy knew a press conference in Palmer's hands was a press conference in safe hands: most of the crime reporters in the media knew Palmer and had built a good relationship with him over many years; they knew he would be totally honest with them, up to a point that did not affect his case or put anybody in danger. If Palmer said: 'That's all ladies and gentlemen, thank you very much,' then that definitely was 'That's all ladies and gentlemen, thank you very much.' Journos new to his press conferences who tried to push him further found a lack of an invitation to the next one.

CHAPTER 17

The press conference went off without Palmer giving away any information that might assist the killer in any way. He didn't want to frighten whoever it was into running and so gave the press the impression that the Squad was still fumbling around in the dark, and that the body at the Waste Transfer Centre could well be a one-off, perhaps even somebody trying to cover up an unfortunate accident. Prior to the Conference, he gave DCI Hardy at Paddington Green a call and asked him to contact the first responder and ambulance crew that attended the laundromat and impress on them to keep quiet about the missing leg.

So he was in quite a good frame of mind as he bounded up the flights of stairs from the media suite on the lower ground floor to his office on the third floor. That good frame of mind disappeared instantly when his sciatica stabbed him in the right thigh halfway up the second flight, reminding him he was over sixty and not sixteen, and sooner or later he would have to have his two dodgy discs seen to. But not today, not until this case had been put to bed, and probably not even then.

In the Team Room Langham, Patel and Trent had returned with their end-of-day reports on the Paddington door-knocking and were stood with Lewis and Claire behind Gheeta's chair, looking at her monitor screen as she tapped on her keyboard. There was an air of excitement that caught Palmer as he entered.

'What is it, what have you got? Some good news from the door-to-door?'

Gheeta turned her head from the monitor screen, her eyes bright with anticipation. 'No guv, nothing from the door-to-door, but quite a bit from the GMC website.'

'GMC?' Palmer didn't understand.

'General Medical Council. You remember DS Lewis said Zerin Awad was called before them and nobody at her work knew why, except they thought it was for a minor disciplinary thing as that was the usual reason nurses were called up there, but she was back at work the next day so it couldn't have been serious?'

'Yes, go on.' He joined the others watching the screen.

Gheeta continued. 'Well, she wasn't in trouble at all. The Council's Disciplinary Committee were sitting to pass their judgement on a surgeon who Awad had reported for sub-standard work.'

'What do you mean 'sub-standard work'?'

'According to Awad's statement to the council, this surgeon had failed to dress wounds correctly after doing two amputations, and that had resulted in severe infection in both cases which had created the need for extensive aftercare in Awad's department. The GMC prosecutor said, and I quote: '*In both cases, only Senior Nurse Awad and her staff's immediate restorative actions had negated the possibility of gangrene leading to sepsis and septic shock, which could have been fatal to both patients.*'

'My word, she really was a Florence Nightingale of the amputee world then.'

Gheeta nodded. 'Yes, but the interesting bit is that the surgeon involved was struck off the GMC list and disbarred from practice, which basically finished their career.' She turned to Palmer. 'Good reason to want revenge on your accuser, eh?'

'Bloody good reason. Who is this surgeon? I think we'd better take a closer look at him or her.'

'Surgeon X.'

'What?'

'According to the terms of the GMC Disciplinary Committee standard constitution guv, and again I quote: '*All those members accused of serious mispractice that go before the GMC Disciplinary Committee are afforded the protection of their personal details unless they indicate otherwise.*''

'Or unless the Serial Murder Squad wants to know who they are,' Palmer said aggressively. He was already picking up his Crombie and trilby from the desk he'd slung them on that morning. 'Where do we find this GMC lot?'

Gheeta tapped some keys. 'Their London office is on Euston Road, guv – bit of a coincidence, eh?'

'Right then Sergeant, you come with me; we are going to the GMC offices now. Claire, in case they prove to be obstructive and start going on about data protection, go upstairs, flutter your eyelids at Bateman and get a warrant to make the GMC hand over the full details of the Awad case, including the name of the surgeon involved. You others wait here until we get that info, and then I'll decide what our next move is.'

The reformed data protection laws infuriated Palmer and most other police officers; if a crime was being investigated, he felt it was the duty of everybody to give the police any information that might help solve it. Unfortunately, the Human Rights brigade held sway with the government, as most politicians had financial and sometimes sexual secrets they wanted to keep, and the Data Protection Laws helped them do that.

CHAPTER 18

'Bit plush this, isn't it guv,' noted Gheeta as they walked into the glass-fronted GMC Offices.

'Public funded, Sergeant – haven't got to make a profit and I bet they didn't get austerity cuts either. Too many friends in high places.'

'Cynic.'

'You bet.'

'Wanna book a nick and tuck whilst you're here, guv?'

Palmer smiled. 'I don't think it's that sort of place, Sergeant.'

They made their presence known to one of the three receptionists and Palmer explained they were looking into a serious crime that involved one of the disciplinary cases. The receptionist asked them to take a seat in the foyer, and pretty soon a middle-aged man with a badge saying he was George – a Senior Investigation Officer, no surname – approached , introduced himself as George, Senior Investigation Officer and asked if he might be of assistance. Palmer cynically thought about asking him if he was the same George, Senior Investigation Officer as the one on his badge, but decided not to.

'I hope you can,' said Palmer. 'We are investigating a rather serious murder case and one of those involved was a witness in a disciplinary case you held recently. Her name is Erin Awad, senior nurse at Guy's Hospital, Amputee Rehabilitation Unit.'

Gheeta showed Awad's face on her laptop to George. He was taken aback.

'Is she dead?'

'She is,' Palmer continued. 'As are two other young ladies. I need full details of the personnel involved in the case that she was called in as an expert witness.'

George, being a legal type, was thinking only of protecting his own back. 'I can't do that. Divulging that sort of information is way above my pay scale, Superintendent.'

Gheeta knew exactly what was coming next. Palmer fixed George with one of his cold stares, the one that could freeze the sun. He spoke slowly. 'It is *Chief* Superintendent, Mr George – *Chief* Superintendent, and may I suggest you go and find somebody in the relevant payscale to furnish me with the details I have asked for, before I put a seizure warrant on every computer in this building and flood it with Scene of Crime Officers.'

George's brain took very little time in realising what a major negative effect that would have on the smooth running of the GMC, and also who would be in the line of fire for allowing it to happen. 'Please wait here, Chief Superintendent. I'll see what I can do.' And off he went into the back offices behind reception.

It didn't take long before a middle-aged lady, grey hair tied in a bun, smartly dressed and slim approached them with a friendly smile.

'Detective Chief Superintendent Palmer.' George had obviously had a word. 'I am Baroness Sharpe's personal assistant. Would you come this way, please.'

She led them into the back office, set as open plan so staff sat at their work stations in alcoves separated by four foot-high dividers, with a long carpeted corridor through the centre leading to glass partitioned offices at the rear where Palmer guessed the senior management worked.

Gheeta moved to walk beside him, holding her laptop open in front of her; she'd done a quick Google search. 'Baroness Sharpe is the big boss, guv: Chair of the Council. Sixty-four years old and worked her way up the ladder from college to being a top traumatic surgeon, and then headhunted into here. '

Palmer nodded. 'Good, should be the right paygrade then.'

The PA led them into what Palmer thought must be the board room, if they had such a thing; a large, long room, well-lit with large windows overlooking the public square at the front of the building. It had a long mahogany table in the centre around which about twenty chairs were arranged, with each having its own decanter of water and a glass for the occupant.

There were only two occupants and neither were sitting. They met Palmer and Gheeta at the door where the PA introduced them. 'This is our Chair, Baroness Sharpe and this is our chief executive Robert Simms.'

The Baroness shook Palmer's hand. 'Chief Superintendent Palmer, delighted to meet you.'

Palmer introduced Gheeta and Simms invited them all to sit together at the far end of the table, which they did.

'Now then…' The Baroness spread her smile between Palmer and Gheeta. 'How may we help you?'

Palmer talked them slowly through the case as Gheeta pulled up the relevant pictures on her laptop to show them.

'And so you can see why we need to know who the person is in the case that Erin Awad was used as an expert witness against. We need to clear this person from our suspect list.'

'Or arrest them for serial murder,' added the Baroness.

'It's a possibility.'

The Baroness took a deep breath and slowly let it out. She looked at Simms. 'Robert, what are your thoughts?'

Simms shrugged. 'I think we should co-operate fully – I can't see any moral reason why not. I know the legal team will quote data protection...' He looked at Palmer. 'And we come against that damn act all the time, but I'm pretty sure the Chief Superintendent has a solid case for asking for the information; and I'm also pretty sure that in a case of such gravity he could produce a release warrant without any problem. So we would have to turn over the papers in the end in any case.'

Palmer liked Simms.

The Baroness stood and walked over to the nearest window, where she stood deep in thought for a minute or so. Turning back, she sat down again. 'Superintendent, let me tell you about the case if I may.' She looked at Sims, who nodded approval. 'That case was without doubt the worst one I have had to preside over in my eight years as Chair. Your victim, Zerin Awad, was instrumental in alerting the Council to the defendant's lack of clinical knowledge and basically damn poor surgery procedures, which may well have caused patient death had Awad not flagged it up. During the disciplinary hearing Awad was subjected to some awful abuse and downright racist taunts from the defendant, who also threatened her and myself with fire and brimstone when the verdict that she was to be struck off was given – security had to restrain her from attacking me. In fact, Awad was offered counselling afterwards but refused it.'

Palmer and Gheeta had quietly noted the use of the word 'she' when the Baroness had referred to the defendant.

Simms rose. 'I'll go and get a printout of all the case papers for you, Superintendent – shouldn't take long, ten minutes at the most.' He left the room.

Gheeta broke the silence. 'Sounds like a pretty horrendous experience, ma'am.' Was *ma'am* the right way to address a Baroness? She didn't know.

The Baroness poured herself a glass of water and took a sip. 'One I hope I never have to experience again, Sergeant. Ever.'

Palmer poured himself a glass. 'What was the defendant's name?'

The Baroness took another sip before replying, as if to give her the strength to say the name aloud. 'Hawke. Doctor Martine Hawke.'

Palmer nearly dropped his glass.

CHAPTER 19

'What have we got then, Claire?'

Palmer hurried into the Team Room with Gheeta, who had emailed Dr Martine Hawke's name over to Claire as they had waited for the case printout at the GMC.

'Not a lot, sir.' Claire was engrossed in social media checking. 'Mind you, she is well respected in her field: Fellow of the Royal College of Surgeons, she's written academic papers on surgery procedures; but she hasn't any social media footprints as far as I can see – no current Facebook, Twitter or Instagram accounts. Although we know she corresponded with Julie Bury on Facebook and Twitter, so she must have deleted them.'

Palmer was disappointed. 'And it will take court orders to get them to unearth anything.' He looked at Gheeta, hoping beyond hope.

'Take too long, guv. I could hack in, but it will take a couple of days.'

'Okay.' Claire put the court order process in action. 'Use Henry Charles, he's a magistrate at Southwark Court – one of the few who's on our side and not the criminal's. Get the paperwork raised and send it to him by courier. I'll give him a call.'

Palmer made the call and Henry Charles was only too glad to assist.

'They'll fight it, Justin – you know that, don't you. Social media sites have no moral compass – they'll lodge an appeal, so it's going to take a few weeks.'

'Yes I realise that, Henry – it won't stop us arresting Hawke on circumstantial evidence, but it will seal the case later on when we go to court with transcripts of her conversations with a victim.'

'Who's raising the order?'

'Bateman.'

'Oh, he's not the quickest, is he.'

Palmer laughed. 'No, but I've got him up-to-date on this case; daily reports have been sent upstairs, so he can't really hold back on this one.'

'Okay, but send the courier to my home address Justin, just in case it doesn't get to the Courts before they close. Are you going to move in on this Hawke woman tonight?'

'Yes, I've got my team coming back from their house-to-house enquiries and we will get it done later on. She's more likely to be at home later in the evening.'

'Good luck Justin, from what you've told me I hate to think what you might find. Take care, old chap.'

'You too Henry, thanks for helping.'

'Anytime – cheerio.'

Palmer ended the call and tapped up his address book on his phone screen and placed it in front of Claire.

'That's where to send the court order please, Claire.'

Lewis, Langham, Patel and Trent walked in. They sat and listened as Palmer took them through the latest happenings.

'Right then,' he concluded. 'That's where we are at the moment, so we are going to arrest Hawke.' He turned to Gheeta. 'Sergeant, get an arrest warrant issued in her name on suspicion of murder. Claire, if we could have the premises on screen please.'

Claire pulled up a road map showing Hawke's house, and next to it a Google Earth map showing it from above. Palmer used a pointer as he talked the team through his plan. 'As you can see, she lives in a detached house: nineteen-thirties style, good front garden with drive to the right and separate garage. Access all around the house is by flagstone paths and at the back a large patio with a summer swing and shed; then a long garden – mostly lawn – of approximately a hundred metres bordered by fencing and shrubs on both sides, and a tall leylandii hedge barrier at the bottom. Her neighbours on both sides have similar properties. Beyond the hedge at the bottom is a row of small council-owned retirement bungalows, which as you can see are separated from Hawke and her neighbours by the hedge, and beyond the bungalows their access lane which joins Hawke's road about half a mile further down. At Hawke's property we will split into three groups – Patel and Lewis circle round to the right of the house and cover any escape route on the right and the back, Langham and Trent do the same on the left. Myself and Sergeant Singh will go in the front and hopefully make an immediate arrest.'

'And then we start looking for body bits – I can't wait,' added Gheeta, showing a grisly expression.

'Okay,' Palmer rubbed his hands. 'It's been a long day already and I don't want to go in there before it gets dark, as I'd like to get up that front garden to the front door and have you all in position around the house without being seen before we make our presence known; so I suggest you all go to the canteen and eat, and see you back here in half an hour.'

The team left.

'Sergeant, you'd better get down to the stores and get stab vests and night tunics for everybody.

Gheeta nodded. Night tunics were heavy tunics that could be slipped on over a normal jacket, with pockets for radio, taser and a front camera fitted and battery charged – so important when a suspect later made false accusations against an officer.

'Claire, are you okay to stay on?'

Both Claire and Gheeta were surprised that Palmer would even ask; he didn't usually, he just assumed people were wedded twenty-four-seven to the job like he was.

'Yes I'm fine, sir. I'll give hubby a call.'

Gheeta held out her hands towards Palmer, as though begging for alms.

Palmer smiled. 'You haven't got a hubby.'

'I might have a hot date.'

'Even if you had a *scalding* hot date Sergeant, it wouldn't keep you away from that house tonight.'

He was quite right.

CHAPTER 20

Inside the small bungalow behind the leylandii hedge, Doctor Martine Hawke sat in the lounge which was bathed in a low red light. She was looking at her surgical tools neatly laid out on a small steel table, beside a longer steel bench on which lay an unconscious young lady securely strapped down. The lady's clothes had been removed and a morphine drip suspended above her on a hook from the ceiling was supplying an injected needle into an arm vein with a steady supply of the painkiller. Even the unconscious state brought about by Rohypnol could be diminished by pain, and Hawke didn't want her victim to wake up during the procedure she intended to carry out.

It was better to operate on a living body as the blood would still be circulating as the heart moved it around; when dead, any incision as large as the one Hawke intended to make would become the point of least resistance, and pressure from the weight of the body's flesh on the arteries would make it leak like a hole in a water main. The body looked like any other body, except for one thing: a thin black felt tip-drawn line that circled the top of the right leg showing Hawke where to make the incision. She stood beside the body and pulled on a pair of rubber gloves. As she picked up a scalpel from the small table, her attention was drawn to the barking of the dog that her next-door neighbour to the main house kept loose in the garden as a four-legged burglar alarm since a spate of thefts from garden sheds in the area a little while ago. Hawke stayed her hand, expecting the barking to cease as the neighbour called the dog in; it didn't cease. Hawke put down the scalpel, removed the rubber gloves, switched off the light and peered through the drawn curtains towards the hedge: nothing to see, but she had better check.

She went into the small rear garden of the bungalow and up to the small gate in the hedge leading to her large garden. The tall leylandii crossed and wove together above the gate after years of neglect, so that a brief glance towards them from the main house wouldn't immediately show the gate from that distance. In the dark she kept herself against the hedge as she looked up across the lawn to the rear of her house. Small flashes of torchlight reflected off the glass of the double French doors from the lounge to the garden; then the light in the lounge came on and figures moved to open the doors. In the light there was no mistake, and the uniform of one of the figures underlined it – the police were inside her house.

She didn't panic – obviously the police had no knowledge of the bungalow being hers, or they would have been there too. The plan she had hatched in her head three months ago was near completion, and she was not about to abort it. The final phase was to be carried out that evening, and there was no reason why it should not be; the young lady on the table could wait. By the end of the evening that lady would have company, and the revenge would be complete. She went back into the bungalow lounge and checked the straps holding the body to the bench – all were tight and secure. She took a pad and some clinical tape from the table and used it to gag the body's mouth; then slipping out of the front door, she got into her car parked in the access lane and drove off.

Getting no answer to his knocking on the front door and ringing the bell continuously, Palmer had used his elbow to smash one of the small panes of frosted glass in the door; not the first time he'd done that to gain an entry, and his thick Crombie made the action pain-free. He cleared the remaining glass and reached through to the door catch, hoping that it would be a straightforward twist knob and not a flat Yale. It was a twist knob, and they were in.

'Gloves on, people – and watch what you are treading on. This could become a crime scene, and I don't want Frome having an excuse to accuse me of ruining it.'

He moved forward, with his torch flashing left to right. Gheeta checked the wall beside the door, found the light switches and turned them on.

'Can't see a burglar alarm, guv. I would have thought she'd have one.'

'Surprising the number of people who haven't – maybe it's a hidden one and goes straight through to a security company control room.'

'We'll soon know, won't we? If a load of local blue lights turn up she's got one.'

They checked the downstairs rooms and Gheeta went upstairs, as Palmer put the lights on in the lounge and opened the French doors for the rest of the team to enter from the garden. 'It's all clear in here,' he told them. 'Go through one room at a time, cupboards and drawers; anything you think might be connected to the case, put on one side.'

It was a fruitless task. Everything was just as you would expect in a normal home – a very tidy home too, so searching was made easy. Nothing of significance was found except a diary on a bedside table. Palmer leafed through it.

'Better put this in an evidence bag, Sergeant; it seems to be a listing of the days she went out looking for a victim.' Palmer pointed to one page with writing on it. 'Look, she says here: *left arm, Greenwich*' on this page, and then a few pages further on: '*left leg, Paddington.*''

Gheeta nodded. 'I bet that date corresponds with the date of the laundromat victim – she had her left leg missing, didn't she? Hang on…' She took her laptop from her satchel and flipped it open. A few taps on the keyboard and her suspicion was confirmed. 'It was; the dates match.'

Palmer flipped the pages forward. 'What's she got down for today?' He opened it on the current date and read. ''*Somerville*' – no body part listed though. That must have been where she was going today, '*Somerville*', wherever that is?'

Gheeta tapped away. 'No place of that name in the UK, guv. Not that I can see anyway.'

'Could be the name of the next victim she's lined up. Let's hope we get to Hawke before anything nasty happens to another victim.

When all the rooms and the loft had been searched, time was getting on. Palmer checked his watch.

'Nine o'clock, Sergeant. Get Claire to give the local boys a call, and get a uniform guard on this place for the night and tape it off.'

'I would have thought Hawke would have come here by now guv, if she was spending the night at home?'

'Yes, so would I. Perhaps she did come and saw us and scarpered – I should have left one of the team outside at the front. I think we ought to get a stop and detain order out on her now. Give Claire a call and get her to raise one – all forces and border control – and see what's happening with the arrest warrant in case she does turn up here.'

Gheeta was about to make the call when her radio pinged; it was Claire.

'Go ahead, Claire.'

'I've got the warrant, but there was a problem.'

'A problem?'

'Yes, when we put her name into the warrant processing program it came up with two addresses for the name Martine Hawke. So I checked the local council rates list and apparently she owns two properties in the borough. You remember the Google Earth scan of the area?'

'Yes.'

'Well, the small bungalow in the lane at the bottom of her garden behind the hedge is also hers, or at least she pays the council rent and rates on it. Could be an elderly relative lives there; the properties are listed as single occupant retirement bungalows.'

'Okay, thanks Claire.'

Palmer was already out of the French door and halfway down the lawn with the rest of the team as Gheeta clicked off and followed.

DS Lewis found the gate; it could hardly be seen in the dark, small and somewhat overhung by the leylandii. 'Gate here, sir.'

Palmer pushed it open and they moved through to the rear of the bungalow. It was in darkness: curtains shut and no sign of anybody inside. He motioned all to be still and whispered. 'Lewis and Patel, stay here. Trent and Langham, come with me to the front – take care, watch your back. We are either going to find a serial murder scene or frighten the life out of a little old lady in her retirement bungalow.'

Gheeta had a feeling it wasn't going to be the latter as they crept around the building to the front. All the curtains were pulled shut there too, and no light could be seen. Palmer crouched and lifted the letterbox, peering through; the small hallway was dark. He tapped on the door, hoping for movement inside. Nothing.

'Anybody home?' No answer.

This door was not glazed, so the Crombie elbow couldn't be brought into play. He turned to Trent.

'What size shoe are you, Trent?'

'Eleven, sir.'

'And you, Langham?'

'Twelve, sir,'

'You win.' He nodded towards the door. 'Kick it in.'

'Sir?' Lanham was a little bemused.

'Kick it in – I'm sure I heard a muffled cry for help. Did you hear it, Sergeant? he asked Gheeta.

'Without doubt, sir – a muffled cry for help.' Gheeta had forgotten how many times she had *heard muffled cries for help'* when Palmer wanted access to a property without having a warrant.

'One good stamp where the lock is should do it, Langham. I'd do it myself, but my sciatica would rain hell on me for a week.'

Langham shrugged; who was he to disobey an order? It took two hefty kicks before the plywood around the lock splintered and the door swung open.

Palmer held up his hands for silence for a moment; no sounds came from within. Gheeta found the light switch and a single hanging bulb glowed deep red, giving a very eerie overlay to the place.

'One room at a time, and don't touch anything,' said Palmer as they moved inside. He slowly opened the first door on the right, which was the kitchen. This time he found the light switch, and the room was bathed in bright fluorescent light from two ceiling strips. 'I think we have got the right place this time.' He pointed to the sink draining board, which had a number of surgical instruments laid out on it: clamps, scalpels, retractors, lancets, rasps, trocars, surgical scissors, dilators, specula and more. Bottles of formaldehyde and other medical liquids and drip bags were arranged on the table.

'Oh my God,' said Gheeta softly, hardly able to believe what she was seeing. 'Oh my God.'

'This has got to be the store-room.' Palmer backed out of the door into the hallway. 'But which room is the operating theatre, eh?'

'Let's hope it's empty, guv. Just the thought of it makes me feel a bit queasy.'

'And me.' Trent felt it too.

'Go and wait in the fresh air,' said Palmer. 'Last thing we want is either of you throwing up in here. You alright, Langham?'

'Yes, sir. I saw enough mangled bodies when I was in Traffic Division on the motorways – I'm immune to it now.'

'Right then, onwards.' Palmer slowly opened the door to the lounge; he found the switch, and again it was the deep red light that permeated the room. Their gaze immediately fell on the young lady tied to the bench and the table of instruments beside her.

'Oh Christ!' Gheeta made her way quickly across to the body and took the pulse, whilst Palmer removed the gag and Langham and Trent pulled off the straps.

'She's alive, guv'

'Okay.' Palmer took off his Crombie and covered the young lady's body as the last of the straps were pulled off. Gheeta sat her up and Trent held her head up.

'What do we do about this?' Gheeta indicated the needle in the arm from the drip-feed.

'Nothing.' Palmer waved his hand. 'Call in the medics and let them decide. We don't know what that fluid is – it could be keeping her alive for all we know.'

Langham took over, holding her in a sitting position as Gheeta radioed Claire to get medics to the scene as fast as possible, and then called in Lewis and Patel.

'Do you think there'll be another one in the backroom, guv?'

'I hope not, I'm hoping it will just be a nice bedroom.'

'I wouldn't put money on it, guv. There's two arms and a leg somewhere.'

'Yes, I was thinking that. Did you notice the marked line on the top of that lady's right thigh?'

'Yes, a guideline for our surgeon's knife by the look of it.'

'Mm, ready to take a look then?' He gave out orders. 'Lewis, stay with the lady in case she wakes.

Trent, keep an eye on the door and when the medics arrive, shoes off and don't touch anything is the order for them.'

He led the others to the door at the end of the small hallway and slowly pushed it open; it was pitch dark inside. Palmer ran his hand up the wall beside the doorframe to locate the light switch; he clicked it on and the same deep red light filled the room. There was no furniture except for two benches in the middle, set three feet apart; each one supported a purpose-built glass tank, six foot by four foot by eighteen inches high. The one on the right had a complete female body totally immersed in formaldehyde; the other had a body minus its head also immersed in formaldehyde.

The sound of Patel making for the front door and retching broke the silence.

'I think we've found our missing limbs, guv.'

'We've found a great deal more than that, Sergeant,' said Palmer as he moved in between the two tanks. 'My God, look at this.' Gheeta and Langham joined him. 'They are reconstructed bodies.'

The bodies in the tanks were made up of several parts from other bodies, all neatly sewn together with black cotton to form the complete female body in one case, and a body minus the head and right leg in the other.

'She's completed one build and is onto another,' Gheeta exclaimed. 'Why do two?'

'Perhaps this complete one was a practice run.' Palmer realised the incredulity of his statement as soon as he'd said it. 'I really don't know. More to the point, where are the bodies these limbs came from? There are no earlier reports of limbless bodies being found are there, so where are they?'

'What's going on, guv? What's Hawke up to?'

'I've no idea, Sergeant. Perhaps the GMC thing sent her off her trolley.'

Langham pointed to the back wall. 'She's working off a plan by the look of it.'

In the dark red gloom, a large poster-like wall hanging of the type used in medical schools showing the human body with the muscles named was fastened to the wall at head height. Gheeta shone her torch at it; the two arms and left leg were crossed out.

'Looks like a 'work in progress' chart; she's marked off the limbs that she's already got. This must be the incomplete body in the tank.'

Palmer had seen something that he couldn't quite make out in the gloom.

'Raise the beam to the head.'

Gheeta did so. What they saw shocked them into silence for a moment or two as their brains took it in.

'Oh my God, so that's her plan.'

They stood looking at an enlarged photo of the face of Baroness Sharpe, stuck on the poster in the head position.

Palmer was thinking aloud. 'First she got the witness, Zerin, and now she's after the judge. It *is* all about revenge.'

'So why the other body? Why complete another body and sew it together?' asked Gheeta, still not seeing the point..

'Remember what the profiler said,' Palmer quoted. ' *This person is showing off to somebody who doubted her, she's saying this is what I can do...* That could be the purpose of putting the first body together: a finished product of her expertise to show how good she is at her job. The person who she thinks doubted her skill is Sharpe, so this completed body is to show to Sharpe.'

'And then?' Gheeta dreaded to think.

'Then she kills Sharpe and uses her head to complete the second build, and her revenge is complete.'

'So if she did come back to the house when we were inside earlier, she would realise we are onto her guv, and panic. Then what would she do?'

'Well she won't come back here, that's for certain – but she might cut her losses and just go after Sharpe to kill her to complete the revenge. Come on, we've some calls to make.'

They left the bungalow as the medics and the local police arrived. Palmer gave DS Lewis instructions to secure it and tape the whole plot off; he had an awful feeling that seeing no limbless bodies inside the bungalow of the woman Hawke had murdered to cut the limbs from to make the first body build could well mean that an excavation of the small rear garden might yield a nasty secret.

It was nice to get into fresh air, and all three drew long breaths of it.

Palmer gathered Langham, Patel and Trent together with Gheeta in a quiet corner, away from what was quickly developing into a very busy crime scene. 'Right then, let's see where we go from here. Let's assume Hawke is aware of our interest and on the run.' He turned to Gheeta. 'Give Claire a call and get her to call DVLA, if they're still there this time of night, and give Hawke's name and both these addresses and see if any cars are registered to her. If they are, then get them onto ANPR camera reporting straight away. If DVLA is shut at this time of night, get her to do it first thing in the morning. Patel, you get hold of Reg Frome and ask him to attend here – say that it's me asking and he'll come, he's up-to-date on the case. I'll get Professor Latin and his pathology boys in tomorrow morning. Langham, you get over to the GMC building and get Baroness Sharpe's address off the night security people there and get over to it and keep a watch outside, in case Hawke pays her a visit. Also get her telephone number and let me have it, so I can alert her to what's happening. Okay, off you all go – and keep comms open.'

The SIO from the local station had arrived, so Palmer handed over the crime scene to him with explicit instructions that nobody entered the bungalow or the main house until Reg Frome and his team had arrived and conducted a thorough forensic search and given permission. The medics had removed the morphine drip from the young woman who was traumatised and put her into the ambulance where an oxygen mask was fitted. Palmer told Lewis to go with her to the hospital, stay with her, and when possible get a statement.

'Mr Frome is on his way, sir,' Patel reported. 'He's got a night team coming too.'

'Good, well done'

'DVLA is shut, guv – answer phone on, but here's the registration numbers of two cars registered to Martine Hawke at these addresses: a BMW 3 series and a Fiesta.'

Patel was confused. 'But if they are shut, how did you get the registration numbers?'

Palmer patted him on the shoulder. 'Don't ask – my sergeant works in mysterious ways Patel, mysterious ways.' Palmer knew that no doubt Gheeta had a back door entry hack into the DVLA computer system that Claire had used to get access and lift the registration numbers.

Gheeta showed an expressionless face of innocence. 'Claire's put the numbers onto the ANPR system as well.'

'Good, let's hope it brings a result. I would really like to know where Doctor Martine Hawke is right now.' He looked around the scene. 'Well, nothing further we can do here, so I suggest we get a bit of shut-eye. Patel, you take over from Langham in the morning at the Baroness's house – give him a call and tell him. Trent, you do the same, and relieve Lewis at the hospital, Sergeant.' He turned to Gheeta. 'Thank Claire for staying on and tell her to go home now; if the number plates show up on any ANPR camera ask control to give me a call.'

'They don't have your number, guv. Shall I give it to them?' There was a twinkle in her eye.

Palmer gave her a knowing squint. 'I meant to say 'give *you* a call' Sergeant, and then you call me.'

Gheeta's radio beeped; it was Langham with Baroness Sharpe's phone number. Palmer rang it and the Baroness's husband answered; thankfully he was aware of the Hawke case and what had happened at the tribunal, and of Palmer's chat with the Baroness.

'Just to let you know that we now have the evidence we need to arrest Hawke, sir, and have put out a warrant for her arrest. But as a precaution I have a plainclothes officer keeping a watch on your home, in case she gets any silly ideas.'

'That's very kind of you Superintendent, but my wife isn't here at present – she's guest of honour at her old college tonight; she's giving a talk on the empowerment of women. I'm not expecting her back until the small hours. If your officer needs anything, tell him to knock – I'll be up until she returns.'

'Where is she, sir? Which college is it?'

'Oxford, Somerville College.'

CHAPTER 21

The *bit of shut-eye* that Palmer had suggested they all got was now not going to happen.

He took Baroness Sharpe's mobile number from her husband and rang it; the phone was off. Thirty minutes later, he, Gheeta and Trent were in a squad car Palmer had co-opted from the local force and were speeding up the M40 behind an Audi S3 Interceptor car that had picked them up at High Wycombe and cleared the way with its blues and siren. The local Oxford police had been notified and asked to get to the college and put a protective environment around the Baroness. Her husband had told Palmer she was in a black Honda CRV and given him the number.

Gheeta was checking the Somerville College on her laptop in the back of the squad car. 'It's a lady's college, no men. Got some pretty famous old girls: Margaret Thatcher, Esther Ranzen, Iris Murdoch, to name but three.'

Claire came through on the radio. 'ANPR picked up the BMW on the M40 at the A40 Oxford turn-off at Wheatley an hour ago.'

Palmer was worried. 'She's well ahead of us then – let's hope the local boys get there before Hawke does. Tell Claire to input Sharpe's Honda's number into the ANPR system.'

Gheeta checked her watch. 'It's nearly eleven o'clock – Sharpe's talk at the College must be over by now, she could be on her way home. What do you think Hawke will try to do, guv – kidnap her?'

'Well that's the modus operandi so far: drug and kidnap. But if she's been spooked by us she might just go for a kill to satisfy the revenge lust.'

'But if what you said earlier about the profiler saying she'd want to show her work to the Baroness before killing her is true, then how will she do that if she knows that we know about the house and bungalow? She can't take Sharpe back there to show off her handiwork, can she?'

'No. Which doesn't bode well for Sharpe, does it?'

'No, I'll keep trying her mobile.'

'Getting foggy outside,' said Palmer, peering out of the side window. 'That's all we need.'

Somerville College is a large three-storey Victorian mansion in its own grounds on the Woodstock road on the outskirts of Oxford. The two squad cars drove into the wide drive at speed and pulled up in the car park at the building's front. Three police cars from the local force were already there, one with its blues flashing. The fog seemed to hang like a heavy shroud over the scene.

Palmer looked at the college building as he, Gheeta and Trent left their car. It was in darkness; whatever social event had been on was now clearly over.

The local detective in charge came over. 'DS Goodman sir, Oxford CID.'

'Hello, Goodman.' Palmer shook his hand. 'This is DS Singh and DS Trent. Anybody around?'

'No sir, all very quiet – in fact, too quiet really.'

'How do you mean?'

'Well the place is empty and no lights on anywhere, but there's a caretaker who has a ground floor apartment and his rooms are empty as well. The front door was open, so he should be around somewhere. A couple of my men know him from being called out when the alarms go off; there's an invisible infrared beam across the entrance that signals a security company, who then ring us. His car is in the car park round the back with one other motor, a Honda.'

'I think we know who that might belong to,' said Palmer, and they made their way to the rear of the building. As Palmer had surmised, it was the Baroness's Honda; it had her handbag on the passenger seat. It was locked.

'Are you absolutely sure the building is empty?' Palmer asked DS Goodman.

'As sure as we can be, sir – all the rooms have been checked, but if somebody wanted to hide I'm sure they could find somewhere, it's a big place. There's a lot of grounds and gardens round the back too, plenty of places to hide there. I'll call in a dog team and see what he can find, shall I?'

'Yes please, good idea.' What Palmer really thought was: *why the Hell haven't you done that already.*

Gheeta tapped his arm and pointed inside the Honda's rear window, 'The back storage section has its cover pulled out and over it, guv. Can't see if there's anything there.'

Palmer looked at DS Goodman. 'Can you get a garage out to open the car?'

'Yes, there's a Honda dealer in town.'

'No need, guv.' Gheeta pulled out her mobile. 'I can do it. Hang on.' She radioed Claire. 'Claire, go into the Honda app program on the mainframe computer could you?'

'Hang on,' came the scratchy reply. There was silence for a minute. 'Okay, fire away.'

'Put in the Honda number I gave you earlier and give me the code.'

It took two minutes. 'One seven K Y seven four six nine R nine L two.'

Gheeta put the number into an app on her phone. 'Okay, got it. Thanks.' She clicked her radio off, held her phone close to the driver's side lock of the car and pressed a number on the pad. The click of the lock opening was clearly audible.

She smiled at Goodman. 'Magic.'

'It wasn't *magic* – what was it? How did you do that? asked Goodman.

Gheeta explained. 'Car security systems are a *bought in* product – the car makers like Honda and Jaguar don't develop their own wireless key systems, they buy them off the shelf from a specialist company that develops them; when a car is registered and given a number, the DVLA gets the code for any wireless lock system installed in it and inputs it onto their registration data for that car.'

'Which you have access to?'

Palmer butted in. 'Sort of, but don't worry about that now. Let's look inside.'

Gheeta went to the back of the car and swung the rear door open.

Somerville's caretaker was hunched in a foetal position, facing forward; he wasn't moving. Gheeta released the storage cover which automatically zipped back into its holding frame against the back of the rear seats.

'Is he dead?' Palmer asked as DS Goodman shone his torch on the body.

Gheeta felt for a pulse: nothing. Then, as she turned his head toward them, the congealed blood around the slit jugular vein glinted in the torch light.

'He's dead.'

'Are you sure?'

'Yes, she cut his jugular artery; takes less than six seconds to die when that happens.'

Palmer took a deep breath. 'She certainly knows what she's doing with a blade, eh?'

'I'll call in the doctor and the morgue van.' Goodman pulled his radio from his tunic.

'Doctor won't do him any good now,' said Gheeta.

'No,' Goodman agreed. 'But the morgue won't take him unless they have a death certificate with the body. Silly rule really, but if he suddenly sat up on the slab in the morgue I'd be in deep trouble.'

Palmer thrust his hands into his Crombie pockets and pursed his lips. 'Well, where are you now, Doctor Martine Hawke – where oh where?'

'And is the Baroness with you?' added Gheeta.

'Bound to be, Sergeant – but what's she got in her mind is the troubling bit. Judging by this poor chap, whatever she is thinking of doing with her prisoner doesn't bear thinking about.'

CHAPTER 22

The Baroness was driving carefully in the fog. They were on the A34 out of Oxford going south; Hawke was in the passenger seat, her arm resting along the top of the driver's seat behind the Baroness's head. In her hand a scalpel glinted as they passed under streetlights that barely threw any light down through the thick fog.

'Go faster,' ordered Hawke.

'I can't in this fog, it's getting worse. Can't see more than fifty metres.'

'There won't be much traffic around, it's late and foggy. So go faster.'

The Baroness felt the cold steel of the scalpel on her neck as an inducement. 'Where are we going?'

'Just keep driving.'

'This is a bit stupid, isn't it – kidnapping me just because a tribunal banned you? What's the point?

'I wanted to show you my work – show you how good I am, and how stupid you were to ban me.'

'You were banned because of your work. You made too many mistakes, you could have killed patients.'

'I've killed seven.'

'What?'

'Including that shit of a nurse that brought the complaint.'

The Baroness felt a shiver run through her body and was beginning to feel very scared. 'What do you mean you've killed seven?'

'Eight if you count the caretaker at Somerville.'

The Baroness decided to play for time. 'I think you are just trying to frighten me. If you'd killed seven people, it would be all over the news. You just need counselling; the stress of the tribunal has affected your mind. I'll arrange a counsellor for you and then everything will work out. Let's face it, you certainly showed you need anger management at the tribunal.' She smiled at Hawke, hoping to build a rapport.

'I've killed seven young women. It's not been on the news because five of them were rough sleepers – nobody to miss them. I killed Zerin Awad; she deserved it, stuck up little nurse. How dare she question my work.' She laughed. 'I put her body in a rubbish bin along with the other garbage.'

'That's six.' The Baroness was now convinced Hawke was mad, and the best thing was to keep her talking.

'And a girl from Manchester.'

'Manchester? Why Manchester?

'She was coming down for an interview to be my PA; it was all arranged before the tribunal. Seemed a shame to dash her dreams and tell her there was no job anymore.'

'You killed her?'

'Yes, she was in the right place at the right time for me.' She laughed. 'The wrong time for her.'

The Baroness was looking for a way to end this journey; she was hoping a car would come the other way in the fog and she could have an accident. She had to get out of the car.

'Why kill these women? What has killing them got to do with the tribunal?'

'I needed their limbs.'

The Baroness was stunned for a moment. 'You needed *what*?'

Hawke was laughing again. 'Their limbs, their legs and arms.'

'What for?'

'I built a body with them; a complete body including a head, all neatly sewn together with bits from different bodies: a leg from one, an arm from another and so on – my masterpiece to show you.' Hawke's mood changed to one overlaid with menace. 'To show you how good I am at my job. How dare you end my career on the say-so of a nurse, how *dare* you! You think you're God do you, eh? Well, now I'm God aren't I, and this is *your* tribunal, and *you've* been found guilty.'

'Is that where we are going, to see this masterpiece?'

'We were, until the police found it. We were going to see it, and I was going to complete the second one.'

'The *second* one? There's another?'

'Of course there's another; you think I was going to show you one and that was that? Just wish you well and off you'd go to ruin more lives, crush other people's careers with a stroke of your pen? Oh no Baroness Sharpe, Chairlady of the almighty GMC, oh no – there's one piece missing from my second masterpiece: the head.' Hawke paused for effect before staring at the Baroness, who was avoiding eye contact. 'The head. Your head.'

'I'm going to be sick, I need to pull over.'

'No, you're not. Keep driving.'

The Baroness had a plan. She forced a retch; being an ex-medical practitioner she knew that if you forced a retch enough times, you would indeed be sick.

So she kept doing it, and a small bit of vomit trickled down her front.

'All right, pull over on the right,' Hawke ordered.

The car halted by the right verge.

'Open the door and turn in your seat. Don't leave your seat, don't release your seatbelt either. Be sick onto the verge, and be quick.'

The Baroness did as she was told; as she bent forward and forced the retches, she made as if to hold her stomach with her right hand which was out of view of Hawke; reaching inside her open raincoat, she found her mobile in the pocket of her jacket and pressed the button to turn it on. She threw a few more retches.

'Right, that's enough.' Hawke was impatient and pulled her back in by the shoulder. 'Let's go.'

The Baroness was weighing up the odds; they didn't favour her. She was thirty years older than Hawke – slower, no match physically, so play it carefully; hope they came into a built-up area where she could get somebody's attention or jam the brakes on and run; maybe hit something so the air bags inflated and Hawke was pinned back in her seat and hope to God to be first out of the car. But that would only work in a built-up area where there were houses to run to, and they weren't in a built up area. All the options were loaded in Hawke's favour.

'We can't just keep driving. If you gave yourself up now, you could claim mental instability due to the tribunal, like I said; you'd get sectioned and you'd get help. If you kill me, you'll get life for murder.'

Hawke smiled. 'I'd probably get nine life sentences then. Shut up and keep driving.'

'Where to? What's the point? Your plan has failed?'

That annoyed Hawke. She stabbed the scalpel through the Baroness's coat into her shoulder; not deep, but enough to hurt and draw blood which the Baroness felt run warm down her arm.

'Aaargh, what are doing you fool!' She clasped her left shoulder with her right hand whilst keeping control of the steering wheel with her left hand.

'I told you to shut up. Next time it will be your throat.'

CHAPTER 23

Gheeta's radio crackled into action; the reception was bad due to the heavy fog. It was Claire.

'... phone... A...,' was all that could be made out. Gheeta clicked it off and rang Claire on the mobile, plugging it into one of the USB ports on her laptop so that they could all hear her clearly through that.

Claire was excited. 'We've got a network reading on the phone you gave me; it's been switched on. I'm running the co-ordinates to place it now.'

'Okay, let us have them ASAP.' She turned to Palmer. 'Shall I ring it, guv?'

Palmer was tempted, but there were odds against that move. 'No, we don't know why it should suddenly go live. If the Baroness is okay she'd ring her husband; could be she's not okay and not even near the phone. Could be Hawke's got the phone and is waiting for us to ring it, which would confirm we know what's happening. No, just give us the area.'

They waited whilst Claire waited for the network to trace the signal.

'Come on, come on.' Palmer was impatient.

A minute went by.

'Have they lost the signal?' He looked at Gheeta, who shrugged.

'Takes a little time to cross reference the co-ordinates guv, but once we lock on it can't get away.'

'The A34.' Claire was back. 'It's on the A34 going south from Oxford.'

Palmer was already running towards the A3 Interceptor parked by the gates. 'Come along, Sergeant –

and you Goodman, we might need some backup from
your lads.'

They piled into the back as the driver and his
partner got in the front.

'Sat nav on, driver. We want the A34 south as
fast as you can.'

Once they had settled, Gheeta went back to
Claire. 'Have you got a positional check yet, Claire?'

'Approaching a place called Sunningwell. They
stopped for a while a few minutes ago but are on the
move again now.'

Goodman used his radio to ask for assistance in
that area; his reception was clear, being near to the
Oxford control room signal. There were two patrol cars
in the area and they were told to head for Sunningwell,
and given the BMW's number with orders to stop it at all
costs.

Three minutes later and the Interceptor passed the
Sunningwell sign.

'We must be catching them quite fast, guv,' said
Gheeta. 'They won't be travelling at our speed in this
fog.'

Goodman took a few calls on his radio and turned
to Palmer. 'I've got two cars on the A34 coming up from
the other direction towards the Abingdon turnoff, the
B4017 – I could stop them there and block the road?'

'Yes, good idea – do that just south of the turnoff;
don't want any locals complaining they can't get in or
out. How far away from there are we?'

'Ten minutes at the most.'

'Then we should be catching Hawke any time
now.'

CHAPTER 24

'What the hell? Stop! Turn the lights off,' Hawke shouted at the Baroness, who obeyed and brought the car to halt.

They peered forward into the dark fog, where a blue flashing light just about permeated through from 100 metres in front of them.

'The police!' Hawke stated the obvious. 'The bastards have closed the road. Okay, turn round – no lights.' She pushed the cold steel of the scalpel into the Baroness's neck as a reminder of her vulnerable position.

The Baroness thought about just driving on, or flashing the lights, or leaning on the horn; but the steel on her neck reminded her that one slash with the blade and she was dead. Best to keep calm and do as she was told, and hope the police could somehow bring this nightmare to a close. The presence of their flashing blues gave her some hope – at least she now knew that the police were after them. She did a three-point turn and headed away from the blue lights before putting the car lights back on. Then there were more blue lights flashing in front as the Interceptor sped towards them out of the fog.

'Keep going,' Hawke shouted at her. 'Faster!'

The two cars passed.

'That was them, guv.' Gheeta swung round in her seat, watching the BMW's red rear lights disappear into the fog behind them. 'That was them!'

The driver did a handbrake turn in the road with the brake pads squealing their objection and floored the accelerator as the car leaped forward after the BMW, and Palmer extricated himself from the weight of Goodman and Gheeta's bodies that had pressed him into the corner with the centrifugal force of the turn. Apologies all round as Palmer punched out the dent in his trilby.

'We can't get away from them, no chance. Give up now – I'll help you! I said I would, and I promise I will.' The Baroness was beginning to fear what might happen if they were stopped; would Hawke lose it entirely and start slashing?

Hawke snarled, 'I seem to remember you helped me once before. That's why we are here.'

A road sign – B4017 Steventon – loomed out of the fog, pointing left.

'Turn left. Go faster,' Hawke ordered.

The B4017 was narrower; just a two-lane A road, unlit. Behind them, the Baroness could see the blue flashing lights of the Interceptor gaining.

'Stay back.' Palmer was leaning forward between the driver and passenger seat. 'They'll know we are here, and hopefully the realisation that her game is over will bring Hawke to her senses.'

'I wouldn't count on it, guv.' Gheeta was sceptical.

'No, I'm not. Where does this road lead to, Goodman?'

'Steventon Village then over the railway and then basically on until it rejoins the A34.'

'Over the railway?'

'Steventon level crossing.'

Palmer's mind was in overdrive. 'Is it gated?'

'Yes, automatic – single barrier.'

'Can you get it closed?'

'No, it's an automatic one; the oncoming train automatically triggers a switch farther down the line and closes it.'

'Can't we get it overridden?'

Goodman checked his watch. ' Probably could from the local station, it's only a few hundred yards up the line; but by the time we get there they'll be long past the crossing, and it's an unmanned station this time of night anyway, so there won't be anybody there to do anything. Hang on!' Goodman checked his watch and smiled. 'The eleven forty-five from London is due through any minute. It could be closed already.'

It was. Lights flashing, bells ringing, the barriers were down. A few cars were stationary on the other side of the crossing, their exhausts visibly adding to the fog as they waited for the train to pass and the barriers to rise.

'Keep going.'

'What?' The Baroness had slowed down and couldn't believe the instruction. 'The barriers are down, there's a train coming through.'

'Keep going, smash through the barriers. Do it!'

'And get hit by a speeding train? No way. If we hit the barrier the airbags will inflate, the engine cut out automatically, and we'll be stuck on the line with a train coming at us: suicide. No way!' She hit the brakes hard, and as Hawke was thrown forward the scalpel flew out of her hand onto the back seat.

The Baroness flipped her seat belt off, opened her door and fell out, scrambling to her feet and running towards the barrier; if she could get to the other side of the tracks before Hawke could get to her, she might put a speeding train between them and give the police time to get there. It was a futile attempt. Hawke was much younger and much quicker. She was out of the car, retrieved the scalpel and caught the Baroness as Palmer's car arrived. She held the Baroness around the neck and twisted her round towards the Interceptor as Palmer, Goodman and Gheeta got out.

'Just stay where you are,' Hawke shouted, waving the scalpel for them to see. 'Any closer and I use this.'

Palmer assessed the situation before shouting back. 'You are Doctor Martine Hawke. We know all about you, we know what you've done, and there is no way you will get out of here. So just let the lady go, put the knife down, and keep your hands in view.'

It was the first law of dealing with a hostage situation: be hard, be firm, be aggressive, and if that fails then start to build a 'relationship' with the kidnapper. This wasn't exactly a hostage situation, but it was worth a try. It failed.

'I'll slit her throat if you come a step closer.'

'That would be a very silly thing to do, Doctor. You wouldn't have a bargaining chip then – no hostage.'

Hawke was slowly edging backwards to the barrier and pulled the Baroness around the end of it to the edge of the line.

Almost unnoticed, Goodman, Palmer and Gheeta were moving closer all the time. Gheeta undid the press stud of the taser pocket on her tunic. On the other side of the crossing people were leaving their cars to see what was happening, and getting too close for Palmer's liking.

The last thing he wanted was a mad doctor slashing at the public with a medical scalpel.

He shouted to them above the din of the crossing's bells. 'Get back into your cars and lock the doors.' They seemed deaf to the instruction. 'NOW! She's got a knife!' That got through, and they quickly did as they were told.

The unmistakable warning blast of an Intercity Diesel Express turned everybody's gaze to its large dark outline, coming out of the fog at eighty miles an hour twenty metres down the track. The force of the displaced air as it sped past blew Hawke and the Baroness apart and down onto the ground beside the line as the lit carriages thundered by, far too fast for the travellers inside to comprehend what they'd just passed. The scalpel flew out of Hawke's hand.

As the end of the train disappeared into the fog again, the Baroness tried to scramble to her feet and run; but Hawke had her by the arm and jerked her back across the track towards where the scalpel had fallen on the ballast between the up and down line rails. She picked it up and moved her hand towards the side of the Baroness's neck, who jerked herself backwards away from it, holding up her hands in protection against the sweep of the blade that sliced across them. A red laser target dot appeared on Hawke's chest and Gheeta's taser dart hit home, delivering a shock of fifty thousand volts. Hawke stood still for a moment, her face riven by shock and pain; the scalpel fell from her hand, she started to shake, and then with the taser wire still in place fell backwards onto the nearest down line rail as the 11.55 freight train from Oxford thundered out of the fog and severed her head.

CHAPTER 25

Night was breaking into day with a cold sun slowly lifting the fog. The B4017 was closed both ends at the A34. At the level crossing a sea of activity was happening under a crime scene tarpaulin stretched over it on poles ten foot-high. Forensics and snappers were hard at work checking the area and recording Hawke's body position and that of the head; both had been covered over but not moved as yet, not until every detail had been recorded. British Rail had closed the line both ways. Numerous police cars, both plain and panda, were parked on both sides of the crossing; some still had their blues flashing. A flatbed truck was lifting the BMW to take it away for forensics and an ambulance was in attendance, as was a black windowless morgue van.

The cuts to the Baroness's hands had been clipped shut temporarily and she had been taken off for surgery to repair them, and to spend a night in hospital where her husband would be waiting; this is the usual procedure for trauma victims, and although a statement would be required by Palmer he could wait until she was released to the comfort of her own home before asking her to recount the last five hours' events.

Palmer, Gheeta and Goodman rested against the bonnet of the Interceptor with cups of very welcome hot tea. He nodded towards the covered head.

'Well, Doctor Hawke got her head in the end, didn't she.'

'Just not the one she was after, guv,' said Gheeta.

'I'd get the body and head into the morgue van if I was you, Goodman; forensics have covered them over so they seem to have finished with them. The press will be here any minute, they'll have been tipped off by now, and we don't want any gory pictures in the morning papers.'

'It's nearly four- o'clock guv, 'said Gheeta. 'Bit late for morning editions.'

'Same procedure as before, sir – got to wait for a doctor to give the death certificate before I can move them,' Goodman explained. 'I've asked for one to attend.'

'If he's NHS we could be waiting here for months.' He turned and looked inside the Interceptor where the driver and co-driver were also sipping hot tea. 'You two okay?'

They nodded affirmatively.

Palmer turned back to Gheeta. 'When we get back to the office remind me to send a commendation letter to their Chief Constable. Bloody good pair of lads.'

'Will that be as well as the commendation letters you'll be sending about me and DS Goodman, guv?' Gheeta had a cheeky twinkle in her eyes.

Palmer took a sip from his cup. 'Tea's not bad.'

Goodman and Gheeta exchanged smiles.

CHAPTER 26

Palmer had arranged to meet Gheeta at the bungalow the next afternoon. They both needed some sleep and he had stood down the rest of the team as well; they could have a couple of days off before returning to their units.

The bungalow garden, front, sides and back, resembled a building plot: large holes and heaps of excavated dirt, alongside a small digger that was carefully removing the soil inch by inch. Along the side of lane which had been closed off both ways, a line of black body bags lay side by side as testament to Hawke's awful deeds.

Palmer and Singh were given boots and face masks by Reg Frome who met them at the lane gate.

'This is definitely your best one yet, Justin. This one will go down in the annals of serial killers. She's on a par with Crippen and Fred West – a real nasty killer.'

'What have we got then, Reg?' asked Palmer.

'Ten. Ten female bodies all with a limb missing – one with its head missing.'

'That ties in with the body parts inside, guv,' Gheeta confirmed from her notes on her laptop. 'Ten different parts,'

'How can ten females go missing with nobody worrying about them or asking questions?' Palmer was astonished.

'Too early to assume that, Justin. Once Latin gets those bodies into his lab and takes the DNA and we get a chance to lift any prints still intact, we might well find that some – if not all – have worried families out there.'

'Only if we get a match.'

'Yes, but there's other things too; three of them have rings on, then there are dental records, physical scars and broken bones. I bet we get most of them identified.'

'And then somebody will have the job of knocking on the family's door.' Gheeta pulled a grim face. 'Not a job I'd like to do.'

'What about the main house, anything in there?' Palmer looked towards the hedge gate to the house.

'No, I've a team inside going through everything, but no signs of any nasty deeds being done there. I've got an archaeological team from the local university coming in later with a ground-penetrating radar buggy to check the lawn area. You never know, could be a load more buried there.'

'I hope not.' Palmer feigned shock. 'This is quite enough, thank you.'

'What about the bungalow?' Gheeta was wondering. 'Going to have to be cheap if it goes on the market. I don't think the estate agent will mention its last occupant to a prospective buyer, do you?'

'It's a council house,' Frome explained. 'We found the assignment documents up in the main house. It's a one-occupant council retirement bungalow, and was assigned to Doctor Hawke's mother twenty years ago.'

'Where is she then?' asked Palmer. 'Hope you haven't dug her up too.'

Frome laughed. 'No, she's not one of the ten. She passed away three years ago, and it seems Hawke kept it to herself. The neighbour's carer noticed all this activity this morning and reported it, and we had a chap from the housing department down earlier. Apparently they are still taking the rent from Hawke's mother's account every month, so Hawke must have kept topping it up. They had no idea she had died. He wasn't very happy.'

'It's a nice quiet spot. Whoever gets it should be happy,' said Gheeta.

'That's why he *wasn't* very happy – nobody will get it. It will be totally demolished and either paved over or planted as a council garden. If they don't do that, the murder memorabilia collectors will be down stealing mementoes, slates and bricks – even bags of dirt.'

Palmer was amazed. 'Are you kidding me?'

'Not at all – that's why they had to completely demolish Fred West's house in Gloucester; it was gradually disappearing as the murder memorabilia lot stripped it bare. The council even had to take the demolished bricks and broken wooden door and window frames two hundred miles away to a waste tip up north. At one stage there was over three hundred West items on eBay.'

Palmer looked at Gheeta. 'Quick Sergeant, get a sledgehammer, knock out a load of bricks and bung 'em in my car boot. *We are going to be millionaires, Rodney!'* he said, in a rather poor Del Boy imitation. 'What about the main house then, what happens to that?'

'The Crown gets that if there are no family, they get the lot – that's the usual procedure if somebody dies without any relatives and no Will.' Frome shrugged. 'So I don't suppose they'll demolish it; worth too much and it hasn't any relevance to the actual murders, as none were committed there. They'll sell it, and the Treasury gets the proceeds.'

CHAPTER 27

'Well done, Palmer.' AC Bateman forced himself to smile as he congratulated Palmer on the result. 'Nasty business.'

He had popped his head round Palmer's office door on his way to a press conference to give the media the news that the case was now closed. Always one to take as much of the credit as he could, he wasn't going to miss the chance to heighten his profile on television just in case his political masters were watching. He had altered the original conference time of 2pm to 5pm, so he'd be seen in all his glory on the evening news at six. 'Anything I should know for the press that wasn't in your report?'

'No sir, all as written. No nasty shocks about to come out of the woodwork.'

Palmer was resigned to Bateman's way of pushing in to take credit whenever he could, as were the heads of Organised Crime and CID.

Bateman nodded. 'Good. I'm going over to see the Baroness later to give her our best wishes.'

'Creep,' thought Palmer.

Bateman spied the crate of Benji's elderflower wine that Palmer had brought in days before, with the intention of dumping it in the large food bins behind the Yard's kitchens. Mrs P. had insisted he remove it from the house so she could tell Benji they had enjoyed it so much they had passed some bottles on to their friends; anything to placate Benji after his episode in the hall.

'Having a celebration then, are you?' said Bateman, nodding at the crate.

Palmer thought: *Shall I? No, I can't.* Then he thought: *Why not?*

'Our neighbour makes his own wine, sir – elderflower.' He rose and took a bottle from the crate and gave it to Bateman. 'Here, I'm sure we can do without one bottle. My wife says it's very good.'

'Thank you, Palmer, that's very kind. We shall enjoy that with our meal this evening – we have our local PCC coming round with his wife. Thank you.'

'Oh, well here, sir – have two bottles.'

'What are you laughing at?' Gheeta asked Palmer when she came into the office just after Bateman had left. 'I saw Bateman leaving, have you given him some info that will make him look daft at the press conference?'

'No, me do something like that? No.'

Gheeta gave him a look that said: *I don't believe you.* 'Right, all the reports from the team members are done; you need to take a look and sign them off so I can get them upstairs for Bateman for tomorrow morning or he'll he hassling us.' She placed a sheaf of reports in front of Palmer on his desk.

'Somehow I don't think he'll be too concerned about our reports in the morning, Sergeant.'

THE END

POSTSCRIPT

On a dark and cloudy night, in a field a few miles outside Allerdale in Cumbria, three figures clad all in black silently rounded up a small flock of sheep, and herded them towards an open field gate that had a livestock transport lorry with its lights out backed up to it from the narrow lane bordering the field. The sheep were soon all inside, and the tail gate pushed up and locked shut.

The figures slipped up into the cab with the driver and the engine spluttered into action. At the same time, police patrol cars and an ARV that had been quietly waiting with their lights out sped towards the lorry from both ends of the lane, where they had been patiently waiting for the loading to be completed. Pulling up and blocking any escape route, the officers made themselves known to the lorry occupants and shouted that they had armed officers in attendance.

It was all over in a few minutes; photos of the lorry and its cargo were taken before the sheep were returned to their field by a grateful farmer, and the lorry driven off as evidence to a police pound in Workington.

DS Lewis had no idea this was going on as she caught up with her sleep in her North London semi' nor did Claire who had passed the number plate and photos that Lewis had given her onto the DEFRA rural crime unit. They in turn had passed it up the line to Cumbria Rural Crime Unit, and they in turn had followed the lorry and its driver for a week before the sting. The next morning the abattoir in West London would be getting a surprise visit from thirty DEFRA Rural Crime Officers and Border Patrol Immigration officers.

****

The Author

Barry Faulkner was born into a family of petty criminals in Herne Hill, South London, his father, uncles and elder brothers running with the notorious Richardson crime gang in the 60s-80s, and at this point we must point out that he did not follow in that family tradition although the characters he met and their escapades he witnessed have added a certain authenticity to his books. He attended the first ever comprehensive school in the UK, William Penn in Peckham and East Dulwich, where he attained no academic qualifications other than GCE 'O' level in Art and English and a Prefect's badge (though some say he stole all three!)

His mother was a fashion model and had great theatrical aspirations for young Faulkner and pushed him into auditioning for the Morley Academy of Dramatic Art at the Elephant and Castle, where he was accepted but only lasted three months before being asked to leave as no visible talent had surfaced. Mind you, during his time at the Academy he was called to audition for the National Youth Theatre by Trevor Nunn – fifty years later he's still waiting for the call back!

His early writing career was as a copywriter with the major US advertising agency Erwin Wasey Ruthrauff & Ryan in Paddington during which time he got lucky with some light entertainment scripts sent to the BBC and Independent Television and became a script editor and writer on a freelance basis. He worked on most of the LE shows of the 1980-90s and as personal writer to several household names. During that period, while living out of a suitcase in UK hotels for a lot of the time, he filled many notebooks with DCS Palmer case plots and in 2015 he finally found time to start putting them in order and into book form. Ten are finished and published so far. He hopes you enjoy reading them as much as he enjoys writing them. Faulkner is a popular speaker and often to be found on Crime Panels at Literary Festivals which he embraces and supports wholeheartedly as well as giving an illustrated humorous talk on the 60s-90s UK crime 'geezers' and their heists for social clubs, WIs and others. With many personal insights! Book him via his Facebook page.

He has been 'on screen' as a presenter in television crime programmes including the Channel 5 Narcos UK series, Episode 2 The London Gangs which you can view on catch up and his Palmer book 'I'm With The Band' has been serialised by BBC Radio Bristol.

*******************.